HOODOO
- A Psychological Thriller

Other books by Christopher John:

The Legend of J.C. Holmes
Peter Fry at Exit 30
Savage

HOODOO

A Psychological Thriller

Christopher John

UNITED WRITERS
Cornwall

UNITED WRITERS PUBLICATIONS LTD
Ailsa, Castle Gate, Penzance, Cornwall.

British Library Cataloguing in Publication Data:
A catalogue record for this book is
available from the British Library.

ISBN 1 85200 070 8

Printed in Great Britain by:
United Writers Publications Ltd.,
Cornwall.

For Alison and Katy.

Special thanks to Joyce for the typing.

Chapter One

People said you should never go back. But he knew different, Hood told himself bitterly. He was sitting high up on the heavily-seamed driving seat of his gunmetal coloured Volvo. His back pressed against a skunk-pattern seat cover.

It felt as if he were purposely driving to his own destruction. Why was he doing this? He had only to find a turning place and swing the car round. In his mind's eye he could see the great arc he would take. And such relief.

Why didn't he do it then? Instead he and the car ploughed on for ever. Was he a prisoner, chained to one direction, incapable of any deviation?

His head hurt. All these accusations had been torturing him since he set out. And the only answer he could give was: he had to go back. 'Oh to hell with you then,' the other voice inside him said impatiently. 'I'm not even going to try arguing with you, if that's all you can come up with.'

Hood nodded grimly to himself. Hell about summed it up. How could anyone in their right mind voluntarily return to the place of their torture and humiliation?

And all for what: to do his duty? There was no one left here for him now - except maybe Ann. Why had that name never left him after all these years? She might have moved away, be married with kids. But just to see, talk to her, yes - hold her.

Her image took possession of him: golden haired, with a figure to die for, joyous - and loving him to distraction. For a while. Then she broke it off - he never knew why. And he married Marjory and was happy in another way till that too fell apart.

Oh Ann, just to have her back as it was before. To make love by candlelight, champagne on ice. The thought was unbearable

7

now that all was emptiness.

His face was brooding, the long sloping forehead creased with pain. The deep set eyes seemed to peer out of a darkness of their own. The cheeks were weathered, hardened like leather. A face that could be taken for handsome but in this light appeared disfigured. It was as if he were holding something in, some great secret or power which when unleashed might sweep away anything in its path.

The car was hurtling forward all the while. There was that strange night darkness inside the car in which only the metal of the dashboard panel caught the light. It was like night flying, that same disembodied, lost feeling.

Along the car flew, past the municipal car parks, the cinema, and then the town hall was in view. The heart of the city, in one large square. All the municipal buildings were there, the law courts abutted it, and the brand new multi-storey police station stood at its bottom-most corner. "Very cosy," he muttered, as he crossed the square and then without a backward glance headed down past the railway station to find his digs.

Hood drove by boarded-up tenements and yards with sheet corrugated iron up-ended as protection against vandals. He was looking for a number - and a building which he had been told, resembled an old school. It was hard, directing the Volvo and watching out under the unevenly spread street lamps.

The doorways were becoming more nondescript the numberings petering out, when he saw it. A large, red brick building with a high, sloping slate roof, windows running right the way round at three levels, and a wide, columned entrance.

He parked the car, and climbed out. The air was wet and muggy, and a whiff of petrol came over from the railway yards. Hood opened the boot and removed his one large suitcase. It was brown and scarred, and a thick leather belt held it together.

He pulled his sheepskin coat closer round his neck, and entered through a wildly swinging door. Once inside Hood stood amid a large, draughty hallway and sought the landlord's door. However, before he reached it he noticed a long shelf and on it a key. His name and flat number 4 were written on a card attached with a piece of string.

Hood mashed the key into his palm and set off upstairs. On the first landing he turned left and confronted his door. The brown varnish was uneven and stained. The keyhole had an old-fashioned plastic cover to it. He turned the key in it and fell into the hall.

From there on the left he found the lounge. He deposited his suitcase in the middle of the floor and switched on the light. There was a huge sash window at the far end. With the long chocolate brown curtains pulled back, it cast a bitter chill over the room. He marched forward and angrily pulled them to.

Turning round his glance fell upon a coarse hessian-covered sofa pushed hard up against the far wall. In the corner was a matching chair overhung by a tassel-shade standard lamp.

On the other side of the room a drop-leaf table and empty bookcase stood faded and neglected near the window. At the end nearest the door crouched an ugly bulbous mahogany bureau. In between a picture of Bude in Cornwall hung over the electric fire.

Kneeling down he switched on the appliance. The coal effect remained unilluminated but the rings did gradually glow orange.

Then, still wearing his sheepskin coat, he sat in the chair. The standard lamp hung lifeless above him but he did not stir to switch it on.

On a night like this, in a cheap flat not all that different, Ann had strode in once, slipped her coat from her shoulders and sat in his lap nuzzling his face. Then they were kissing, rolling over and falling together on the floor, laughing. Then more kissing and making passionate love as the electric fire rings glowed.

He thought he had a tiny, crumpled picture of her somewhere which he'd kept from way back. He fumbled in his pockets and pulled out the contents. No picture, but there was the gun. All the way he'd felt it pressing into his side as he drove, reminding him of its presence.

He shouldn't have it, of course. All firearms had to be returned after issue, but this one had slipped through and he'd kept it. A Browning small calibre job. Not that he cared so long as it fired. If he ever needed to use it, he'd be eyeball to eyeball when he pulled the trigger.

He turned the gun this way and that, felt its weight, aimed it at the window, looking along the sight. Then he lowered it again, thinking.

He lifted it again and pointed it at his heart. He raised it higher, to his head. His arm remained raised, like a statue. The moment

9

lengthened, on and on. There seemed no good reason either way. Pain was living, pain was dying.

He put the gun down, like the suffering patient who decides to live and the pain in his sick body returns.

But he couldn't stay there, looking at his unopened suitcase and the forlorn room. He was going out into the city. After all, that's what he'd come for. What was the name of that pub Ann used to frequent when not seeing him? - Slumming it, she said. The Newsroom, that was it.

Chapter Two

Pushing down with his hands Hood lurched from his chair, till he stood swaying in the middle of the room. He felt giddy and pressed his palm to his forehead. Then he took it away again. The nausea was probably just hunger. He hadn't eaten since breakfast. Such had been his turmoil about returning to the city, his stomach hadn't been able to keep anything down.

Buttoning up his coat he swept out of the flat and onto the landing. All the rooms off were quiet; the carpet a thin brown streak to the stairs. There was something discouraging about all those doors closed to him, uninterested in him, uninviting. Well, this city was going to hear from him. He'd set it about its ears before he was finished. But meanwhile he needed to eat.

Outside the drizzle had stopped and there was only the wind, a wet slap in the face, as Hood turned making for the city centre.

The pub on the next corner was The Newsroom. The smoked glass prevented him from seeing its interior, and so there was nothing for it but to investigate.

Hood pushed the door open. Light was reflected through its purple stain glass showing a gold cup overflowing with wine. He carried on inside. The bar was heavy, dark stained walnut, with upright moulded columns all the way along.

Around the walls he saw framed music hall bills, yellowing newspaper headlines and photographs.

Hood ambled over to the bar. "Do you do any food?"

"What does that look like?" Julie the barmaid muttered, nodding at the card menu fixed with a drawing pin to the bar. Then leaning on the pumps, she looked away, bored, chewing.

She was a streaked blonde, her hair a mass of tight curls. She wore a low, orange T-shirt and ripped jeans. On her feet were dainty ankle boots. She had a habit of swivelling her hips, while staring down her nose at the customers. Her eyes were insolent, hard and bored. Her stare said she had found nothing and no one to like so far, and saw no prospect of this changing.

"I'll have the hotpot."

"Wait a mo." She strutted through a door to the rear, and then a few minutes later strolled back.

"It's all gone."

"All?"

"All. Are you deaf or something? And the cod's off too. You'll have to make do with sandwiches. Cheese all right?"

"Do I have any choice?"

The barmaid picked up another nut, chewed it, scowled sarcastically and wrote down his order. "Be a few minutes."

Before Hood could ask her to bring the sandwich over to a seat, she said, "You can come and get it in a few minutes." Then she turned her back on him.

Hood stood there, his eyes boring into her back. Her shoulder blades twitched. She tried to ignore him, wait for him to go, but she could sense him there. Wriggling, she switched her weight from one foot to the other. But she knew he was still there.

Her control snapped. She swung round, and then stopped with a jolt. His eyes seemed to have receded till there was darkness in their sockets. Subdued she fetched the two sandwiches and placed them in front of him. Hood shook his head and smiled. Then he took a bite of his sandwich. It stuck to the roof of his mouth, a stale musty taste. But without spitting it out, all he could do was chew messily. He gulped. Then he remembered he hadn't bought a drink to wash it down with. Leaving the half-eaten remnants, he ordered a pint. Julie pulled it without looking at him. Paying her, Hood glanced down the room.

And there he saw her. At least it looked like her. Picking his pint off the bar he walked down unselfconsciously to have a closer look. "Ann!"

The woman looked up from her half-full glass and then leaned backwards.

"Good God after all these years. William Hood. Well as I live and breathe."

"May I sit down?"

"Surely, make yourself at home."

It was a table near the far end wall of the pub. All that lay beyond were the kitchens and the toilets. Ann had her back to the wall and the alcoves obscured her from view, except from the bar itself.

Hood looked at her, remembering. Her face was now fat, her cheeks slabs, like those seen in distorting mirrors. She had put on weight in other places as well, and wore a voluminous floral patterned dress. A red bandanna at her hair-line made her look like a gypsy.

But her eyes had that same embracing yellow-green, reminiscent of cornfields and summer sun.

"I never expected to see you on my first day back," Hood began.

Ann shifted her shoulders and took a pensive sip of her drink. "Come back? It's too early to go into why. Save that for later. How are you Bill?"

The lines tightened on Hood's face. "Holding together." Something between a dry cough and a laugh followed it.

"Always the stoic, serious and unbending, eh Bill? What are you doing now?"

"I've got a new job starts tomorrow, as a matter of fact. Book-keeper for a man called Slattery. He seems to run most things round here."

A shadow seemed to fall across Ann's face. Impulsively she reached across to Hood's arm.

"He's bad news, Bill. Please be careful. If you hadn't just arrived, I'd tell you to turn round and go straight back again." The upset made her cheeks quiver.

Hood patted her hand. "I'll be OK. I'm only working for the man, in a very low capacity. Probably never meet him."

"Keep it that way." A savage, hunted look came over her face. Then she tried consciously to smile. "I'm sorry, you're quite right. You've got to work for someone. All bosses are bastards. Shall we drink to that?"

They both took a quick sip and then placed their glasses down simultaneously. Somehow this embarrassed them. To break the silence, Hood took up with: "And how have you been?"

"Oh you know - acquiring a fuller figure." She almost did a pirouette in her chair. "And I'm on the council now."

"No!"

Ann laid her hand flat on the table top. "Unbelievable, isn't it? But it just kind of crept up on me. I was unemployed, looking at four walls. Anyway every time a children's crossing was needed or a pensioners' club, I seemed to end up doing the shouting. So they elected me - the poor fools." She chuckled, as if she couldn't quite believe people could vote for her without being conned.

"I bet it keeps you pretty busy."

Ann nodded. "That was the idea, originally. Simply to get out of the house. But it's blossomed since then." Abruptly however, the optimistic flow dried up, and she took another quick, nervous sip of her drink.

Then she turned troubled eyes to Hood. "By the way, I was sorry to hear about your family. It all seemed to happen at once, didn't it?"

Hood sighed at the memory. "Thanks. Yes. It feels funny coming back and no mum or dad waiting above the shop. Or Marjory . . . " he didn't, couldn't, go on.

"You still look undernourished," Ann chided him to get over the moment. "I'll have to build you up with thick broths and . . ." Then she realised what she was offering and wanted to unsay it.

"Don't tell me you cook now?"

Unwillingly, Ann responded, joking, "Oh you'd be amazed. I keep saying things like that don't I? What's so amazing about a fat, middle-aged woman who drinks alone?"

"Hey, you're not fat. You were always beautiful. I remember seeing you in the ballroom on New Year's Eve, oh how many years ago?"

"Please Bill, you'll make me blush. And that's ancient history. I'm fat and relieved, to be honest, no longer to be competing to be glamorous."

And yet the tilt of her bandanna, the swish of her brightly coloured dress partly belied this. "And for God's sake don't say I'm still a fine looking woman. Eyewash."

"You'll never change to me." It was half truth, half lie. He found himself all the while he was looking at her, imagining her as she had been. It was as though he could compensate for the distorting mirror; he would find her just as she was, her large boned, powerful beauty.

"Buy me another drink, would you?" Ann asked him. "This one's all dried up."

"Of course." Hood picked up her glass and his own and went to the bar.

How strange, after all this time, and she still excited him like no one else. He must be careful how he acted with her. She might have a husband or lover tucked away at home. But he had to see her again. She was the only good thing left in this hard city.

"Ice?" Julie's voice cut in on him.

Hood turned to repeat the question to Ann. "Ice . . ." His voice tailed away. She was gone. On the table were left only two wet rings where the glasses had been.

He waited a little while, hoping she had only gone to use the ladies. But really he knew she had sneaked out at the back.

So much for romance. Well he wasn't the romantic type, was he? Still he wished she hadn't run away, out on him. Tonight of all nights. What an end to a beginning.

Chapter Three

Propping at the bar, slowly Hood downed his pint. There was nothing to stay for, now that Ann had gone. Suddenly the evening had gone flat. He realised how disproportionately much those few minutes with Ann had meant to him. He knew he mustn't build it up in his mind to be more than it was - a casual reacquaintance. And yet Ann bolting like that had lent it a dramatic frisson.

He wished she wouldn't put herself down, giving up on her appearance. Why had she done it? Being large-boned, in the past she had always fought to keep her weight down. It seemed deliberate, a rejection of her own desirability and of men. This public life of councillor; was it a fulfilling and adequate substitute?

He longed for further conversation with her. It was so long since he had enjoyed such an interest in another person, which wasn't the professional absorption with the criminal mind.

In the meantime however, he had an appointment to keep with the Assistant Chief Constable. Russell had the reputation of practically living in his office, and so Hood felt confident about calling on him at this late hour. Besides, he had had strict instructions to present himself on the same day as his arrival in the city.

He had no reason to stay at the bar, and yet he dallied. From where he stood he could see the table at which he and Ann had sat, and feel the afterglow of that meeting. Ahead with the Assistant Chief Constable lay the taking up of duties, the commitment to living and working in this city again. Only the thought of Ann made that palatable. He'd had other, personal reasons for returning but seeing Ann had made him question them. But he mustn't let her make him soft, or weaken his resolve. If he allowed that, his whole justification for living would disappear.

Pushing his pint glass away he nodded to Julie the barmaid and walked out. She snatched it up and stalked away, excitement and fear having ebbed away and resentment taken their place.

"Pig," she mouthed after him as he pushed the door open and went outside.

The night air had chilled, and whipped at his face as he struggled to find his sense of direction. He walked past row after row of terraced property, some boarded up with ugly green planks nailed across their windows and doors.

Then the road widened and the city's central square came into view. A splash of red across the sky appeared behind the town hall providing a garish backdrop. The new police headquarters was a multi-storey block of black-tinted glass and towering rectangular concrete columns. Whether intentionally or not it had an over-powering and sinister air.

Hood had been warned to avoid the large public entrance and instead found the hidden way in, at the rear near the car park. Pressing the security code buttons he waited for the door to spring open and went inside.

There were packages and liquid containers stacked up near the stairs, for this entrance was used as a dumping ground for deliveries. Hood headed up the staircase, wishing that the lifts weren't on the other side of the building.

At each floor he read off the number and panted. How often would Russell want to see him? It would crease him, to do this several times every week.

Eventually he reached the top floor and entered the hall leading to Russell's office. It was bare concrete, cold and draughty as if the decorators had forgotten about the top of the building. Hood shivered. It was like visiting the top of a multi-storey car park.

Bringing his breathing under control he rapped firmly on the door.

"Enter."

Hood twisted the knob and went in. Russell in full uniform, was sitting stiffly upright in a high-backed, black swivel chair. He gazed seriously at Hood, his face large and wide with a full, black beard. His eyes were questioning, a little misty, sensitive to any offence. Then he risked a smile, edgy, uncertain, almost raffish. He liked to show his teeth.

The desk in front of him was immaculate, a golden mahogany

on which sat several small piles of papers with no sheaf out of place. A virgin-white blotter in a leather surround sat at his elbow.

The flimsy partition office walls were covered with certificates, and visual planners which contained many little coloured arrows and markers. The wall coverings were so cluttered that Russell appeared cramped, hemmed in, by his own decorations.

Russell extended a hand. "Please relax and sit down."

Hood took the bare wooden chair facing the desk. "Thank you, sir."

Russell leant back for a moment and then pounced: "You took your time."

Hood stared back at him. "You said any time on the day of my arrival, and that is today. Sir."

Russell twisted to one side, and passed his hands over his eyes. "Yes, well all right. And you don't need to say 'sir' all the time. It's just that I judge a man by his keenness."

Hood let that one pass by, before coming back with: "I'll do the job for you to the best of my ability sir . . ." the word came out anyway, and Hood let it lie.

"Yes, well you come highly recommended, I can tell you that. And by God you're going to need to be."

Russell rose, and walked around his desk to sit on its corner. "I asked for you personally. I need someone I can trust absolutely. You will report to me, and me alone. Do you understand?"

Hood replied, "Yes," judging that a nod would be insufficient.

"Security on this one has to be airtight. It must be a closed operation. Every time I've moved against Slattery in the past someone on the inside has blown the whistle on me."

Russell, uncomfortable, rose and walked behind Hood, and then round to the other side till he was half looking out of the window. "But this time it will be different. Because I'm putting my own man inside: you. Under cover you will infiltrate Slattery's organisation and report your findings only to me. That way there will be no slip-ups, and you will deliver Slattery at last into my hands."

Hood sat impassive, wondering if all this was supposed to impress him.

Russell watched him soaking up the words like blotting paper. Finally he could hold back no longer. "You do know about Slattery?"

18

Hood nodded unblinking. Ann's assessment suddenly came into Hood's mind and he wondered if it coincided with Russell's.

Rattled Russell launched in: "I've made a study of the man. You see, criminal psychology is a speciality of mine. Slattery is a classic case of a gangster who has over-extended himself. He has interests in hotels, casinos, health clubs, massage parlours. All with legitimate façades. But underneath lies prostitution, illegal gambling, extortion, drugs, the whole works. I've waited a lifetime to nail him. He is the last big fish to catch in this particular pond."

Then Russell swung round, his face now grim and bitter. "If only they'd given me the resources earlier. Instead all I've had is endless carping from the Chief Constable. 'When am I going to get results? When will Slattery be put behind bars?' "

Russell's eyes were unseeing now, concentrated on his own stress and pressured career.

Gravely Hood said, "I won't let you down. I've a hundred per cent record. I always get them in the end. They say I put a sort of jinx on them."

Russell exhaled loudly. "You'll need to. Both our heads are on the line, with this one."

Then he wandered off again around the office, flicking through papers pinned to the wall, then moving off like a butterfly to examine a chart.

This irritated Hood but he tried not to show it.

Eventually Russell brought his attention back to Hood. "Well that's about it. You'll learn about me quickly enough. I give dedication and I demand it. I live this job twenty-four hours a day. It's not a job, it's a way of life to me, a mission. A moral crusade against the evils in society. Are you with me?"

"Certainly."

"That's my man. I knew I wasn't wrong. I'd back my judgement of people against anyone's. Well get started tomorrow, and keep me posted - any time day or night. But you must never be seen. Remember this is a closed operation."

Then Russell turned his back as if absorbed in thought, and Hood understood that the interview was over. He rose, went out, and closed the door behind him.

Then in the cold concrete of the hallway he let out his breath deeply and shook his head. Russell was either dedicated or

19

barmy, or maybe both.

What was it about Russell's tone and sentiments that made him squirm? After all he agreed whole-heartedly with any drive to clean up the city. So what was the matter? Guilty conscience? Maybe.

Somehow he couldn't bear to be on the same side as Russell. Perhaps it was the sanctimonious tone or the air of desperation. Whatever, there was a crack, a flaw, in Russell's façade. It reminded him of his own. That was the trouble. And it made him angry.

However, despite his feelings, he had a job to do. He only hoped that Russell put his support and commitment where his mouth was. To be abandoned, a scapegoat, to men like Slattery would be the end. They'd tear his heart out.

Chapter Four

Slattery watched Hood from behind the venetian blind of his office window. He'd always wondered what an undercover policeman would look like. It only surprised him that the police top brass had taken so long to think of it. He'd always suspected that one day this would happen. It was a good job his informant was so reliable.

He was tempted to go straight away and greet the new recruit personally, as he usually did. It would be fascinating to watch Hood dissemble and see how long it took him to try and wheedle his way into Slattery's confidence.

Hood was being introduced around the accounts office now. Slattery moved to one side and pressed down a spar of the blind to obtain a better view.

It was Hood's height and bearing that impressed him at first. The man looked to be well over six foot and carried himself like a commander. His saw-tooth, woollen suit was clearly not new but its cut and the way it hung were of fine quality.

Hood's long face intrigued him. It had a sort of ravaged handsomeness, as if marked by pain.

Despite the situation Hood seemed to betray no shiftiness or nervous twitches. He spoke to each person with polite dignity, gave a brief smile, and listened carefully. His eyes took everything in to their deep recesses, without being obvious about it. His high, strong cheekbones, a ledge beneath his eyes, gave him a hard, battered expression. His only tic was an occasional gnawing of his fleshy lower lip.

Slattery noticed the slow-motion grace with which he moved around the office. But a tension, an anxiety was also building in him, to find his place, his desk, and be still.

21

Slattery realised his quandary. It would be hard and regrettable if Hood had to be killed.

Then he saw Cobham the Office Manager slide across and introduce himself to Hood. Both men glanced towards his office and quickly looked away again. Slattery let the the spar of the blind drop. He was obviously about to become the topic of their conversation. Wandering back to his tilting, black leather, executive chair he lounged there, and let them get on with it.

Cobham, a florid, effusive man in his early thirties was leaning well over Hood, till the latter motioned him back a little. He wore an eager expression, his curly hair falling over his forehead in a quiff. His shirt sleeves were rolled up.

"I see he's not been out to give you the once over yet. Probably watching from behind those damn blinds."

Hood seized the obvious opportunity. "What's he like?"

Cobham clicked his tongue, searching for the right word. "Very . . . paternal. Likes to think of us all as his family. It doesn't do to resist that. I saw a bloke once at an office party refuse Slattery's offer of a drink. It didn't go down well at all. He takes care of everybody. Any personal problems, he's there. He can be very sentimental as well as tough. Personally I think he wet nurses this lot too much, but that's only my opinion."

"And outside work?"

Cobham was flattered and allowed himself even more time. Hood could sense that Cobham was unpopular and long-winded, and welcomed a newcomer with whom to become expansive.

"Hard to tell. A big family man. There are all sorts of stories about shady dealings but nothing has ever come near the firm here. To be honest I don't think he's got the energy to mastermind half of what he is accused of. Sleepy old buzzard whenever I've seen him. One foot in the grave."

Hood sucked his pen and became thoughtful. The silence lengthened as he looked into space. Eventually Cobham became uncomfortable and drifted off, expressing the hope that they could talk again soon.

Hood busied himself at his desk-top computer, which forestalled further meetings with staff. He wanted to acclimatise himself to his surroundings. Certainly Slattery had spared no expense in giving his staff a landscaped office, with desks, their rich wooden finish gleaming, in cosy clusters. There were head high, undulating partitions over which cheerful faces would pop up and exchange words. Potted plants flourished in warm corners. There was a pleasant buzz of activity.

The door to the main office swung open. Hood glanced away casually from his computer screen and to his astonishment saw Ann standing hesitant on the threshold. She wore a wide-spread yellow, PVC raincoat and with her swathe of blonde hair appeared like a ray of the sun.

Hood was dumbfounded, after all that Ann had said about Slattery. He longed to ask Ann what she was doing there.

But she purposefully set her sights on Slattery's office and marched straight ahead, not seeing Hood or anyone else. The Office Manager made a lame, half-hearted attempt to intercept her but she was already through the doorway to Slattery's office and slamming shut the door behind her. "Des, I have to see you."

She had caught him unawares, lounging in that swivel chair. She'd like to knock him out of it.

He turned his knowing, green eyes on her, a tinge of anger at their turned-down corners.

"Not now, not here." He smoothed down his carefully parted, silver-grey hair with his hand.

"Yes here and now. We've got to straighten things out."

"No. I'll call you."

"You always say that. You never do. How do you think I feel coming here with everybody watching?" Ann's head was tilted back to show off the hurt to her pride.

Reluctantly Slattery climbed out of his chair, with the nimbleness of a long, lean body that was in good shape, enviable for a man of sixty. "I don't know what you want of me."

Ann's face became urgent. "Get me out of this mess. Only you can."

"You exaggerate. I'm only a businessman."

Ann snorted and her face filled with baffled fury. "You can have whatever you want - as always." She stood hands on her hips, legs splayed.

Slattery eyed her, lust and distaste fighting it out behind a dispassionate gaze. Quietly he said, "We can't discuss it here. What would the staff think? I really will call you. Now you positively must leave."

He took her arm and opened the door for her. In a clear voice he announced, "Mr Cobham will see you out. I'm sure we can find a solution to your difficulty."

Reluctantly Ann allowed herself to be ushered, her cheeks burning, out of the main office.

Slattery paused in the doorway, looked around, and his gaze alighted on Hood. He swung round to face him. "Do forgive me. I've broken my principle of always greeting new employees personally. Please come inside." And he stretched out a welcoming arm.

Stiffly Hood rose and walked across the room and into Slattery's office. How did Slattery know Ann? It had taken all his resolution not to acknowledge her and intervene.

He went and sat on the opposite side of the desk from Slattery.

"Welcome aboard. I desperately need a mature person with sound book-keeping experience, I can tell you. All this new fangled computer stuff is beyond me, I confess it. But meat and drink to you, eh? Good, of course it is."

"I'm just finding my way around the system at the moment."

Slattery beamed, as if to remove any insinuation of a criticism. "Of course you are. Take all the time in the world - as long as the books balance at the end of the month." He laughed again, a hint of nastiness there.

"Oh I always get it right in the end," Hood assured him. "I never give up till I have."

Slattery nodded approvingly, while massaging the back of his neck. "If there's any training . . ." the phone rang, interrupting Slattery's flow and irritated he picked up the receiver. He listened, and the irritation was massaged away. "Of course darling. If you've promised the children then they must go. I'll drive them myself if necessary. Yes, look I've got to go now, we'll talk later. Yes, love you too." - "Grandchildren." He mused fondly.

Then he looked at Hood again. "Well, I think that about takes care of everything. If there's anything you want, you know where to ask."

"Oh yes, I know where to ask."

Hood stood up and walked out.

"Shut the door behind you, there's a good chap."

24

Slattery was then left alone. He exhaled and walked over by the far wall, leaning on a filing cabinet.

He should never have permitted Hood into the business. He felt a premonition of disaster. The man was hungry for a conviction. No softness there. Hood couldn't be bought off.

It was like having a caged animal in your own home. Some day Hood would break out and run amok.

"Damn him." A red line was forming along the ridge of his forehead. He kicked the bottom drawer of the filing cabinet.

Things had been going so well. He was at the top. His business was flourishing and provided for a growing family of sons-and daughters-in-law and his grandchildren. They all looked to their papa.

He could afford to take things more easily now, drift gently towards retirement - if it weren't for people like Hood nosing around.

It was no good, something would have to be done about Hood and quickly. Then he smiled, broader and broader. He had the perfect excuse.

He knew of someone else, an important client, who would like to see Hood taught a lesson. Very well: one lesson could serve both their purposes.

Reaching for the phone he dialled and waited. "Hello, Joe? I've a job for you. A warning. A working over, nothing too drastic - yet. Man named Hood, just started here. That's it, yes. Keep me posted."

Replacing the receiver, he stood and thought for a moment. Was he being hasty? Some people wouldn't like it if Hood was to disappear so soon. It might look suspicious.

But Joe knew his stuff. He wouldn't go too far. Hood would still be able to crawl into work. On his knees, where he belonged, the dirty spy. Revulsion filled Slattery. He didn't know if he could stand it, letting that man sit yards away from him in the outer office, plotting his downfall. Every move he made, every letter, every phone call would be seized upon.

An image gripped his mind of Hood strangling him, slowly, till he was choking unable to breathe. All his family were standing around, watching, helpless. What a nightmare!

Hood had certainly got under his skin. This was a battle of wills. He mustn't let some second-rate police nark get the better

b

of him. He must win - it might be the last great battle of his life, to safeguard his empire. He must have something to pass on to his grandchildren.

Chapter Five

Sitting alone in his room after work, Hood had time to brood. It was something he worked at, something to which he devoted a lot of time. Because in these periods of intense quiet and solitude he could build up a sort of pressure, and concentrate his mind on his enemies.

Like Slattery. He would be an elusive target, with his vicious charm and iron paternalism. But the secret to Slattery was in the changeable quality in his eyes. One minute relaxed and fatherly, the next defensive and panicky, the next hard and vengeful. The man was on the run - from himself and his own empire. But he would fight a tiger of a rear-guard action, with all the cunning it had taken to build it up.

Hood needed a picture of him - maybe from police files or the newspapers. He always worked with a picture of his quarry. That way he found he could know better than the man himself the way he thought, and anticipate.

Hood passed a weary hand across his face. That was enough of Slattery. He stood up, stretched, and switched off the light beneath the tasselled shade of the standard lamp. Then he walked up and down beside the long sofa by the wall. The chocolate curtains at the far end hung heavy and uneven, blocking out the moonlight.

He hated the thought of Ann resorting to a man like Slattery, for whatever reasons. She had strode in like someone making herself do something abhorrent. She was a disappointment. After all these years to come back and find the only person left he cared for, so gone to seed. Her hair was a sandy-coloured mop without texture or shape. And her girth.

He couldn't understand it. In the old days she had been

besieged by admirers. That was partly why he had accepted her loss philosophically. He had assumed a better man had won. Evidently not.

He sighed and walked over to the empty bookcase, forlorn, and then on until his back was to the electric fire.

But if others were a disappointment, what about himself? What had he achieved, coming back? He was starting from scratch again in this bug hole, in the city which was the scene of his past failure.

Only once a day, maybe, did he permit himself to use that word of his past life - because it was so true. And yet it had not been his fault. But somehow that didn't diminish the pain.

From being a community leader, with a family and roots he had become a refugee, run out of the city.

Somehow, after resisting tooth and nail every inch of the way, the final defeat had been all the more shattering. It would have been better to have avoided the conflict and never taken them on. His parents, his wife Marjory had all said that. They had maintained no good could come from a protracted struggle against enemies who were invisible but malevolent.

However he had to go all heroic, with talk about standing up and being counted; letting the rest of the community see that he could not be pushed around.

And he and the family had all stood firm - for a while. But they found that you can't live in fear for ever. Being hated eats away at you until finally you crumble. Or until, like Hood, you can feel only hate in return.

Every day, at certain times, he could feel it coming on, the hate. His jaw would set, teeth clench and his forehead tighten as if someone was twisting a cord around it. His breath would come fast and his chest heave and a pain would settle in, low down.

He thought of it as his 'hate pain', the trigger that reminded him, lest he was forgetful of the cause for which he was living now. And yet in all this time, despite his best efforts, he had never discovered the identity of who he was hating.

He could imagine, put various faces to the enemy, but he didn't know.

It gnawed at him so badly sometimes, he felt he would go out of his mind if he didn't find out. Returning to the city, to save his sanity he must find the answer.

Hot pain was reaching up his back now. He felt behind him, and realised his legs were scorching from the electric fire. Quickly he jumped away and massaged them, trying to smooth away the discomfort.

Soon it would be time to leave for The Newsroom. It was strange that he had begun spending his evenings there. Thank goodness he had never taken Marjory. He didn't think he could stand being reminded of their time together.

He thought of Marjory, with those dark humorous eyes and the lashes which could flutter over them so provocatively. Her short, swept-back black hair, which waved like a plume either side of her clear white parting. Marjory, with her tall full figure. And her arms, curvaceous and tanned, ready to embrace him.

She had all the kindness, warmth, and fun to give. With her he had even learned to laugh at himself, not to take himself so seriously all the time. And he had let her go, for a principle. No, that was too grand, too easy; for his pride, a cussedness, a refusal to admit they were beaten, a willingness to let hate and anger and fear devour them. Or rather him, for she pulled out before, she said, it engulfed her too.

At the time he had railed against her, called her coward for selling them both out, chicken, weak . . . but now he would have given anything not to have said those things, to be able to take them back.

Because those words, more than the enemy, had destroyed their marriage. She would never forgive him, and he didn't blame her. He couldn't forgive himself either. The enemy had achieved more than they ever probably anticipated - they had destroyed the love between him and Marjory.

How could he ever put it right when he had so degraded her? Accusations like those he had made were not retractable. They stood for ever, an indictment, between them. What use were protests now,that he had been wrong?

He wished he could get his hands on those who had done this to him. He'd make them suffer. He'd lost the love of his beautiful Marjory. What could be worse than that?

His hands twitched to retrieve the gun from its hiding place beneath his clothes, third drawer down in the bedside cabinet. He longed to do something desperate with it, turn the gun on someone, press the trigger, feel the relief of the explosions. Blow someone's head off. But who?

It was hopeless, a sick, vindictive fantasy, full of self-pity and disgust. He must escape his own company, get off to The Newsroom. Loving, working, talking were the only things that helped when he was in the depths of despair.

Chapter Six

Later that evening found Hood, calmed down, leaning on the bar of The Newsroom nursing a pint of bitter. His sheepskin coat sagged open, under which he wore a ribbed, cream Aran sweater and warm brown wool trousers. His shoe rubbed back and to on the polished gold foot-rail below. Despite himself he was early. He supposed he should count himself lucky Ann had agreed to meet him at all. But he'd badgered her over the telephone until she said yes.

He still couldn't get over the sight of her as she had swung through the office to see the very employer, Slattery, she had warned Hood against.

And why did she drink regularly in The Newsroom, at a table which could not be seen from the entrance?

He longed to know more about her, but at the same time did not wish to be drawn into mutual confessions. About the story of his own life he preferred to keep silent.

Looking down the bar, he could see no sign of Julie, the rude barmaid. Either it was her night off or she had been sacked, because a thin, tired man with an anxious expression was the only staff around. The barman wore striped trousers and a frayed shirt, open at the neck.

Hood found that he missed the rude one; it would have been a challenge, a bit of excitement to cross words with her again.

"Another beer please," he called down the bar.

The barman jumped guiltily and moved from the spot where he had become rooted. He hurried to fill the pint, spilled some, and hastily placed it before Hood.

Taking a sip Hood wondered if all this was the effect of his own personality, but he saw the same pantomime repeated with two regulars at the other end of the bar. Each time the barman was aroused as if out of a trance, and then there followed suspicious movements as if he were covering some heavy secret.

The light in the pub was diffuse, spreading from the orange glass covers over the imitation gas lamps attached to the walls. On high shelves all around Hood noticed rows of faded hard back fiction, without dust jackets. He laughed to himself as he pictured a newcomer entering the pub and finding total silence with everyone immersed in one of those books. Except of course that they were too high up for anyone to reach them.

Instead customers had to make do with reading the play-bills and framed newspaper pages on the walls.

Though renovated it seemed that parts of the pub might have simply slept in their original decor ever since Edwardian times. It was a nice thought anyway. Hood wondered who in the past had watched their own reflection in the large tarnished mirror with its huge gilt frame.

Then in the mirror he saw Ann. She startled him yet again, for revealed beneath her open coat was a pink sari-style dress with voluminous folds. She had a pink bow in one side of her hair.

Without a word she walked straight past him and down to the table at the far end. This time Hood noticed how the seat she took abutted onto a green and cream pillar, a colour scheme which was repeated round the far wall. In the corner nearby was a gas fire hidden behind a mesh cage. Unpredictably it would suddenly whirr into life and emit hot air in suffocating waves before clanking to a halt again. Up above a fan droned.

"Gin and tonic, please." Ann let her suede coat fall from her shoulders and rest on the chair back. Then she adjusted the long sleeves of her dress, and the top so that a fold of fabric covered her neck.

Hood returned with her drink, and sat down, his own drink opposite hers on the table.

She sipped and said, "I nearly didn't come. But when you want something, you don't let up do you?"

She smacked her lips. "That I do remember from way back."

Hood leant away on his bar stool and looked at her, then around them. Why did she dress so exotically? She couldn't have done more to draw attention to herself. And yet then she insisted on sitting in the most out-of-the-way corner in a back street pub.

32

Ah well, he'd learned to be patient over the years. One day he'd find out the whole truth.

"I wanted to see you," Hood said simply.

"Cobblers. You wanted to know why I appeared in Slattery's office this afternoon. Oh I saw you, lurking in the corner, thinking I hadn't noticed you."

Hood shrugged. "OK. So what's the story?"

Ann looked away. "I don't know if I should tell you. But what the hell? Since when did I have any privacy in this city. I went to Slattery for protection. He's the only one who can guarantee it around here."

She took a long sip of her gin and tonic and asked for another. Hood signalled to the barman. He didn't want to break her concentration. For her brow was furrowed and the callous and caustic note in her voice was changing to something more plaintive.

"Do you know what it feels like to be hated?"

As Hood nodded, she put her hand up to prevent him agreeing too quickly.

"I mean really hated, to the marrow, and down the years. A sort of unrelenting obsession. I've lived with that - well it seems for almost as long as I can remember. I suppose it must have begun in the misty days before I took up politics, but that was the turning point."

As the barman reappeared with another drink, she reached for her glass knocking the tonic bottle sideways. Hood caught it and set it upright again. Ann watched him sagely, waited then continued.

"I mean there I was, middle-age spread staring me in the face, and nothing but the four walls for company. So one day I said to myself, 'listen girl you've got to get out and make a life for yourself.' So I became involved in the local school, then the hospital, and before I knew it was elected councillor."

She grinned, proudly for the first time. "Me. I never thought I could pull it off. I was popular - at first. Got pedestrian crossings laid, things like that. But then there were changes at the town hall. Suddenly one lot were out, another lot in - leather jacket poly-technic lecturer types. And oh how you had to toe the hard left party line, or else."

She could see that she had Hood gripped, and smiled again in

33

grim satisfaction. "Well it's become very nasty indeed. I can't begin to tell you the stunts they've pulled - the abuse, the intimidation. I'm even frightened to go to council meetings. For two figs I'd jack it all in, but there's a few old dears depend on me. And hell, why should I? I was elected, wasn't I?"

Hood leant forward and gripped her hand. "I'll do anything I can to help. You know that."

Ann smiled gratefully through tears. "You were always like that, a rock to depend on in the old days. I've sometimes wondered over the years what would have happened if I'd encouraged you, if we'd got together."

Hood smiled and then winced in memory. "You threw me over, I remember that. I never really knew why. I was . . . well let's say hurt."

"One day I'll tell you, but not now. Anyway you were probably better off with Marjory. I thought you two were a fixture, so right for each other."

There was a pause then Hood said, "So did I."

"Do you want to tell me about it?" Ann placed both her hands over his. Her large oval eyes swam with sympathy.

"I can't," was dragged out of Hood.

Ann nodded in reproof. "You were always the same. Kept things bottled up. You'll have to unload one day, or you'll burst."

Hood shook his head. "I'm OK, I can cope. As long as I can function, get the job done. Then it doesn't matter what happens to me."

Ann became angry and shook his hand with her fist, to and fro. "Of course it matters. Don't you think I've wanted to lie down and die sometimes? But I don't, I get dolled up outrageously and I go on the town. A poke in their eye."

"And you end up in the corner here, where you can't be seen from the door."

Ann glared at him, then put her hand on her hip contemptuously. "That's not a very gallant thing to say. OK so sometimes I prefer some peace and quiet and my own company. Go on beat it, if you want to."

Hood stared back at her. "I never said I wanted to leave."

"No, that's right you didn't." Then her eyes fell, with an appeal to him. "Bill, will you take me home?" Then before he could answer she wafted her hand as if to remove a misapprehension.

34

"Just as a right guy? You see I'm frightened every time I leave the house. I'm afraid while I'm out, and I'm afraid of what I may find when I get back. Will you come in with me and see everything is all right. And then say good-night?"

She looked upwards and there was desperation in her eyes. "God, what a way to have to live! Terrified of leaving your own doorstep. This is what they've reduced me to. But not for much longer. I'm doing something about it. I don't know what yet, but something."

Hood placed his hands on her shaking shoulders. She was swaying so much he wondered if she was about to have convulsions.

But eventually the distress subsided, and Hood pulled up her coat from the back of her seat and placed it over her shoulders.

Then he guided her in front of him and through past the stained glass front door.

So her enemies were doing the same to her; turning that old familiar screw, waiting for her to crack and give way, another victim of their remorseless pressure. Well, he was back to put a stop to all this.

All right, so there was only himself - and Ann. But revolutions had been started with as few such people. If only his under-cover work wasn't such a drawback, with the secrecy it required.

And then he thought again. Had he learned nothing from the past? He remembered all that he'd said to himself earlier in the evening, in his lonely room.

Would he be doing Ann any favours by encouraging her to resist, and supporting her? Wouldn't she just be hurt all the more in the end, the way he had been?

But against every lesson he thought he'd learned, Ann's appeal stood and couldn't be ignored. She wanted and needed his help.

What was he supposed to do?

Then again, could this hate campaign against Ann be the same people who had driven him out of the city those years ago? It seemed far-fetched and yet the similarities could not be ignored or wished away.

Ann and Bill stood together on the chilly street corner as the wind whipped around their legs.

"If you go with me down here I'll fetch the car," Hood suggested.

Ann looked up and down the street. "It'll take ages, with the one-way system. It'd be quicker to walk."

Hood gave in and took her arm. At a good pace they followed the way round the bottom side of the city square. It seemed to Hood that Ann was putting as much distance as possible between herself and the town hall opposite.

The white lettering was slipping off the red brick pub farther along, and then they were passing the end of the pedestrianised shopping area. The wind blew paper bags up and down it, cheerless in the empty cold evening.

"Heavens it's nippy," Ann commented, pulling her coat more firmly around her.

"Sometimes I dream of living in a warm climate. I even got brochures once. Cyprus, Malta. Somewhere like that. It'd be wonderful, wouldn't it?"

Her face looked years younger, wistful with longing, and Hood felt himself falling in love with her all over again.

There was that unusual combination of sympathy and spirit in her eyes. When the fear left her mind, she sailed along head back, hair blowing in glorious profusion, bright colour to her cheeks.

Hood nodded, then asked, "Why not get away? Maybe not abroad, but somewhere, where you'd be safe and appreciated. I did - for a while." He wondered if he was such a good example to quote.

Ann cast him a quick sideways glance as they strode along. "But you couldn't keep away for ever could you? This is my home. I've always lived here. Why should I be driven away? Besides - I tried it, did what you said, for a short while. I was no better off. Wretchedly lonely. Scared the men off as usual. So in the end I came back. Better the devil you know, I suppose."

Hood gripped her arm more tightly. "You could try going away again." He longed to add 'and I could help you,' but he couldn't throw up his work here, when he'd barely got started.

Ann shook her head sadly. "No, I'm sorry Bill. I'm stuck here for good or bad. But it was a nice thought. No one's cared about me like that for a long time."

Embarrassed they both then looked away and plodded forwards.

They were on one of the avenues leading from the city centre now. Sooty trees lined the verges and the terraced property

36

seemed to stretch for ever, broken up only by the occasional corner newsagents and fish and chip shop. Like racing cars the traffic roared past the windows between one set of traffic lights and another.

On end of terraces huge hoardings displayed advertisements or were derelict, unlet boards.

Off-licences appeared regularly like watering holes. Video hire outlets, petrol stations and take-way restaurants dominated the neighbourhood. The residents might not get any peace, but they'd hardly be lonely or uncatered for.

Hood was beginning to wonder how much farther, when they entered a pedestrian underpass, a huge concrete semi-circular pipe.

Disgorged from the other end they walked along by the canal for a little while. The railway bridge arched overhead, then they cut down a back entry and found the street where Ann lived.

The terraced houses were set well back from the road, each with its own low wall fronting on to the pavement. The houses had two bay windows with a cream coloured slab beneath each.

The date '1909' had been set by proud workmen into the brickwork of the end house.

Some were well kept with varnished oak front doors, tidy gardens, and shiny ornaments in front of fresh, bright curtains.

Others were down-at-heel, with overgrown gardens, rubbish piled up in heaps, peeling front doors, and furniture jammed against windows. Two were completely boarded up.

Hood felt Ann tense as they began to walk up the street. Instinctively he grabbed her arm. She was trembling. The colour had drained away from her cheeks, and she looked steadfastly forward so that he could not see her face.

"It's just up here, number 27," she managed to say, trying to preserve an appearance of equanimity.

Her pace slowed, fearful of what she might find.

Patiently Hood walked with her to her garden gate. He could see one or two strange black marks on the lower brickwork of the house, but otherwise it looked perfectly normal.

In fact the front door appeared brand new, and the window frames had recently been replaced.

Ann looked up at the house with a mixture of pride and fear. She walked down the path and pulling out her key from her bag inserted it in the lock.

Hood heard her intake of breath, saw her pause to gather her nerve, and then she went in over the threshold. That seemed to decide her and hastened her into action, for she was then gone for several minutes.

Hood lingered on the doorstep, feeling awkward and redundant. He was about to set off when she appeared again in the doorway, beaming with relief.

"You can go now, Bill. What a silly woman I am. Everything is fine. I'm sorry to have worried you, and dragged you all the way here. Would you like a hot drink before you go?"

But he could tell the offer was only made in gratitude. Soon her euphoria would be replaced by dog-tiredness.

"Some other time. I'm glad to see you home safely. I'll be off now. See you soon."

Ann nodded, grateful. "Yes, thanks Bill. Tonight's meant a lot to me. Really." Then she shut the door, happy to be inside and secure, for the moment.

Thoughtfully, Hood set off down the street the way he'd come. Then he shook his head. He knew all the symptoms by heart - the nervous expectation, the palpitations, the fear of what she might find when she arrived home. He knew it all so well himself, from years gone by.

But what could he say to her? Everyone was different. She might crack under the strain, she might not.

He'd be the last person to undermine her confidence or will to survive, but on the other hand he knew the effect such long-drawn out attrition had on people.

Slowly he turned at the end of the street, down the entry and headed for the underpass. The concrete bunker seemed waiting to swallow him up.

He had progressed half-way down, when two men advanced towards him. Hood shrugged and continued, but his intuition warned him about their bulky and aggressive stance.

When he was feet away from them, they stopped.

Both wore thick black leather bomber jackets with metal studs and tassels. Their hair was cropped short, and razored half-way up at the side.

One reached across and grabbed Hood's lapel. "We have a message for you," he sneered. "Stay away from Ann, if you know what's good for you. Go back to where you came from."

Hood wheeled away and slapped the man around the ear. The other ran forward, head down, and butted into Hood's midriff trying to bowl him over on to the ground. But Hood backed with him, his height enabling him to keep his balance. Then with both fists he smashed down on the man's head. His assailant collapsed onto the ground.

But his friend had jumped Hood and was hanging on to his shoulders. Hood swung this way and that, but couldn't dislodge him.

The other man, picking himself up off the floor, let fly a punch which caught Hood on the cheek, almost breaking the bone. Then finding Hood still not down, frustrated he began furiously kicking him, pell-mell, lashing at his vulnerable legs and thighs.

Enraged, Hood suddenly swung his head down and catapulted the man from his back on to the gravel. This obscured Hood from the other assailant, giving him time to run for the far exit. His battered legs felt as if they were on fire, as he made them go faster and faster.

But still his two attackers were gaining on him. The tunnel seemed to go on for ever. Hood glanced back behind him and could see the two men's faces eager to work on him again.

This incited him to make one final effort as a street lamp came into view at the far exit. He could hear the pounding feet behind him. But he forced his body on till he emerged into the night.

If only he could make it through to the traffic and lose himself. The men were racing towards him. But with a final effort he flung himself between two lorries and then dodged around a weaving motor cyclist till he reached the other side.

Turning he could see the two men, winded, watching angrily from the other side of the road. They'd given up.

Turning again, Hood staggered away.

Chapter Seven

Hood stumbled along, his sense of direction gone. His body was sore all over from the mauling he'd received. His jaw hurt from where the punch had landed, throbbing like the worst toothache he remembered. Around his stomach the muscles felt all knotted and constricted where the head butt had caught him. His thighs and legs felt scalded with the imprint of weals left by vicious kicks.

How bitterly ironic that under-cover he had suffered a worse beating than in any police raid. But who had set those men on to him? Slattery? It seemed too obvious to be him.

Who else knew of his arrival in the city? Perhaps a secret lover of Ann's had seen them together in The Newsroom. Jealousy could have exploded into violence.

Anyway, the thing to do now was not to speculate fruitlessly, but find his way home.

"Never a taxi around when you need one," he complained as he tried to find his bearings.

The roundabout he had just passed seemed familiar and if he took a left fork . . . He tried this, and hit a dead-end. Retracing his steps was painful and he cursed his bad luck. This time he tried a road almost parallel to the first, and found he was heading across the city centre shopping precinct.

Apart from two down and outs camped in a shop corner swapping bottles, he was alone. They hailed him but he ignored them and continued on.

Eventually he came out by the red brick pub with the broken white lettering. The town hall stood majestic, its flag fluttering, across the square. At the far end was the Police Headquarters, but that could offer him no help or comfort at the moment. It was

40

frustrating to have to pass it by and continue on skirting The Newsroom pub until he finally had his flat in sight.

His legs hurt so much he thought they must cave in beneath him as he limped the final yards to the front door. Then he pressed inside and dragged his screaming frame up the stairs. Fumbling with his key he let himself into the flat.

Without even bothering to find the lights, by touch he felt his way into the lounge and collapsed on to the sofa. Its hessian covering felt rough against his face but he didn't care. Just to take the weight off his body, to let it mould itself to the cushions.

In the dark he lay letting his body have its say, letting the pain seethe out of it and the bruises form.

So this was what his return to the city had let him in for. He grimaced, but even that change of expression hurt his jaw.

One side of his face felt as if it were on fire. He must take something for it, whatever the pain of getting up.

Stumbling across the room he switched on the light and then went through to the kitchen. He found some pain-killers in a jar kept by the cereals and swallowed a couple down. Without water he almost choked on them but finally they slipped down. Then returning he searched in a cupboard for a bottle. There was a half of whisky left. Knowing he shouldn't, he nevertheless took a swig on top of the tablets. Anything, to assuage the pain. He needed relief. He was desperate.

Lying back on the sofa he tried to empty his mind, but still it kept questioning away. Who was behind the attack? Ah, it was hopeless. He was in no state, or frame of mind, to find out. Nor, working under-cover, could he use his police contacts. He was hamstrung at every turn.

All he could do was lie there, licking his wounds. It was infuriating and embarrassing, that those two thugs should have given him such an effective working over. But if he ever got his hands on them again . . . he'd break them, crush them into little pieces, make them wish they'd never been born.

The room was stuffy. The chocolate curtains had a dusty, sickly aroma of their own. He leant on one arm. Were the tablets beginning to work? His jaw seemed to be numbing a little. Maybe that was the whisky. The shooting pains through his body also seemed to be less frequent.

He'd perhaps manage to drag himself through to the bed in a

minute. Then over-night he'd give healing a chance.

The phone rang. He waited, was going to ignore it. But then suppose it was Russell or someone important like that. He cursed again and forced himself up in a sudden harsh movement. Then like someone shackled he staggered across to the occasional table and picked up the phone.

"Yes?"

"Bill. Thank God." It was Ann's voice, high pitched. "Please, you must come over. I'm so . . . help me."

Hood switched the phone to his other ear. "Slow down, Ann. What's the matter?"

"Outside, men are swarming all over the place. I just know someone's on the roof. They'll be in any minute. Oh Bill, what am I going to do?"

"Call the police. Ann, I can't come over. I'm bushed. Honestly. Are you sure it isn't some lads just fooling around?"

There was a pause then a wail. "Bill! Don't you understand? I can't stand it. They're after me. They'll overrun the place. You must come now. I only want you. The police would just laugh at me. I know them."

"Ann, I . . ." he tailed off. She'd never believe he couldn't make it. Quickly he finished: "I'll drive over. Be there in a few minutes. Sit tight."

"Thanks Bill." It was the most heartfelt gratitude he'd ever heard.

All he needed to do now, was to force, to cajole his protesting body into the car.

Behind the wheel of the Volvo Hood tried to sit up straight and not tense his stomach muscles. But the effort sent pains up his back, and his arms ached from gripping the steering wheel.

Ann had been right when she said that via the one-way system it would be a long way round to her house. Hood found himself skirting the back of the Law Courts, past two schools, then along the ring-road which ran alongside the brewery with its big shiny, steel tanks.

He was forcing himself to concentrate and forget the pain, but his anticipation was acute as he peered out looking for the pedestrian underpass and railway bridge as signposts.

Frantically he yanked the steering wheel as he threatened to overshoot the turning and get caught up in the next section of the one-way system. That would have been too much, to go all the way round again.

Reducing the Volvo's speed to a crawl he entered the end of Ann's street. He wound the window down. The breeze had dropped now, and all he could hear was the distant rumble of traffic and the odd car horn.

He parked a few houses down and climbed out. There was no movement on the street. Perhaps these men Ann spoke of, were round the back.

Stealthily Hood moved down a side entry and worked his way along behind Ann's house. Everywhere was quiet. A cat nimbly crossed along the wall in front of him and down.

He walked up the garden path, looking carefully to left and right, but nothing. Little tufts of dock leaves and nettles clustered at the edge, and a rhododendron bush was sprouting in the corner.

He advanced up to the back door and knocked. "Ann, it's only me, Bill. Can you open the door?"

There was a scuffling sound and then the door opened to reveal a dishevelled wild-eyed Ann. She peered out past him, looking into the night. "Have you seen them? They could still be out there. Come in quickly, Bill."

She almost dragged him inside and shut the door behind him. The smell of washing soda assailed him, a childhood memory, and made him queasy.

He followed her inside to the living-room. There was a pine bureau against the rear wall and matching bookcase full of cookery books. The wallpaper was a light blue textured pattern and the theme was continued in the floral cotton covers of the three piece suite. There were lamps everywhere. Two provided up-lighting in corners; there was a strip-light over a painting of a Spanish village scene and there were spot-lights in the other two corners of the room.

In the centre of all this, like an illuminated target stood Ann. The concentration of white light made her look ashen. In vivid contrast she wore a red, ribbed cardigan and black ski pants.

"Are they still out there? Did you see them?"

"No, I saw nobody. Why not sit down. You're all right now."

Ann sat on the sofa with Hood beside her. She put her hands to her face.

"It was awful. They were swarming all over the place. I

43

thought they were going to come through the doors or windows any minute. They kept calling me horrible things. Horrible."

Hood looked about him and through the window. "Well they're gone now, whoever they were."

Ann stared upwards, the tears drying on her cheeks. "You keep saying that. You must have only just missed them."

"Yes."

"Bill." Her tone was brittle. "You do believe me, about them? I'm not making it up."

Ann jumped up and stood with her back to the electric storage heater.

"Can't you say anything but 'yes' and 'OK'. All right, I'm sorry I dragged you out if you're going to be sulky about it."

It was Hood's turn to be stunned. "Who said I was being sulky? I'm here, aren't I, though I feel like grim death. I answered your call. But there's no trace of anyone. You said you were in terrible danger."

Ann put her hands on her hips, her eyes fiery, glaring down at him. "I didn't invite them, you know. When gangs of men come surrounding the house, surprisingly enough I find that pretty scary. Of course I wouldn't expect a man to understand. All you men stick together."

Hood began to feel picked upon and used, and gave a long sideways glance of helpless incomprehension. "Hang on a minute. Don't bracket me with everybody else. I've just taken a beating on your account." He'd promised himself he wouldn't mention it, and regretted the moment it slipped out. But he couldn't take it back.

"So that's my fault as well? Always the same. I remember in the old days, you blaming me, telling me where I was going wrong."

He should have known he would get sarcasm not sympathy. It was his turn to rise, his shoulders braced. "Well it's a pity you didn't listen, isn't it? I have heard some pretty unsavoury rumours about you since I came back."

Ann walked straight up to him, eyes blazing. "What rumours? If I've a past, I've earned it and paid for it. I'm not ashamed of anything I've done."

"Not even of being a slut?"

Ann heaved back and slapped him hard across the face. The

44

pain shot like a fiery band across his jaw. He staggered, yelling out.

"There. And good riddance. Coming in here, after I asked for help, and calling me dirty names." Angry tears began coursing down her cheeks.

Hood forced himself to raise his head, even though it felt as if it was coming off.

"You ugly old bag. You don't think I could care for you now, you fat tub of lard. Take a good look at yourself in the mirror. You disgust me."

"Not half as much as you disgust me, raking that up. I know what I look like. And something else - I couldn't care less. I stopped worrying what men thought of me ages ago."

"Oh yes but you'd let them pay. That crowd outside - is that what they were waiting for?"

Ann stood back from him and surveyed him with contempt. "All because you can't have me - though you'd like to. You'll never change. You're a woman hater and cruel with it. Deep down you're a coward and a failure. Go on, beat it. I never want to see you again."

"Never would be too soon," Hood growled, and fingering his agonising jaw stepped back through the kitchen and out into the garden.

No wonder she planted nettles. They must make her feel at home.

Chapter Eight

As he drove back to the flat Hood's mind was in turmoil. While his pained body jarred at him, the same question harried away at his brain: how could it have happened? How could a mission of mercy have been transformed into a barrage of insults?

The spacious car interior felt lonely; the dashboard suddenly foreign to him. Even driving itself seemed an alien, strange experience as if he might suddenly forget how to do it.

He mustn't crash the car; that imperative thought kept hammering away at him. Get home, that was what mattered. Once there he could go over things, make sense of them, find out how he'd let things go so wrong.

Wearily he followed the one-way system round, noticing the landmarks mechanically in reverse order to earlier that evening. Somehow the schools, brewery, warehouses all seemed to be ugly, forbidding hulks against the night sky without beauty or symmetry.

When he parked outside his flat he flung the car door open and jumped out without bothering to lock it. Who would want to steal that heap? he thought. If they did, they were welcome to it.

Once inside the flat he poured himself a whisky and sat in the armchair. The lamp behind him gave a fuzzy illumination to the room. He must get some books for the bookshelf, he reflected. His mind needed occupying and reading would help.

He sipped at his drink and sighed, long and deep. His left side felt stiff and bruised and he tried to decide whether it was pain or simply fatigue working its way up.

How could he have repeated to Anne all that smutty talk he'd heard about her in the office? He hadn't meant to do anything of the kind. His intention had been to support and comfort her. And,

46

what else? He thought this over. Was there more, some ulterior motive?

He tried to remember, to reconstruct his intentions from earlier. As he worked his way back, a realisation came to him. Despite, or maybe because of, his injuries he had thought he would bed her. It was as simple as that. The whole evening had been a prelude, leading up to it, and her call had only reinforced that impression.

It had been self-delusion to think he only wanted to help and reassure her. But it had not gone that way.

Somehow her hysterical manner had put him off. And all these men pestering her. If they did exist. Why? Were they like bees round a honeypot? That is what had sparked things off, that impression.

He twisted to one side, but the thought was unavoidable. He had been jealous. The thought of all those men queuing up for her favours was unbearable.

Yet she had protested her innocence, maintained these men were part of some hate campaign. He had conveniently forgotten that part. If it was true, he had let her down more terribly than he could ever have thought possible. But all he could think of was her and disappointed clients.

What was he to her, and what did he want to be? Certainly not a client. That disgust which riled up in him when he was with her, boiled up again. If she, the only person left from the old days in this city, had been corrupted too, he would despair. He felt that in such a case he wanted to punish her, kill her for what she had become, for letting him down finally and inconsolably.

And yet with another part of his mind he saw the unfairness of all this; treating Ann as a scapegoat for all his accumulated disappointment and frustration with life,

She who had seemed to represent a possibility of renewal, survival, had turned sour on him. But it was his own fault. He had demanded too much, acted as judge and jury on her without giving her any real chance.

Why was it that he always seemed to destroy those he loved for not living up to his expectations? Hell-fire, he didn't live up to them himself, so how or why should anyone else? He groaned and buried his head in his hands. What a God-awful mess.

Why was he so angry that she was not the same as before, but over-weight, cynical, suspicious? Was it because she reminded him that he wasn't the same either? That he had let himself and everyone else down until he had been able to stand it no longer and fled the city all those years ago. If so, he shouldn't pick on her, but on himself. Well, the gun was waiting.

He swallowed his spittle. That damned gun. He was sick of thinking of it and what he might do with it. If he had any guts he'd throw it away.

Then he stiffened in his chair. No - it had another use. He was saving it for the man who had directed all that hate towards him five years ago. And when he'd found him, he'd let him have it, and damn the consequences.

Hood rose and prowled the room, easing his joints. What an unsavoury customer he had become. It almost surprised him that people couldn't look inside him and see all the deep-seated murderous urges, the hate, the distrust, the self-disgust all churned up together like some evil-smelling brew.

There must be other ways of living besides his lonely, obsessive, vengeful one. Ann seemed to offer an alternative with her sensuality, flamboyance, all the things he missed and craved. But he had thrown them back in her face, miss-applying his so-called principles. Haggard he wandered back to face the door, indecisive. The words he had spoken to Marjory had destroyed things between them, could never be rescinded. It looked as if history was repeating itself with Ann.

Could she ever forgive him - how could any woman? Oh why did he keep doing this?

It was too much, he had to go out before he started banging his head on the walls. No matter that his bones ached and his bruises cried, he had to go - anywhere.

Donning his sheepskin coat again, Hood stumbled out into the night. A fine drizzle had set in and walking along was like taking a shower. But he didn't mind; anything just to distract him and make him feel connected to the real world out there.

The Newsroom was all locked up and the lights dim as if they were doing their last clearing up. He passed by the smoked glass windows and felt a yearning for the quiet emptiness that lay within.

But he realised that inside he would have been alone with Ann's ghost at that far isolated table, which would only bring on the horrors again.

So he steadfastly went on till he reached the corner of the city centre square. The Police Station was to his right. Even if Russell was still there, what could he tell him? He had only been on the job a day. Russell could hardly expect results in that time.

No, he was driven to move on, skirting the square, the rain plastering his hair to his skull. But he felt better; the water seemed to refresh him, and clear his head.

At the far end of the square stood the Law Courts, dark and shut, all judgement suspended for the day. Then beyond them were department stores and furniture shops. He passed in front of their windows but could work up no interest. He had no home to furnish, no one to share a home-making.

Instead he moved off again, his foot scuffing some paper boxes in the gutter. A light in the building on the opposite corner caught his eye.

It was sandwiched between an Estate Agent's and an Insurance Office. Then he remembered from the old days: the Labour Club. Why, he had frequented it in the past. He even had his old scruffy membership card somewhere.

The light attracted him, and he saw that the door was open. He dragged himself up a flight of stone stairs, then entered a linoleum covered corridor.

Through a glass door he came upon an open area and hesitated. A table with leaflets and a coin box stood to one side. Behind it on the right was a door, and on the opposite side another.

Trying to remember the geography, he took a chance and opened the right hand side door. It was a smallish room, empty, with a bar on the left. There was heavily scarred and cracked wood panelling on all three walls, and bench seats covered in scuffed purple upholstery followed the walls round.

Limp, green cotton curtains hung at the windows on the far side, and there was a large maroon carpet with a geometric design.

High backed wooden chairs with smooth green coverings stood arranged round five, black ash tables.

The marks of wear were evident everywhere - on the chair backs, the panelling, the fraying and finger marks on the curtains. This was a room used by no-nonsense men, who liked to rest weary backs and knew no delicacy of touch.

c

Cigarette burns were indented on the table tops and made black marks on the carpet.

A man appeared behind the bar, polishing a glass.

"Can I help you? We've just closed you know."

Hood turned to face the man. He was smallish, with thick arms around which was wound elastic to hold up his shirt sleeves. His stomach was pot bellied and he wore a fat kipper tie over it. His face was large, his jaw quite long, and his eyes were alert, lively, outgoing. Slicked back dark hair receded from his forehead.

"Oh come on. I've just dragged myself up all those stairs. I'm beat. Just one drink."

Bouncing back and to on the balls of his feet, the man looked first doubtful then grinned. "You are, and all." Then he was suspicious again.

"Are you a member?"

"Got my card here somewhere." Hood fumbled through his wallet, searching for the dog-eared piece of card, probably out of date by now. Still it was worth a try.

But the man was waving him to put it away.

"OK. But don't make a song and dance about it. One quick drink and then that's it. Bitter?"

"Thanks." Hood's chest heaved. He really needed that drink.

The barman had put the newly cleaned glass under the beer pump. He glanced up for a second.

"My name's Charlie. I'm on here most nights."

"Bill," Hood replied. "I'm just back in the city after a spell away. Thought I'd look the old place up." Charlie nodded and taking Hood's money passed the pint across.

"Used to be a regular here? That must be a while ago. I've been here, oh how many years?"

"It was," Hood agreed hastily, and took a gulp from his pint.

He looked up to see Charlie beaming appreciatively. "You look as though you enjoyed that. I like a man who likes his pint. Between you and me, some who come in here, I don't know why they bother."

Hood leaned on the bar, drank, and thought for a moment.

"I suppose you know all the regulars?"

Charlie nodded. "Like I said, I'm on most nights."

"You on the committee or anything?"

Charlie shook his head and began to mop the bar. "No, not me.

You can keep all that heavy political stuff. It gives me a headache. I'm happy as a barman, that's all."

Hood took another drink. "I know what you mean. Politics can bring a lot of grief."

"You said it. You should hear my wife go on sometimes. She's really keen. It's like a party political broadcast in our house some nights. Leave it out, I say. Give us some peace. But you know women." He winked, and pulled himself a short from the whisky optic. "I think I'll join you. Want to hear some funny stories? I've got a million of them."

Inwardly Hood winced but forced himself to smile in encouragement. He laughed at two ancient jokes and that seemed to satisfy Charlie.

"You're all right Bill. Some come in here, chins down to the floor, dead miserable. I can't be doing with that. I say, if you want to be sad stay at home. Leave your troubles there. This is just a good place to meet, the beer's cheaper than the pub, and you can get a decent game of pool. So forget the politics and enjoy yourself. That's what I say."

Hood nodded. He was nearing the end of his drink, and couldn't easily prolong his visit. But he hadn't learnt much yet.

He wandered across from the bar and looked up at a photograph on the wall.

"What's this?"

Charlie followed his gaze and then turned away again dismissively. "Our glorious ruling group on the Council."

Hood looked closer then laughed. "Whose the sour puss in the middle?"

Charlie didn't need to look again. "That's Monica Rigby, leader of the Council. She's my wife."

Hood almost spat out his mouthful of beer.

"I'm sorry Charlie. No offence."

Charlie waved away his apology, solemnly. "It's all right. I agree with you. God, if she would just lighten up. It's politics all the time with her. Another Council meeting tomorrow night. She won't be home till gone ten. Plays havoc with your home life. I tell you, sometimes it's like screwing the parliamentary Labour Party."

His vulgarity came with a twinkle in his eye, and Hood laughed good naturedly with him. "Well anyway, Charlie, you

51

don't seem to let it get you down."

Charlie looked straight back at him. "You can't, can you? My old dad always used to say, 'don't let the bastards grind you down,' and I don't intend to. Keep your pecker up, ducking and diving and a little bit of what you fancy does you good. Get my drift?"

The clichés were coming steadily but Hood felt no inclination to demur. Charlie had raised his spirits; for that he could forgive a lot, even third-hand platitudes.

"Well Charlie, I've got to go now. I'm dog tired. Thanks for bending the rules and letting me have that drink.

"My pleasure. Come in anytime, and ask for Charlie."

"See you."

"Bye Bill."

Hood replaced his glass on the bar, and went out of the door. Then it was down the corridor and carefully navigating the stone stairs. The drizzle seemed to have ended, and Hood breathed in the freshened air. Charlie didn't seem a bad chap. Bit over-talkative. And those awful jokes. But he was good entertainment value, and he might well eventually turn out to be a useful informant. But all in good time.

He was pleasantly tired now, and felt better than he had all day. For once he should sleep without rocking.

Chapter Nine

Next day Hood found it hard to concentrate on work. His mind kept harking back to Ann and last evening, and his desperate need to put things right. But he had barely a minute to himself, and certainly no time or opportunity to contact her. A few times he looked at the telephone but then rejected the idea. She would only put the receiver down on him. No, he had to see her face to face.

Meanwhile Slattery seemed to be keeping his distance. There had been no comment about Hood's bruised face and pained movements, though he was sure his colleagues had noticed and were whispering about it behind his back.

He was beginning to become familiar with the accounting system and how Slattery's business empire worked. Each part had its own balance sheet and financial target. It was Hood's job to monitor expenditure and flag up any excesses or losses.

It all seemed above board. In fact Slattery seemed to be adhering to all the best accounting practice. If there were any shady deals going down, then Slattery was making sure they were well disguised and went in the books as legitimate transactions. The odd thing was that Slattery, although keeping largely to his own office, was not particularly secretive or absent. There were no hurried phone calls to eavesdrop or disreputable-looking visitors quickly ushered out. Slattery himself did not disappear unexpectedly for undisclosed meetings. He was circumspect. His diary was practically an open book.

In fact Hood was despairing of getting any evidence against him. But he knew that soon Russell would be jumping up and down expecting results, and Hood would have none to show him.

It was imperative therefore that he turn up something. He had to stay in the city. He had promised himself to find out who was behind the original hate campaign that drove him away, all those years ago. But there was another reason now: Ann. He couldn't walk away from her troubles any more. She was becoming part of him, maybe the only good part, and he couldn't throw that away.

After work he called at Ann's house but there was no reply when he knocked. Disappointed he drove back to his flat. There he ate a steak and potato ready meal. But parts were not cooked through properly and he ended up throwing half of it away. Then the hours seemed to drag by and he soon tired of sitting staring at the walls. He wondered at one point if the fire was giving off a strange, over-heated odour but after investigation decided he must be imagining it. The weather had been milder with occasional showers and so he donned his anorak and headed for The Newsroom. He was vaguely hoping that Ann might happen to come in, so that he would not have to convince her to meet him. But when he entered, there were were only a few regulars and the surly barmaid Julie he had encountered on his first evening. This time she wore a blue blouse with ruffles down the centre and a tight black skirt which buttoned up the back.

"Pint please."

"Give me time," she muttered over her shoulder as she moved a box of crisps along the floor. Then she straightened up and saw who was speaking.

"Yes - sir. Would you like it in a glass or over your head?" But she was grinning.

"I'll take it anyway it comes."

She pulled him a pint and passed it across.

"One for yourself?"

Julie nodded and took some coins from his outstretched palm. "Thanks. You're a funny fella."

"My friends think I'm downright hilarious." Hood took a gulp of his drink.

She put her hand on her hip and cocked her head to one side. "No, I can't figure you out. I don't think you're on the make with me but there's something. Here, you're not a copper are you?"

Hood spread his hands wide. "Me? Do I look like one?"

"Dunno. But you have a funny habit of weighing people up. Gives me goose-pimples."

"It's my strange power over women."

"Likely story. Buy me another drink later and I'll tell your fortune."

"I already know it."

"You're no fun. I could change it for you."

"I bet you could, at that."

She went away to put the money in the till and Hood took the opportunity to find a seat in one of the booths. She was getting a little too near the truth with her lucky guesses and he didn't want them broadcasting. The paint was flaking off the top of the table, and he picked away at a strip with his nail. Then conscious of what he was doing, left it. His mind needed occupying. He thought Ann might still arrive, but as the evening wore on he realised it was a forlorn hope. The clock above the bar showed nine-thirty. Then he remembered. Was it Ann or Charlie had told him? There was a Council Meeting that night. It should be breaking up soon. If he hurried he might intercept Ann, coming out. Rising, he gulped down the last third of his pint, and placed it back on the bar.

"See you."

Julie glanced across at him. "Off already?" There was a tinge of disappointment in her voice and then she dismissed it. "Don't fall under any buses."

"I'll try not to. Kindness to a customer?"

She winked at him and laughed low but raucous. "That'll be the day. See you."

Hood grinned and then went out into the night. It was mild but clear and dry. He left his anorak half open and strolled round the square. He cast his eye over the red brick of the town hall, with its grey slate roof and entrance archway like a church. Lamps, set among the shrubbery of its gardens, illuminated the building with an orange glow. Its central clock tower cast a giant shadow across the square.

As he approached he noticed a handful of hangers-on around the foot of the town hall steps. He joined them, happy to be amidst a throng for a change. He caught the ends of political gossip but the names mentioned meant little to him. Then a council porter in purple livery appeared, and people began spilling out through the revolving doors at the top. It became a stream, then a torrent like a football crowd swarming away from a match. He spotted Ann's face, half covered by a violet head-scarf, bobbing up and down in the crowd. Then she appeared to stumble and disappeared for a moment. Hood pressed forward to help and be near her. She seemed to half right herself, then he heard her say, "Stop it, get off. Don't push me." Then she went down again, and Hood saw a man spit over her. It landed on her head-scarf in an ugly wet mark. A fist came down on her shoulder and she cried out in pain. "Help somebody. Get them off me." By this time Hood was wrenching his way through the crowd and then was standing over her. He glared at the silent men around him.

"You cowards. Come on, who wants some of this?" He showed his fist.

Then a woman's voice called out from higher up the steps, "What's all this? What on earth is going on?"

Hood, like everyone else, looked up. There stood a smallish woman, fair haired, late thirties, with a pinched face, spectacles and wearing a duffel coat over black trousers. She seemed irritated, annoyed, and effortlessly had their attention.

Ann meanwhile was freeing herself and straightening up. "You ought to know," she told the woman.

The other proceeded down the stairs with a surprising lightness of step.

"I don't know what's been going on. Are you all right?"

Ann stared up into her face, angry and defiant. "Just about, Mrs Rigby. After your bully boys have stepped and spat all over me. Scum," she burst out.

Monica Rigby came down the last few steps to face her. Her face was drawn and little lines formed across her cheeks. Hood could see the grey of tiredness under her eyes.

"I'm sorry if you've been hurt in any way, but this has nothing to do with me. You'd better watch who you're accusing, because my patience is wearing thin."

"You!" Ann moved towards Monica then thought better of it. "You . . . dried-up stick of a woman. Getting these men to do your dirty work. Picking on other women. I don't know how you can sleep at nights."

Monica turned away. "I don't have to stand here and listen to this. I've made it clear that I have no truck with intimidation of any kind. Is that enough for you? There's no use getting hysterical."

Ann then lunged at Monica and in the nick of time Hood

56

sprang across to keep them apart.

"Mrs Rigby, isn't it? I think you'd better leave. I'll take care of Ann."

As Monica's friends led her off she called back, "You'd better. She needs putting away, accusing me. Everyone knows her background."

"Why, the little upstart. She says these things because no man would look at her except that good-for-nothing husband of hers. And he skips in and out of other women's beds. So there!"

"Ann, for God's sake stop it. Let her go. Don't make an exhibition of yourself."

Ann snarled. "She's one to talk. It's all true." Then she recollected who she was with. "Where did you spring from? And let go of my arm. Last night I said all I was going to say to you."

But Hood hung on to her grimly. "That's as maybe. But I've not finished with you. There are things I want to say to you, if you'll just get down off your high horse and listen."

"I don't seem to have much choice. Now let go of my arm."

They walked on a bit further along the square, and Hood released her. She massaged her arm. Then she began rubbing her back and elbow where she'd been punched.

Hood was concerned. "Any damage?"

"I'm just checking. No, I don't think so. But it hurts like hell. Those louts. This happens after every Council meeting. How can I stop them?"

"I'm sorry I ever doubted you. I was blinded by - well jealousy."

Ann gave a hard laugh. "It's a bit late now, isn't it, after what you said last night? The names you called me."

"I did, and I shouldn't have. I could tear my tongue out. You're above all that."

Ann regained some of her composure and dignity. "Oh, so you recognise that. I'm not some slut, some piece of dirt? You despise me but still come pawing after my body."

Hood looked down. "You're quite right. I've treated you abominably. All I can say is sorry. I want to help."

Ann's resolution failed her and tears came from her eyes. She clung to Hood. "Oh why did you have to say that? Look what you've made me do. All for a little kindness."

"I know." He held her close.

Then she grasped his anorak tightly. "This isn't a trick is it? I couldn't bear it if it was." Her eyes were staring wild, desperate, in appeal. "Tell me you'll stay, that you're not going to disappear or ignore me in the street."

Hood looked straight down into her eyes. "No, I'm not going away, and I won't desert or deny you. You have my word."

"Thank God." She was shaking. "Take me home, would you? If I don't get there soon I think I'll fall down. It's the reaction."

"Sure. Be home soon. And this time I'll make certain there are no men waiting. You'll be quite safe."

"Thanks Bill. What a turn up, seeing you tonight after last night. Maybe my luck's about to change after so long."

"You can count on it."

Hood only wished he could be as certain as his words implied. However, looking at her, he knew he must do something. The strain was taking an awful toll on her. She looked grey, weary, and there were marks on her face. She'd been through more than anyone could reasonably stand.

Chapter Ten

After several days on Slattery's case Hood felt complete frustration. He wasn't getting anywhere. Working under cover only hamstrung him.

He couldn't apply his talent, with the technique he'd perfected over the years. Hound your enemy; get to know him as well as you know yourself. Wear him down by constant vigilance. Follow his movements, dog his footsteps, exploit his weaknesses, his fears, until he is practically begging to confess to you. Hood knew all about the art of psychological warfare. Some criminals swore that he had put a hex, a voodoo on them as if he had stuck pins in their effigies.

He used to say to them: "Why prolong the pain? You know I'll get you in the end. The waiting must be terrible. Confess and it's all over. It'll be a relief, back in prison with all your mates. Like old home week. And no more me breathing down your neck."

But he could use none of this on Slattery. He had to stay a polite distance from his boss; never interrogate him, only try and draw him out. He had to be self-effacing, humble. And that was what really hurt.

He was losing his identity, his self respect; a stool pigeon, an office hack trying to get the goods on his boss. Russell would have the glory. He, Hood, would probably be shipped quietly out of the city afterwards.

But this was pure speculation, for what did he have to show for his efforts? Hearsay, stuff which Russell himself could have picked up around the city's pubs and clubs.

Slattery's leisure empire apparently fronted for drugs, extortion, and prostitution rackets, but he had always managed to distance himself. Fast on his feet, that was Slattery by all accounts. They said he had the 'teflon' factor - nothing stuck. It seemed there were some very highly placed people behind him.

To survive and prosper in this city it was essential to be on good terms with Des Slattery. His social calendar was full, at least until recently. Some wondered if his health was failing.

Hood was sensitive to the thinness of his report. But he couldn't put it off any longer: Russell was waiting for him.

The city square was bleak and empty as he crossed it, to be swallowed up in the Police Headquarters building. The lights were dim on the stairs, and his heavy footsteps echoed as he trudged ever upwards.

When he entered the office, Russell was peering gloomily out of the window. It was streaked with rain and misting up.

"Ah Hood, and not before time. Sit down."

While Hood took the stiff-backed chair in front of the desk, Russell returned to his watching. What was he hoping to learn about the city spread out below, Hood wondered? While he waited Hood turned his attention to the desk opposite With amusement he saw that Russell had acquired a neat red plastic 'desk tidy' to hold his pencils, rubbers, pens, paper clips and rubber bands. Everything today's modern policeman needs, Hood mused.

Then Russell slowly turned and walked stiffly over to his desk. He sat down and the thick black leather upholstery creaked. He moved his buttocks to get comfortable, and it creaked again. He searched Hood's face for a smirk, but Hood managed to remain deadpan.

Russell clasped his hands out in front of him. Hood watched the knuckles going white. After a few seconds Russell was compelled to ease the grip to allow blood circulation.

"Well what have you found out?"

Hood went through his general knowledge of Slattery's business interests, his circumspect behaviour, lack of public meeting with unsavoury characters, and the model state of his accounts.

Russell laid his hand flat on the desk and scowled as Hood finished. "So in fact he's whiter than white, and we've nothing on him." Petulantly, he turned sideways in his chair. Hood could see the dark hurt in his eye, and the careful trim of his full black beard.

60

"I didn't say that. It's clear that Slattery uses his leisure outlets as fronts for many illegal activities. But finding evidence is a different matter. The man seems to have made a life's work out of being careful. He leaves no loose ends hanging around."

Russell swung towards him again. "Then it's up to you to find some. Gain his confidence."

Hood's face went stony. "That's easier said than done. Slattery is very particular about who he confides in. He spends most of his time with his family. Recently he's been socialising less." Hood paused before going on, wondering if it was wise but felt compelled. "Besides, he may be on to me. A few days ago two thugs jumped me, tried to beat me up, and told me to leave the city. They could be from him."

Russell's face was horror-stricken. "How could Slattery be on to you? You haven't told him this, accused him of setting them on to you? I hope you're not losing your nerve."

Hood shrugged his shoulders impatiently. "No, of course not. But I think it must be a strong possibility he was behind it. If so, I might just as well pack my bags right now."

Russell took offence at Hood's decisive tone. Wagging a finger he said, "I'll say when it's time to pull you out, and not a moment before. The very idea. Your defeatist tone disappoints me. This is a rough city. A couple of thugs pitch into you, and you jump to all sorts of conclusions. They could have had other motives. Are you telling me everything?"

Reluctantly Hood responded, "They did say I should steer clear of Ann . . . Renshaw."

Russell's eyebrows went up. "Ann Renshaw?"

"Yes, she's a councillor and an old friend of mine from way back. We had a couple of drinks together, that's all."

Russell began fingering his beard, playing with the tufts at the bottom. Then he smoothed it out.

"This is very indiscreet, Hood. She's a well known person in the city. I should say notorious. Do you know her background?"

"I think so."

"Oh do you? Well let me put you straight about her. For years she worked as a common prostitute. We had several runs in with her. It's rumoured she was, and still is, on Slattery's stable - though God knows she's getting past it. How she ever got elected with that record, I'll never know. But there it is. Stick well clear of her. She can only do you and us harm."

Hood fought not to argue with his superior and defend Ann's name, but the colour was rushing to his face. "I thought it was good for my cover to take up with her. And as she knows Slattery, she may prove useful in gaining information."

Russell was becoming tense, irritable, and began taking items from the 'desk tidy' at random, twisting them in his fingers.

"You can use her as an informant without going to bed with her."

"I think that's most uncalled for. My private life is private."

Russell stared back at him, slack jaw sagging. "Oh do you? Well you've no private life while you're under cover. Just you remember that. And I'm telling you to keep your distance with the Renshaw woman. She's nothing but trouble. If you let your relationship with her jeopardise this operation I'll break you. Is that understood?"

Hood scowled back. "Yes, sir."

"Good. Well I suggest you get back out there and start doing more of what you're paid for. The information you've brought me tonight I could have picked up in any bar in the city. You'd better get into gear on this one, and start digging. That's all."

Dismissed, Hood stood up, saluted and left. By the straightness of his shoulders and steadiness of his tread, he tried to convey the contempt he felt for his treatment by his superior officer.

Russell gnawed his finger nail as he gazed at the door now slammed shut. He could imagine Hood striding down the stairs, cursing him and determined to do his damnedest to prove his superior wrong.

Why was it the man made him feel inferior, as if their positions should be reversed? He had as good a record as Hood, better. In fact if he hadn't been held back, he could really have modernised policing in this city. But no one listened to him; the phone never rang. He was isolated up here, with no support from the top. And always there was that 'glass ceiling' to his promotion.

He shifted in his seat and then stood up. Well no one was going to edge him out of this position. If they'd only give him the resources. But one under-cover man: Hood.

Besides their whole tactic was wrong. He'd lived with Slattery's presence for years. He'd understood his every move; he was predictable, known. With Slattery in place crime had set and limited dimensions; remove him and you left a vacuum which syndicates of organised crime would surely fill.

One old fashioned gangster, a bit of a gentleman, he could cope with, live with. But the unknown; quite frankly it terrified him. The syndicate might be the ruin of him. Better the devil he knew. So let Hood burrow around, wear himself out fruitlessly, and then Russell's superiors would realise he was right in the first place and bury the investigation.

Uneasily he paced, trying not to let his certificates on the wall catch his eye. OK, so it was tough on Hood, but he'd had to import the best, to make it look good. Hood would get over it. He was made of steel, he endured, his face showed that.

What was he feeling guilty over Hood for? Hood had taken up with Ann, hadn't he, and no doubt would disregard Russell's warning over her.

Hood and Ann. He felt his scalp tingle. Gripping the side of the desk he took deep breaths. Them together. He tried not to imagine it, but the cruel image forced itself on him. He gagged as if under torture.

That slut, that prostitute, he cursed. But then he relaxed into terrible yearning. Ann from all those years ago.

Why did her name have to keep cropping up? Why did his crusade against prostitution in this city have to target her?

She who had teased him, stroked his beard, let him take her to dances and for walks by the lake. Ah those walks and tea afterwards. It was heartbreaking to think that was all the love he was ever going to get, if you could call it love.

One kiss. He remembered it, under that spreading willow tree in the park. He'd caught her off-guard; maybe that had been his only chance.

But he could tell she didn't really respond, return his passion. And then a week or so later it was all over. Him forgotten in favour of other lovers, light-hearted with easy manners.

How could a few weeks of bliss, so many years ago, be so indelible? Many things had happened to him since, advancement in career, new colleagues, but he couldn't forget her. He didn't want anyone else, even though he'd seen what had become of her.

If only she'd come to him, at any time over the last few years. He'd have picked her up out of the gutter, treated her as a lady. But she never had; instead she'd gone to people like Slattery and done them favours and their friends and clients, which she had so firmly denied him.

Why not him? What was wrong with him? He took out a mirror he had hidden in a drawer. He examined himself full face, then each profile. He liked to think he had an authoritative appearance, his beard gave him an earthy masculine air, his eyes had warmth, he had no scars. His features were in proportion - what more did the woman want?

Slamming the mirror down, he scowled, then his lips twitched in despair. He must get a hold of himself. Anyone might come in.

He pushed the mirror away in the drawer and pulled out some papers to lay on his desk.

It was as if he'd introduced them, Hood and Ann. He'd brought them together. If Hood were her salvation instead of himself he'd - blow his brains out.

Whether consciously or not Hood seemed determined to outdo him. First his woman, then no doubt his job. He barked a laugh. Hood as Assistant Chief Constable. He returned to gnawing his nail. The trouble was, it could happen.

The Chief Constable was easily impressed. Suppose against all the odds Hood pulled it off and nailed Slattery.

Who would receive the credit, the glory? Not him, his superiors would see to that. No: Hood would be the hero of the hour, succeeding where Russell had failed all these years.

Hood must not succeed. Russell clasped his hands together and tightened them over his desk. If necessary he'd break Hood - fine man or not. This was survival time.

Chapter Eleven

For days Hood worked hard at keeping Slattery's books, rein-forcing his cover. He was going to nail Slattery - for Ann's sake now that he had discovered how she'd been abused.

Then after work there was tea alone. A tin was warmed up on a ring and then eaten on a tray in his armchair. He was thinking of buying a TV to overcome the boredom.

The phone rang. He picked up the receiver from the occasional table and, mouth full of spaghetti, spluttered, "Yes?"

"It's me, Ann." Her voice sounded desperate, choking.

Immediately Hood cleared his throat and sat up, tray balanced awkwardly across his knees. "Yes Ann, what is it?"

"I'm sorry Bill. I tried not to phone, not to bother you. But I just can't go on."

With one hand Hood put down the tray by the side of the chair. "That's OK. What's happened?"

There was a silence, as if Ann were trying to gain composure and then an exhalation of breath before she resumed: "It started on Monday. A man rang and said they were going to come round this week and finish me off - set light to my house with me inside it. I was terrified. I rang the police. They've watched the house off and on ever since but they can't sit out there 24 hours a day, seven days a week." She gulped, "It's Thursday Bill and I'm at the end of my tether. It's the waiting, knowing that they'll come. I can't sleep. I can't eat. I think I'm going mad."

Hood wanted to hold her and comfort her, but it was so frus-trating to be on the end of a telephone. "I'll be right over. Don't you worry, we'll think of something. I won't let them get you."

"You'll come over now?"

"Yes."

"God Bless you. I didn't know who else to turn to."

"That's what friends are for. I'll see you in a few minutes."

"Please hurry." Then Ann rang off. Even though a few minutes could hardly be crucial, she longed for his reassuring presence.

Hood replaced the receiver and stood up. Then bending down he took the tray through to the kitchen, and placed the dishes in the sink. They could wait.

Then going into the bedroom he pulled on an old brown corduroy jacket over his grey pullover. Finally picking up his sheepskin coat off the hook behind the door he was ready and set off.

He was becoming used to the drive and managed the journey in a few minutes. The long street in which Ann lived was deserted. There were several cars parked up and down it. The library opposite was shut. One or two street lamps were out of action. That was normal. An electricity sub-station gave a monotonous background hum, but otherwise there was no sound.

He crawled the Volvo along and then manoeuvred its wide girth down a side entry near Ann's house so that it would be inconspicuous.

Then he climbed out and walked back to her house. Again he looked around him, but there was no sign of anybody.

If only he could drop his 'cover' and organise a police stake-out. They could use infra-red cameras, and put the searchlight on these bastards and frighten the life out of them. Turn the hunters into the hunted, that was the technique and he'd never known it fail. But he couldn't use it, and he clasped and unclasped his hands.

Then it struck him: he couldn't but Russell could - and would. At their next meeting Hood would somehow extract an undertaking from Russell to protect Ann. He nodded vigorously to himself and felt a little better about his part in all this.

Then he knocked. Within seconds Ann's face peered round a crack in the doorway, then she opened the door fully. Quickly she glanced up and down the street and ushered him inside.

Even in the dimly lit hall Hood could see the toll all this was taking. Her eyes seemed sunken and rounded by grey rims. Her clothes hung baggily and she was stooping.

They embraced and she led him inside. It was so cosy that no one could have imagined that she was the object of violent threats.

She pulled her hand through her hair. "I must look a mess. Still who cares, that's not important now is it?"

"No of course not. You look fine," he lied.

She leaned against the table that stood beside the wall near the window. Along its edge nearest the wall, were lined up little ornaments: figurines. animals, and delicate Chinese wood carvings under glass. Pride of place was held by a bonsai tree, a firm and perfect specimen in miniature.

"What am I going to do Bill? Sit here and wait? If I go away I don't think I could stand the thought of coming back to a smoking ruin."

Hood tried to stay calm and sat on the sofa, hoping this would encourage Ann to do likewise. "I'm sure it won't come to that. They're probably bluffing. But I'm here now and we can see it through together."

She looked at him gratefully but still troubled, with reservations.

"Yes, but for how long Bill? I can't expect you to sit here with me for ever, holding my hand, listening for every sound outside. That's how I spend my time now. Pathetic isn't it?" She turned away but there was fire in her cheek rather than tears.

Hood was glad to see her pride and anger flare up. "It's nothing of the kind. You've borne up amazingly. Most people would have given in long ago."

She looked at him ironically. "Believe me, I've thought of it. Throwing it all in. Telling the doctor I need help. But I don't and I won't." Then she laughed at her own sterling speech. She stopped.

"Don't stop," Hood told her. "You keep right on going. That's the spirit. We'll show them."

Ann wandered across and impulsively stroked his head. "Oh that's just bravado and you know it. OK for a few minutes but you can't keep it up hour after hour, day after day. That's where they've got you. You never know when they will strike - except that they will. They can choose the time and the place."

Hood grabbed her arm and pulled her half down towards him. "We'll fight them, we'll find a way."

Ann locked his eyes with hers, watched his hard pupils, his irises grey-green. "You mean like last time - when they drove you

67

out of the city?"

He relinquished his grip on her arm and she came and sat beside him. It was cruel but true. Who was he kidding?

"Tell me about it Bill. You never have. What really happened, back then?"

Hood turned to her. "You're sure you really want to know? It's not a very pretty story. I thought you'd been depressed enough."

"I'd like to know Bill. I'm a big girl. You can't dishearten me any more than I have myself. I'd like to think we'd shared similar troubles. It would help me. Really."

Hood took a deep breath. "Well OK, if you're sure." His mind went back; he could picture the shop, its lettering, its shelves, the peculiar smell of wood, oil, of rags stained with turpentine and paint.

"Well, we had the shop. That is Mum and Dad started the business. Then when Marjory and I married we largely took over the running of it from them. When I say shop, it stretched way back like a little warehouse. We stocked everything the handyman could ever need. This was before the big chains really took over the market." Mentally he walked those passageways again, saw the shelves piled high, the check-outs, the motors and heavy tools piled against the walls.

"At first we thought we were unlucky. Overflows, blocked drains, raining in, electricity cuts, that kind of thing. But then it seemed to fall into a pattern, every few weeks." He sighed and it hurt him to remember, to continue.

"I was active at the time, like you in the community. I suppose I offended a few people but nothing had prepared me for what followed. There were threats, dead animals left outside the premises. Broken windows, disgusting messes left inside. Then my parents house was burgled, they were threatened, my father hit over the head in the street."

Hood looked down, the pain livid across his brow. "I don't think he ever really got over it. Anyway, a year later he was dead. I think they killed him. Mother lingered on a few years but she was never the same after he died." He thought of that single, marble headstone and the grave he couldn't bear to visit.

"I talked big talk with Marjory, lots of bravado as you call it. But all the happiness was drained from our marriage. I could think of nothing but fighting them, hitting back. But it was all empty. How can you fight an enemy who never reveals himself, never ever says why? To this day I don't know who was behind it. I have suspicions, but I don't know." He ground out the last word and Ann saw how this ignorance had tortured him.

"Anyway, Marjory talked of being sensible, keeping our sanity and selling up the business. But I was adamant. No one was driving me away. So we argued. We were at loggerheads. She stood it as long as she could in this hate filled atmosphere and then she left. She said I'd become a monster and she couldn't live with me. Then they'd really won."

"Don't Bill." Ann put her arm around his shoulder. "You were no monster, you couldn't be. Stress does strange things to people. They cope in different ways. It was just sad that Marjory's way was different from yours."

Hood's head came up, his handsome, square features anguished. "But why did she go - and why did she never come back? Never contact me. That was what really hurt. Because I threw in my hand in the end anyway; sold the business, moved away. She could have joined me. Why didn't she?" He was gnawing his fist.

Ann embraced him more tightly. "I don't know Bill. Did you ask her?"

In comforting him, Ann felt happier, more fulfilled and released than she had in months. And as Hood looked at her he saw, though harrowed, the younger Ann shining through.

They nestled down together on the sofa, temporarily forgetting the terrors and dangers outside. The blue floral pattern covers felt smooth and snug, like a bluebell glade. Minutes went by and both tried to prolong this hole in time, this oasis.

Together they curled up, silent, daydreaming, enjoying the warmth and security of the other.

But Hood was getting pins and needles in his arm, and reluctantly had to disturb Ann. She straightened up and stretched to relieve a kink in her back. They found themselves returned to the real world, spell broken.

"What a pity!" Ann murmured, "I was just getting to like it, curled up with you beside me. I suppose I'd better make some tea for us. Like some?"

Hood nodded and flexed his right leg. While Ann was through in the kitchen, he surveyed the room. She'd done her best to cheery it up, with all the lamps, the Spanish painting, the knick-knacks, the bright pine furniture. Her home put on a brave face as she did herself. How cruel that it should be under threat, siege. Ann was reluctantly at war, her home the battlefield while millions lived in peace.

She returned with two mugs full of tea and passed one to him. Then like sentries they settled down to drink and wait. During the evening Ann occasionally offered to put on the radio or TV, but they both preferred the silence. It seemed at least to intensify their togetherness.

All the living-room lamps were on now, while it was pitch black outside. Ann was trying to read a magazine, while Hood was staring into space.

Ping. Hood turned quickly like a dog sensing a cat nearby. Where had it come from? He listened carefully. Ann was looking up from her magazine, wonderingly. Ping again. This time he pinpointed it as coming from the window. Something light had hit it. Like an air rifle pellet?

He moved to the window.

"Don't open the curtains. They'll see us, if there's anybody out there," Ann implored him.

Crouching, Hood slipped off the sofa and crept down below the window, until he reached the corner. Then by barely touching the curtain, he could peer through the side.

It was hard to make out anything. There was the huge, rectangular bulk of the red brick library opposite. The odd street lamp, he could identify.

Then a thud made him jump and his heart pound. A lump of mud had attached itself to the window. Looking around it, he could see some lights moving, swaying about. What were they? He peered harder, and Ann clasping his shoulder looked too.

Another thud. This time the mud did not stick and fell off, leaving only a dirty mark.

The lights were now visible as flames, higher now and swaying less. They formed a little forest. Then Hood knew: he turned to Ann. "They're carrying burning torches out there. Ring the police quick."

Keeping low, Ann scampered to the phone. Trembling her finger struggled to dial 999 but she managed it and blurted out the address. Then she slammed the receiver down, and rushed to be

70

beside Hood. She didn't feel safe alone anywhere else in the room.

The flaming torches were stationary now as if the men were having a meeting. A scrabbling sound came from above.

"Oh my God," Ann cried, "they're on the roof."

Hood strained to listen. "I'm not sure. I think they're just throwing stones up there."

There was a crash. Hood covered his own and Ann's face with his arms. Seconds later they looked. A brick had come straight through the window and was lying beside them. A common house brick, bits of earth and mortar still clinging to it.

Ann screamed. That seemed to alert those outside, and a cheer went up and then sounds of running. Hood was straining to go outside.

Ann hung on to him with powerful hands. "Don't Bill, they'll kill you. Stay here with me. Don't leave me."

Hood returned her grip and they waited. Nothing seemed to happen for a while and then the torches seemed to move off a little.

Breathing deeply Hood and Ann desperately hoped the attack was over and their ordeal at an end. But having moved back the torches paused. More murmuring.

Then a swish. A torch sailed through the air and banged against the remains of the window.

Hood and Ann swayed back. The torch slide down the window and fell on the ground outside. Two more torches came through the air and fell short.

"Lousy aim," Hood muttered.

They waited but no more came through the air. But the smell of burning was becoming stronger. Was it from the torches lying on the ground outside, they wondered?

However, it seemed closer and stronger than that. Tearing himself free of Ann's grip Hood slithered along below the window to the lounge door. Reaching up he opened it and staggered through.

Smoke was filling the hall. Pulling a handkerchief over his nose he crawled on his belly towards the door.

A torch had been stuck through the letter box and flames were licking the inside of the door.

He quickly slithered back, towards the kitchen.

71

Ann called to him, "Bill, where are you? What's happening? Is the house on fire?"

"Just the front door," he called back. "I'm getting some water."

Ann, keeping low, ran to join him. Together they filled basins and bottles with water and threw it on the torch and the front door.

There were explosions of steam but little else. The flames licked higher undeterred.

"We've got to do something," Ann cried, "it'll reach upstairs at this rate."

Hood tried to think. He ran upstairs and grabbed some bedding from one of the rooms. Then he ran pell-mell down the stairs. He threw a blanket over the stuck torch. This helped to douse it and control the spread of the flames.

Ann was still bringing more water and sloshing it about, gradually weakening the power of the fire.

Then there was a crack. They both whirled round. Hood was back into the lounge. A lighted torch had come through the broken window and was lying where they had been sitting on the sofa.

Ann joined him, appalled. "We could have been killed."

Hood rushed forward and grabbed the handle of the torch. For a moment he was bewildered as to what to do with it. He swung it round.

"For God's sake, don't do that. Watch where you're going," Ann railed at him.

Hood ran out with it to the kitchen and then unlocking the back door threw it out onto the path.

Surprised, angry faces stared back at him.

"My God, they're round the back," he muttered in despair at being surrounded.

He tried to slam the door shut but in his haste it snagged on the uneven floor. He saw torches and batons waving towards him. Dragging the door back and to, he struggled to free it. If a torch came in through the gap, the kitchen would be an inferno.

With a screaming, wrenching sound of torn draught excluder, he freed the door and slammed it shut. Then he leant against it, his heart pounding. He felt a thud against the door, and then another. Anxiously he hoped the weapons were bouncing off.

Then he heard Ann's voice, shrill down the hall: "Bill, Bill what are you doing? Where are you?"

Could he risk leaving the door? He listened a little longer. He had to; Ann needed him. He couldn't leave her all alone at the front of the house.

When he returned, Ann was putting out the last of the flames over the front door.

As they worked together they could hear loud laughing and jeering, but apparently receding. Despite their anger they prayed that perhaps at last their assailants were going.

Then came a roaring sound. Both panicked for a moment and clutched each other in their terror. But the siren made their faces light up. Recklessly Hood grabbed the smouldering door and yanked it open.

Two policemen were climbing out of a patrol car. They wandered suspiciously up the path. "Had a frying pan fire, have you?" one asked.

Hood did not know if he was joking or serious.

"What a mess," the other policeman muttered.

Ann came out to join Hood. "And where the bloody hell have you been?"

Hood turned and grinned at her. That was telling them.

d

Chapter Twelve

It was the early hours of the morning. Hood sat in one chair, his arms hanging loose over its sides. Ann sat in the other, her legs drawn up under her, her face heavy, brooding and desperately tired.

"Well, we've done as much as we can," Hood commented to break the eerie silence. His voice had a mechanical tone as he forced himself to speak.

Ann nodded, dull and lifeless.

The front window was now boarded up, after the police had contacted a firm with a 24-hour call-out service. The sofa looked naked, with its burnt cushions deposited in a corner of the kitchen.

Through from the lounge the hallway and stairs were smoke damaged and the front door badly charred. The charcoal smell hung everywhere, a sickening pall.

Hood heaved on his chair and suddenly stood up. Without movement he knew he would stiffen from tiredness and depression. "Come over to my flat. I can't leave you here, the state the place is in."

Roused a little, Ann looked around her and rubbed her eyes. She felt that she just wanted to sleep for ever.

"It's OK, Bill. I think I'll just stay curled up here." She didn't really want to, but it was the easiest option, course of least resistance.

Hood approached but gave her room, trying not to pressure her. "Please Ann. You'll freeze in that chair and the smoke is no good for your lungs. Besides, I'm not leaving you alone tonight."

Ann smiled at him. "Good old Bill. I haven't thanked you, have I? I couldn't have got through this night without you." She paused and thought before going on: "It would have finished me off. I really would be a basket case by now. Instead I'm just . . . pissed off and awfully, awfully tired. I don't think I can move."

Hood leant over and slowly pulled her out of the chair. She seemed to uncoil, legs from under her, body straightening, until she was upright. Even then she wanted to lean on him. It felt good, not to have to support herself alone.

"All right, I'll come." Then she broke out with an angry cry: "Look what they've done to my lovely home. I spent ages getting it right. Yes, take me out of here. I can't bear it." She threw some clothes into two bags.

Hood grabbed her suede coat from a hook down the hall and placed it over her shoulders. She nodded in gratitude and pulled it more closely around her.

Then together they forced themselves to approach the front door. Blackened it was distorted and cracked, edged with burnt splinters.

"Maybe we'd better go round the back," Hood urged her.

"No, let's open the bloody thing. I'm not creeping out the back way."

Reluctantly Hood wrenched on the door and managed to drag it open without shearing off too much wood from the surround.

Head down, Ann bustled through and Hood followed her, forcing the door shut behind them. They walked down the path trying not to look back and to ignore the daubings on the brickwork and the unsightly board across the window.

Ann was shivering as they walked down the road and then up the side alley to Hood's car.

They drove in silence till they reached Hood's flat.

Once inside Hood sat Ann down in the living-room while he made her a hot drink.

Then: "If you'd like to take the bedroom I'll kip down on the sofa here," Hood offered.

Ann, bleary eyed, looked at him over her coffee mug. "Don't be silly Bill. Let's go to bed. To hell with the niceties, I'm too damn tired. But don't expect anything."

In the cold bedroom they both quickly undressed to their underwear and then climbed into the narrow bed. Its confines forced them to embrace but neither was complaining. They fell asleep that way.

In the morning Hood tried to slip out of bed without disturbing Ann. He had slept badly whereas Ann, through dogged tiredness, seemed to have gone the night without waking.

Gathering up his clothes, he dressed quickly in the kitchen. The cold made him hurry. In his haste and discomfort he was still seething from last night's events.

What a cowardly bunch of men, to pick on a lone, innocent woman and callously try to destroy her home, her sanity. His mind was full of revenge and retribution. He wanted to make them suffer for what they had done to Ann.

And if that Monica woman was behind it, then he was even more sickened. For one woman to put another through this kind of hell for some political spite, was beyond his comprehension.

Dark waves of hatred were breaking inside him. In this black mood he might do anything. He pressed hard against the walls of the kitchen, fighting it. Then slowly the feeling ebbed away.

He crept silently back to the bedroom doorway and looked in. Ann's blonde hair was cascaded on the pillow and her face relaxed in sleep. He noticed worrying hollows under her eyes, and in her cheeks. Maybe under the strain, she just wasn't eating. That had to be put right.

At that moment her eyes opened. She was surprised for a moment at her surroundings, but on seeing Hood, reassured. She even managed to smile.

"Morning Bill. What time is it?"

"Just after eight."

Ann yawned. "Lord, I must get shifting. I've so many things to do today."

Hood put his hand up. "Now you just stay there. You need pampering today and I am going to see you get it. The house will still be there."

Ann knew he meant: 'now it's daylight, it's safe'.

Without much resistance, Ann lay back on the pillow. It was nice to be fussed over, for once.

Hood rubbed his hands together. "Now: breakfast. We have cereal, toast, coffee or I could pop out to the shops if there's anything else you fancy.

"No, no," Ann pleaded with him, joking. Then a coughing fit caused him concern till it suddenly ended. "It's all right. I was lying at a funny angle, that's all. Toast and coffee would be fine."

Hood felt almost schizophrenic as he placidly went about making breakfast, having only minutes before been contemplating violent revenge. It was a relief to be looking after someone else and he relished preparing Ann's breakfast tray.

He placed it on her knees as she sat up in bed, and rested her back against the headboard. Hood moved her pillow up so that she could sit more comfortably.

"Now, have you everything you need?"

Ann smiled, impatient. "Yes Bill, everything. Now go and get your breakfast. Your coffee will be getting cold."

Thinking that she might wish her privacy, Hood returned to the kitchen, and leaning against the draining-board ate his breakfast in thoughtful silence.

Then he heard from outside a shuffling of feet followed by a knock on the door. Putting down his coffee mug and swallowing his last finger of toast he moved from the kitchen. Wiping his sticky fingers on the handkerchief in his pocket he went to open the door.

Outside stood Monica. She was wearing a quilted anorak, polo neck lamb's-wool sweater, blue flannel trousers and Doc Marten shoes. Behind her wire spectacles her eyes were resolute. Her whole bearing showed that she meant business.

"Can I come in?" she almost snapped. Hood was so surprised, taken aback, that he acceded without thinking.

However, as she stepped past him hurriedly, Hood sensed the tension in her. She was making herself do this, appear in control.

She paused in the hall, unsure where to head next.

This gave Hood the opportunity to overtake her and ask, "What are you doing here?"

Monica looked about her, sniffed, unimpressed by her surroundings.

"I should have thought that was obvious. I just heard about the fire. I went there immediately but with no answer, I came here. Ann is staying with you, isn't she?"

Hood was becoming angry with her for taking so much for granted. "You can think what you damn well please. You've got a nerve, coming round here after what happened last night."

Monica looked straight back at him. "I know I have."

"Why for two pence, I'd wring your neck."

"Oh cut that out. Do you honestly think that if I was responsible, I'd be round here this morning?"

"You might, to crow."

"Do I look as if I am crowing? Use your eyes, that's what they're there for."

Hood paused and thought. It was true that her attitude though belligerent was not gloating.

Hood leant back against the door jamb to the kitchen. "Well all right, so what do you want?"

"I came to see Ann. Is she in there?" Monica said, pointing to the bedroom.

"She is, but she is resting after her ordeal."

"She'll want to see me," and before Hood could stop her, she marched into the bedroom.

Ann, seeing Monica at the end of the bed flushed and put down her cup, and then the tray.

"How did you get in? Bill, what's happening?"

Hood, following after Monica, said over her shoulder, "She just barged in. Do you want me to throw her out?" He was thinking it would give him some satisfaction to chuck Monica into the street.

But torn between weary resignation, and curiosity Ann said, "No, let her stay. I want to hear her excuses."

Monica unzipped her anorak and moved to the corner of the room. "Don't patronise me, Ann. I came here as a favour. I didn't have to, and don't make it hard for me."

Ann's features widened. "Well pardon me for living. Your thugs tried to burn me alive in my own house last night!"

"That's a terrible thing to say. I would never condone anything like that."

Ann plumped her pillow behind her, and sat up straighter in bed, defiant.

"Nevertheless, it's true. Your people were behind it."

"You have proof I suppose? You saw them, recognised someone?"

"I didn't have to. This has been going on for months, and you know it. Take that incident on the Council steps. That was your gang again."

Reluctantly Monica turned to face Ann properly again. "I acknowledge it could have been - against my knowledge and my wishes," she added hastily. She wanted to come close to Ann but

78

dreaded a rebuff. "I'm sickened by all this too, and I give you my word I'm doing everything in my power to stop it."

Ann gazed back at her, amazed at the effrontery. "How many times have I heard these same promises from you before but nothing ever happens? And I go on suffering." A tear escaped, despite clenching her eyes. "Damn you. Why can't you people leave me alone? This vendetta, it's wicked, it's cruel . . . so senseless."

The colour had drained from Monica's face and her hands were buried in her pockets. She felt herself succumbing under the weight of Ann's accusations.

Lamely she tried again. "I came, not because I had to, but I felt I owed it to you to try to help, to reassure . . ."

Ann pulled the pillow out from behind her and threw it. "You want to clear your conscience. Well you can't. I don't forgive you. Not ever, for what you've done to me. I hope you rot in hell."

Stiffening, Monica zipped up her anorak again, and slowly turned down her polo neck where it had rucked up.

"There's no talking to you. I'm sorry you feel that way. I'm offering to set political differences aside and be your friend." Then to Bill: "Talk some sense into her." She dropped her voice, "Crazy old tart."

But Ann heard.

"Ladies," Hood interposed, as it seemed all this might lead to blows.

Then to Monica: "I think you'd better leave while the goings good."

Ann was half out of bed by now, lurching drunkenly towards Monica, finger-nails out.

"Let me at her," she screamed, "I'll tear her eyes out, the frigid cow."

Hood grabbed Monica by the arm and propelled her through the doorway into the hall. Then it was to the front door.

Monica was breathing heavily, as was Hood himself. "I don't know how you stand her," Monica told him. "Always flying off the handle like that when you try to help."

"She's had a lot of provocation. We both have," he replied.

"Well try and make her see reason. I don't want us to be enemies." She looked him in the face, and Hood recognised a special feeling behind her words.

"I'll do everything to stop this intimidation. We've all suffered from it over the years, you know. Ann's not unique." Then she pulled the zipper of her anorak right up to the top. "I gave up valuable time to come here. I hope it wasn't wasted."

She turned, and her small determined, brisk figure clumped down the hall.

After he closed the door, Hood wandered back to the kitchen and considered whether to make some more coffee. He'd let Ann alone for the moment, he decided, and allow her time to calm down.

He didn't know whether to believe Monica or not. But it would have taken amazing nerve for her to be lying. Unless she really felt guilty and ashamed.

He reset the button on the kettle and spooned some more coffee on top of the remnants in his mug. There was another knock at the door. Quickly he moved to answer it, aiming to intercept Monica before Ann could get to her.

But when he opened the door it was to find Charlie Rigby standing on the threshold. He looked smaller than Hood remembered and his long flat forehead was glistening. He must have run up the stairs. A grey waterproof jacket hung loose on him and he wore light, blue sports trousers. He could have come straight off a golf course.

Charlie flashed him a quick, exhausted smile while he gathered his breath. Then he was ready to talk, one arm resting on the wall outside. "I wouldn't blame you if you slammed the door in my face. Only mind my fingers."

Then he held his hand up, fingers bent as if amputated at the knuckles.

Seeing Hood's impatience he hurried on: "Just my little joke. To lighten things up. Sorry. Only Monica was so agitated, I had to come up and see. Have she and Ann had a barney?"

Hood nodded, then added, stepping out into the corridor, "For goodness sake, keep your voice down. Ann is furious."

Charlie backed off, hands up. "OK. Don't set her on to me. I don't want any trouble. I told Monica to make peace with her. No good?"

"Let's say Ann didn't believe her. I'm not sure I did either."

"Don't say that Bill. Man to man: Monica is sincere, but she's in deep with some very heavy people. Things don't change over night."

"These attacks on Ann have got to stop. That's the bottom line."

Charlie bit his lip. "I know. I sympathise. I'm doing what little I can. But there's no need for you and I to fall out, is there?"

Hood looked at the eager, bobbing face. Slowly he came back: "No, I suppose not. Now I must get back to Ann."

"You didn't mind me coming up."

"No, that's OK."

"See you in the Club?"

"Yes, sometime. Goodbye."

Charlie forced himself not to overstay his welcome and retreated down the corridor, apparently pleased.

Hood turned his back and promptly forgot him as he returned to Ann.

Chapter Thirteen

Hood checked in on Ann again. She was still seething, the bedclothes gripped in a knot around her waist.

"Please Ann, try and take it easy. Just rest. I'm off to work now, but I'll call in at lunch time. You'll stay here until then?"

Sullenly Ann nodded. Hood came across and kissed her. She gripped his arm fiercely for a moment then let him go, lassitude beginning to take over.

She slid under the bedclothes and turned her face to the wall.

Hood padded out and made sure he had everything he needed for the office. He was heading for the door when the phone rang.

Damn, he thought, he'd never get to work at this rate and Slattery demanded punctuality.

Irritated he changed direction and stalked through to the living-room. He picked up the phone. "Yes?"

A voice at the other end announced: "Is that you Hood?"

Hood recognised Russell's curt tone. Reluctantly he replied, "Yes it's Hood . . . sir."

"About time. I don't like having to chase you. What's all this I hear about you and Ann Renshaw in a house fire?"

Hood was angry. He resented more explanations but was forced. "That's right, I was with her when some thugs started laying siege to the house. We could have been burned alive in there."

Hood could hear Russell's excited, impatient breathing down the phone, waiting for him to finish.

"Yes but what were you doing there? I explicitly told you to avoid her. Are you incapable of following simple instructions?"

Hood transferred the receiver to his other hand and wiped his freed palm on his trousers. "With respect, sir, I couldn't simply abandon her. I love her. She needed my protection."

Russell was exasperated. "Your personal feelings are no concern of mine. Drop her. She's interfering with your work."

"I can't sir. She needs police protection. She's being persecuted."

"Who by?"

"I don't know," Hood finished lamely, baffled.

Russell was dismissive: "You've no idea! And yet you're willing to let her jeopardise the whole operation."

"Quite frankly one man under cover like me, isn't going to nail Slattery. We're just playing at it. You need the fraud squad, a flock of auditors going over his books if you really want to get him."

Russell's fist came down on the top of his desk. He was almost too upset to speak. "When I want your opinion I'll ask for it. Do the job you're paid for and stop messing about with that Renshaw woman. I'm deeply disappointed in you Hood."

"The feeling's mutual . . . sir. The sooner I'm back in my old division the better. I never asked for this transfer."

With that Hood put the phone down.

Russell was incensed that Hood had broken off a phone call from him, the Assistant Chief Constable. The nerve of the man. He'd totally ignored Russell's instructions over Ann.

Hood was out of control, disobeying orders, showing no respect for the uniform. He must be brought to heel immediately. But how, with so much at stake? Russell quailed from confronting Hood himself, but he knew someone who could. It was distasteful but necessary. He couldn't put it off any longer. He had to see the man.

Scratching his beard he rang a phone number he kept secret and left a message on an answering machine. It was in a simple code, devised for emergencies.

During the next few hours Russell tried to concentrate on necessary paperwork, but his mind kept wandering.

Why hadn't Ann turned to him instead of Hood? All these years he'd waited, expecting her one day to walk through that door, beg his forgiveness and ask his help. Just a sign from her, that's all it would have taken, and he would have protected her with his life. But she was too stupid to think of him and the help, the love, he could give. In all these long, fraught, lonely years she'd never thought of him once. Whereas he - he couldn't get her out of his mind.

It was so pointless, dwelling on someone who had only been a casual relationship so many years ago, but he couldn't help it. She, her memory, was all he had. And it was only right that she should suffer in her own way as much as he had. Only right.

Glancing at his office clock he roused himself, and walked across to take his peaked cap from the hook behind the door.

Then he clattered down the back staircase and out to the compound. He found his Rover and settled himself inside it. He always felt better, more in control, when behind the wheel.

Edging the car out by the tightly packed mass of vehicles, he turned through the gate and began following the ring road round. He pressed on at reasonable speed, not wishing to draw attention but impatient to arrive at his destination.

Finally he pulled up outside a burnt-out pub. Arson seemed to be increasingly popular that year. Climbing out of the car he gazed up at the blackened roof beams jutting up into empty space Only a handful of slates had remained in position.

Part of the near-side wall had collapsed, revealing the plaster rendering. Half-way up the beams were intact, reaching to the distorted window frames scorched and twisted.

Russell walked round the back, treading over broken brick, ash, and charred timbers. Even more of the wall had collapsed and one quarter was only shored up by a strong though blackened beam. Crouching down Russell staggered through the gap and was inside, holding his cap on to his head.

Then he rose from a stooping position to see Slattery thoughtfully trying to prize apart two chairs which had become moulded together. Then brushing his hands he gave up.

"You got here first." Russell couldn't help envying Slattery's light grey suit with the hand-stitched lapels and the delicate strands of blue and red that ran through it. To wear a suit like that so easily, for it to hang with such grace.

Slattery turned round and sniffed. "I thought I'd better inspect the property. After all that's why we're supposed to be here isn't it?"

"All right," Russell agreed, impatiently, and they walked round together.

"It's a bloody mess," Slattery commented, gazing up at the sky through the slats of blackened beams.

84

"Yes."

Then Slattery brought his gaze back to earth. Russell always made him feel uncomfortable, in a bored sort of way. He never felt afraid, but rather awfully tired as with an irritating but close relative.

"You wanted an urgent meeting. What couldn't keep?"

"Hood, that's what."

"Oh." Slattery looked baleful. He didn't really want to talk about Hood.

"I can't control him." Russell blurted out this admission, to his own surprise.

"I thought that was my job. I keep him bogged down in mundane accounts, wear him out."

Russell stiffened, annoyed at this diversion. "Oh you're quite safe. I mean him and Ann Renshaw. The way they're going we'll hear wedding bells soon."

"And you don't like the idea?"

"Too right, I don't." Russell puffed himself up, and strutted around the broken bricks and piles of shattered glass. "She can't want him - and she's not going to have him either."

Slattery walked across to him. He would have put his hand on Russell's shoulder if it hadn't been covered with epaulettes.

"Why not let bygones be bygones? This thing of yours with Ann is well past its sell-by date."

Russell's eyes filled with hurt pride. "She'll come to her senses one day. She just needs a little help."

"What do you want me to do?" Slattery's voice was weary.

"Break them up."

"We've tried that. Bruises don't seem to make any difference. Only draws them closer together."

Russell began slapping his white gloves into his palm. "Well find another way. Anything."

Slattery scratched his neck as the obvious question went begging.

"Why don't you withdraw him from the case and send him packing, back to where he came from?"

Russell was stung. He was not that obtuse. "I can't. They won't let me," Russell's voice rose, "the higher-ups. They say I haven't given Hood a fair trial. They really want your head you know. You've no idea how I've covered for you. You really owe me."

Slattery sensed the reason: to Russell he was a gentleman, the acceptable face of crime. He even co-operated with Russell's sometime crack downs, to salve the man's conscience. He gave Russell the respect he couldn't find elsewhere. Russell had to be indulged.

"All right, I'll see what I can do. Fit him up, embezzlement maybe."

Russell's frown was becoming pronounced. "Yes, well don't go into the details. I don't want to know. Hood has to be taken out of circulation, that's all that matters."

Slattery felt less than whole-hearted about this. True, at first he had bitterly resented Hood as a police spy and would even have seen him dead. But lately he had grown to like and respect him. Hood had natural authority and talked no nonsense. Just the kind of man he needed for his new, legitimate operation. Maybe when all this was over he could use him. Every man had his price.

How to compromise Hood and then use him for his own ends - that was a conundrum.

Hiding his reservations he patted Russell on the back. "Leave it to me. You go first. I'll give you a couple of minutes, then follow."

Russell tipped his peaked cap and began picking his way over the debris. He banged his head on the low gap, to emerge dazed out into the street.

Erect, though swaying, he walked stiffly to his car, hoping no one had noticed his awkward and embarrassed exit. Gathering up the shreds of his dignity, he drove off.

Chapter Fourteen

Home from work, Hood tried to banish his misgivings about everything and appear cheerful. When he entered the living-room he found that Ann had decided to do the same. She was wearing a pale yellow cheesecloth top, a long autumnal-print skirt, and sandals. Her face was rouged and she was forcing a smile. She looked awful. Despite herself, the edges of her mouth kept turning down and puckering. Over her eyes was a hard sheen like glass.

"I'll make some tea," Ann announced and half rose from the sofa, catching the hem of her dress on the hessian.

But Hood waved her back and sank down in the armchair. "How are you feeling?"

"Oh I'm OK," she came back in a bright, brittle voice. "I must have gone off again after you left and slept really heavily; it took me a long while to come to."

Hood nodded. "It probably did you good. I bet you've not been getting much sleep lately."

It was Ann's turn to nod. "That's the truth. I've been getting so dog tired. It does that to you doesn't it?" Absently she began picking at a thread on her cheesecloth blouse. Then she looked up. "Have you had a busy day?" she asked out of politeness.

"So, so. Going through invoices can be pretty tedious at times, but I get by."

"I should think you'd want something more . . ."

Hood saw the need to head off this line of enquiry. "Maybe. Perhaps I'll look around. But I was lucky to land this job. There aren't that many good jobs going."

"That's true." The conversation began to lag, into desultory silence.

Ann seemed to be relaxing into her own thoughts. Then suddenly she came out of them.

"I want to go home - tonight."

Hood sat bold upright. "Tonight? Are you sure? Think of the mess you'll find. You can stay on here as long as you want."

"I know and I'm grateful, but I mustn't impose. I've got to face it sooner or later. Besides, I can't leave the house unoccupied. It's mine and I'm keeping it."

Hood rose and bending over her, clasped her hands in his. "I understand. Of course you can go back anytime. I'll stay there with you if you like."

She looked up at him. "It's very tempting, but I've lived all these years on my own. They're not destroying my independence. I'd die first."

"Good for you," he said, and leaning forward kissed her. "When do you want to go?"

"Could we do it now while I'm feeling brave. I don't want time to change my mind. There's no use putting it off."

"Whatever you say. Just give me a minute to change out of this suit and I'll drive you."

While Hood was in the bedroom changing, Ann sank back against the sofa head-rest and looked around at what she was leaving behind. The flat was certainly no luxury apartment. How could Hood bear it? On his pay he could afford somewhere better. It was all very odd.

Take this room: the imitation coals in the electric fire didn't even illuminate, giving a curiously dead, chilled effect. The hessian was such a cheap, uncomfortable covering. That squat bureau - precisely what shape was it? It seemed to jut out at all angles. And then to frame it all, those bilious chocolate curtains.

She laughed, it was so bad - and so like home now after a day. But she felt she was invading Hood's privacy. He must have some reason for living like this. Was he indifferent to his surroundings, or punishing himself in some way?

Rising she wandered across and looked at the cheap print of Bude, Cornwall. The dust and dirt told her it came with the room. There was no personal flavour to the flat whatsoever. It was as if Hood were squatting.

Oh why didn't he hurry up and finish changing? She wanted to get into the bedroom and gather up her few belongings. The sooner she cleared out, the better.

But she felt a pang. Wasn't she letting the grim surroundings keep her from the man she loved. She tried the words again: 'the man she loved.' Was it true? She didn't know. Desperation was pointing her in that direction, but she distrusted such motives.

She couldn't let herself love him. Consider what her track record was. Not one successful relationship. Zero. Every single one had foundered, the man almost always losing interest, disappearing, apparently without reason. One minute everything would seem to be going well, and the next - finish. Without so much as a goodbye or apology.

She couldn't risk investing her heart in a man again. Besides it wouldn't be fair on Hood. He wouldn't know what he was taking on, and she couldn't tell him. It was all such a mess. Better to leave it as good friends. Heaven knew she could do with those, maybe more. Friends helped you survive; lovers, well - they were exciting but then gone, not dependable like friends.

"All right, I'm ready," Hood shouted, and emerged from the hall. He was wearing a heavily cabled Fair Isle sweater and hound's-tooth check trousers, over his brogues. "Shall we go?"

His smart appearance took her by surprise, and she said, "I'll just collect up my things and then I'm ready to clear out." She paused, feeling that the words sounded harsh, ungrateful. "I mean I'll be ready to go."

"Take your time." Hood sat down in the chair and made himself glance through the newspaper.

A few minutes later Ann reappeared, all her belongings in two carrier bags, one in each hand.

"I'm ready."

Flinging the newspaper aside, Hood rose. "Oh Ann." It all seemed so wrong, so hard. She looked pathetic with those two crumpled bags in her hands. He took her in his arms and squeezed her tight. "Don't go Ann. Stay with me. I love you. We'll be good together." Then he was kissing her, taking her breath away.

She dropped the carrier bags and gripped him, moulding her lips to his. She was so hungry for love and affection.

They mauled each other, hands working over each other's body. Occasionally Ann stifled a wince and Hood affected not to notice.

He took her hand and led her to the bedroom. "Now Ann,

please."

"I shouldn't. I'm leaving."

But her desire and need were as great as his. "But listen Bill, before we start. It doesn't change anything. I'm still going."

"Whatever you say, only stop talking. I want you so much."

"And I want you. Don't you ever doubt it." Despite her feeling of guilt she joined him in the bedroom. No matter where things led, she had to have him, a lover, now. She'd waited so long, too long, for this to happen.

Quickly they undressed and climbed into bed together. It was so different from last night, when in terror she had clung to him non-sexually, like a child, and gone to sleep almost immediately.

This time they were both keenly awake, ready to enjoy each other's body. Although it had been long for both of them since they had made love, they both tried to use the most considerate caresses they remembered.

And then their bodies locked and they rolled over first on one side of the bed and then on the other, laughing and ecstatic.

"Oh God," Hood cried. "This is marvellous, so good. I love you. I could eat you."

"You are, you devil.Where did you learn all that? Here I'll give you some." And she turned her attentions on him.

The relief from pain, disappointment, and stress was so colossal they felt they couldn't bear it. Just to be this happy if only for a few seconds, prolonged to a few minutes. This happy.

But no matter how often they said it, thought it, clung on to the moment, still it began to evaporate.

They lay, Hood with his arm around her shoulders, Ann with her head on his chest, her fingers smoothing down his hairs beneath her cheek. They were both staring into space.

"You can't go now, not after what's happened." Hood kissed her temple.

"I have to." Ann's tone was sad.

"Why? I don't see it."

"I told you before we started, it couldn't make any difference. One moment of passion won't make me stay.'

Hood stirred a little, away from her. "Don't. It was everything, for me at least."

Ann lifted her head and gazed into his hurt eyes. "For me too. But I won't go back on my word. It was a promise to you also.

One day you'll thank me."

"Oh yes, when we're both back in our lonely separate rooms. Well great." He pulled the bedclothes aside and climbed out, searching for his garments on the floor.

"Don't spoil everything Bill, please. I only said I have to go home. The rest can be the same. I want to be with you."

"Well you've a funny way of showing it. Come on, get dressed will you, then I can drive you home."

Nonplussed Ann reluctantly began looking for her clothes. So much for romance. Well what did she expect; she had killed it, hadn't she by her refusal?

No! He couldn't expect her to give up her independence just like that and move in with him. Suppose he turned out to be like all the rest - as he seemed to be doing now? Where would that leave her? With an empty house burnt to the ground no doubt.

She dragged on her underwear and then her cheesecloth blouse all scrunched up in a ball. Well it always looked creased anyway, she reflected, as she pulled it on. Then she was into her skirt adjusting the waistband, and she looked almost as she had before. Where had all those moments of passion gone? They seemed like a dream now.

"Ready?" Hood's tone was impatient, unhappy, foiled.

"Yes, I'm ready. Where are my carrier bags?"

"Oh yes those." He helped her find them.

Those sad little articles had made him feel so protective. Ann seemed so vulnerable. Well he wouldn't be taken in again so easily.

He clumped ahead of her along the hall, down the cold stone steps to the front door of the building, and then out to the car.

"Hey," she called out, "slow down. I can't keep up."

Hood muttered, and then opened the car doors.

"Aren't you going to hold the door for me?" Ann asked.

Sourly Hood climbed out again and going round the side of the vehicle held the door for her.

Once she was inside he slammed it hard and went back to the driver's seat.

"Right?"

"Right. Go on then."

Chapter Fifteen

On the outside of Ann's house there were grim reminders of the assault the other evening. There were scorch marks round the door frame and blackened brickwork. Daubs marred the area below the front window which was covered by a large brown board with orange lettering. Some slates had been disturbed from the roof, and lay in cracked pieces on the lawn and pavement.

Ann inhaled deeply and then very deliberately took her key from her bag.

"Let's see if I can get the door open." She managed a grin.

Hood stood behind her as she turned the key in the lock. Then with some pushing and working the door back and forward, she managed to drag it open.

The stale odour of smoke imbued the hall. Inwardly Ann groaned: would it last for ever, a pall clinging to the fabric of the house like an infestation? She made herself walk through to the lounge, all in shade; if it were only blinds drawn across, instead of an ugly board.

There was the black scorch mark on the carpet and the damaged settee, with its ruined cushions discarded in the kitchen. She gasped as she remembered choosing it specially for its soothing blue floral pattern and the way it seemed to sigh pleasurably beneath her when she sat down. Now it looked disembowelled, with bits of stuffing hanging out.

Then Ann sagged down in one of the chairs, dropping her carrier bags at her feet. She shook, turning her head away.

Hood came over and knelt by her side. "Hey, what's this? Come on, keep your head up. It's not so bad. We'll soon have the place tidied up. A new piece of carpet and sofa, and you'll never know the difference."

Ann smiled through her tears and caressed his cheek with her hand. "I know, I'm just being silly. It all suddenly came over me. I suppose I've been bottling it up. You're quite right - it could have been a lot worse. It's just coming home to it all."

"I know. That's why I wanted you to stay at the flat. I could have cleaned the place up really spruce for your homecoming."

"No, you're so good. I couldn't let you. You've done enough as it is."

"Nonsense. Shall I make a brew for us?"

"Would you? I'd be so grateful."

As Hood went through to the kitchen, Ann sadly surveyed her living-room and wondered if she'd ever feel safe and happy there again.

Hood found the kitchen an unexpected mess, with burned pieces of the vandals' torch still lying in the sink. He tidied up and carried the remaining debris out into the yard.

Then he set about making some tea. Seeing the mess made of her home had upset Ann even more than he'd thought.

Their recent argument seemed a far off, pointless thing now. She had a home, here, and it needed rebuilding, re-establishing with his help. He realised she could never face life or love confidently again until that was done.

Balancing two mugs on a wooden tray with an orange blossom pattern he carried it through to the lounge.

Ann took a mug off the tray as it was proffered to her, and settled down to sip it.

Spilt drops landed on her carrier bag but she didn't seem to notice She was distracted again, and Hood found himself using his own thoughts for company

"Bill."

The words brought him out of his reverie. "Yes?"

"I've something very difficult to tell you. I've thought about it endlessly, should I or shouldn't I, and I've made up my mind. You must hear it."

Hood bristled. He sensed it was going to be a continuation of her rejection of him begun at the flat. He tried to prepare himself, tell himself it didn't matter, it had only been a quick fling to relieve his loneliness.

"Bill, I've got cancer."

The words seemed to go past him. He wanted to recall them to make sure he had heard them correctly.

"You've . . ?"

"Cancer. I've known for some time now. The doctors have done their tests and there's no doubt. I felt you had a right to know."

Hood was appalled - and yet she wasn't throwing him over, she trusted him enough to tell. "I see now why you didn't want to impose yourself on me, living in the flat. But I wouldn't have minded - I don't mind now!" he added emphatically.

"But I do," she came back at him. "I have my pride and I'm not inflicting myself on you as a burden. When the time comes I'll go into a hospital - or a hospice."

The shock showed across Hood's gaunt face. "Hospice! Ann it's not . . . incurable? Please God don't say that, or believe it. If the doctors have told you that, we'll find other doctors. There's always hope."

Ann had suddenly become calm, and reaching across laid a hand on Bill's shoulder.

"Don't get into a panic. Nothing's cut and dried. It's not incurable, although it might as well be.

Hood had never before heard such a bitter, defeated note in Ann's voice.

"Why? Tell me."

"No Bill. There's no point in going on about it. We've just got to accept it, and live on the best way we can."

But Hood wouldn't be side-tracked. He rose and stood over her. "Now what was it you began to say and stopped? I want to hear all of it. I've a right, don't you think?"

Ann became angry, feeling badgered. "Don't glower over me Bill and sit down. I can't stand people trying to intimidate me. I'll tell you when I'm good and ready, not a moment before." Suddenly she sounded like a crotchety old woman and despite themselves they both smiled.

Rebuked, Hood resumed his seat and tried to keep his voice calm and low.

"All right Ann, now please what is the whole story?"

Ann paused, still hoping to forestall his questions but then realised it was no good. He had to know the whole truth. Sighing, she began, "The doctors told me I have a very rare form of leukaemia. I can't remember all the technical jargon, but something like only one in ten cases is like mine."

She watched sympathetically as Hood's face dropped and his anxiety heightened. Yet there was something brave and gallant in his bearing, not wanting to let her down. "Don't worry, it's not all bad. There is a treatment and it has worked - well, slowed down the disease's progress anyway."

Hood looked up eagerly, grasping at this hope. "So when do you start on it? Is that what all this is building up to? You're going into hospital?"

Ann shook her head. "It's not that simple. The treatment isn't available in this country. It requires hugely expensive drugs and I think they use special lasers. I don't know. Anyway I can only get it in America."

"America?" Hood thought about it. Then: "Well if that's what it takes. Your health is all that's important."

Ann was becoming impatient, and pulled at her skirt twisting it this way and that. "Bill, I can't go to America. I can't afford it for one thing. You can't get this on the NHS you know."

"So how much is it?"

Ann hesitated before telling him. She knew he'd want to help raise the money and that it was hopeless. But she'd been carrying the knowledge round alone too long. The burden had become insupportable.

"Four hundred thousand pounds. That was the figure I was told. For a six month period of treatment, with room, nursing care, drugs, the laser treatment, everything. Four hundred thousand." She spoke the words as if they fascinated her, as if the price tag on a miracle.

Hood whistled. "That's a hell of an amount! I've never heard of so much for a treatment. Are you sure these doctors know what they're talking about?"

Ann nodded.

Hood was thinking furiously. "If we could just have some time - a year or two - we could save and maybe organise an appeal in the city and get donations. With you being a councillor that should help and maybe the council would . . ."

Ann put her hand up to interrupt him. With infinite sadness she said, "It's too late for all that Bill. I've only months. Resign yourself, like I have. Besides there are probably hundreds of American men and women who have first call on the treatment.

It's out of the question. I just wanted you to understand."

Hood stood up. "Resign myself, nothing. There must be a way. We can't just sit around and wait for you to . . ."

"Die," Ann completed the sentence for him. "What else is there to do? Believe me Bill, I've thought this through from every angle. I've added up all the money I have and could raise and it's not a tenth of that. The banks won't help - I've tried. I don't even own this house," she added bitterly. "I've a millstone of a mortgage round my neck. Oh Bill what am I going to do?" She shivered and Hood moved across and folded his arms around her.

"We'll think of something, my darling. We'll think of something. They're not taking you away from me so soon after I've found you. I won't let them."

But there was despair inside him as he contemplated the impossibility of raising that kind of money. He cursed his poverty.

Chapter Sixteen

Hood felt numbed as he drove back to his flat. Everything seemed unreal, including the city outline around him. The strange, dilapidated frontages to run-down shops, in garish pink or orange looked like stage props. The huge advertisement hoardings only added to the emptiness with their phoney cheerfulness. How could all of this have befallen one person - the one person he cared about in the whole world: Ann? He trembled as he whispered her name out loud, so vulnerable and precious did it seem.

What was life trying to do to her?

It felt like some cosmic conspiracy to destroy her. She who had done so much good in the world. It wasn't simply unfair, it was downright cruel, malicious. He tilted his head back in despair for a moment, his forehead almost touching the dark green ribbing of the car's inside roof.

Finally he arrived back and parked up. He sat for a full minute, unmoving, then climbed out. He couldn't face his thoughts cramped up in that desolate living-room. Walking was the only solace.

Setting off left down the street from his lodgings he passed a pawnbroker's and an old fashioned barber's shop complete with striped pole. Then round the corner at the bottom was the railway station and the marshalling yards.

He walked along by the railing that flanked the line and then up the gradient to the squat grey brick bridge over the railway. Looking down he gazed at the maze of lines spread out below. Odd rusting wagons sat, cast offs, on forgotten sidings.

He leant on the parapet glad to halt and rest. What was he to do? If there was really a chance, he'd raise the money somehow.

e

But were the doctors telling the truth: did this cure exist in America or was this another cruel trick to be played on Ann? He must stop thinking like that: they wouldn't tell her untruths.

He gnawed on his thumb, hoping the pain would produce an idea. Where was he going to get four hundred thousand pounds? He had no property, no assets.

"Oh God." He looked about him, helplessly.

Ann's life in the balance and he couldn't come up with the bits of paper needed to save her. What kind of man was he? He pondered that. A detective with a reputation for never letting go, never giving up, dogging a trail until he obtained a conviction. Well this case required its own dedication, its own perseverance. There could be no giving up on this. Ann's life was at stake; that was all that mattered.

Yes, but how? He was lost for an idea, for inspiration. Then a cold band settled across his brow and he turned away from the parapet. Think, think, he told himself bitterly instead of all this wild emotion.

Where did people usually get money from: banks. He'd try them in the morning. Just because Ann had failed there, didn't mean he couldn't succeed. All right, without assets as collateral it was a long shot but he had to try it. After all he had a long and distinguished employment record. That must count for something.

Then there was Slattery. Hood flinched from approaching him, but knew that if all else failed he must be tried. A contribution would be no problem to a man like that. And he might feel an obligation to Ann. Damn it, he ought to, having blighted and exploited her for so many years. Hood pictured himself grabbing Slattery by the throat and squeezing a promise of money out of him. The image did him good, but he knew in reality it wasn't the way.

Still, one day, Slattery would be punished. Suddenly Hood wondered if Slattery had anything to do with this hate campaign against Ann, but then dismissed the idea. It was politically motivated, wasn't it, and Slattery didn't seem a political animal.

Hood walked on down by the Fire Station and then passed a Quaker Meeting House, a polite spruce little building behind a small well tended garden. He looked longingly at it for the peace that might lie inside.

Thought of the hate campaign had brought him back to the malignancy that was destroying Ann's life. Some people seemed more vulnerable than others, meant to be victims. And Ann wasn't the cringing, self-destructive type who brought it upon themselves. She was large, vibrant, outgoing, for a good time - and still she got hers.

He wanted to protect people like Ann. That's why he'd been a community spokesman in the past, why he was a policeman now. But it was no good. Convicting villains didn't stop the evil, and the victims still suffered; their property not recovered, their peace of mind shattered. He couldn't forget Ann's expression as she sat in the chair and looked at the destruction round her.

He clenched and unclenched his fingers. If he wasn't careful the problems of the city would engulf him. He must stop trying to put the world to rights. The image of poor, ineffectual Russell sprang to mind and he rebelled against any resemblance. God forbid he should become like him, looking down from his lonely room on the tenth floor, issuing orders that were ignored, trying to clear up a city by proxy, and failing.

Ann was the only cause worth fighting for at the moment. He realised how much he had invested in her. She was the sun to his cold moon. He must save her. And there was selfish reason: he would be saving himself too.

With a course of action decided upon, Hood felt happier - and impatient. He wanted the banks to be open for business at 11 o'clock at night.

Instead he had to settle for going straight home and to bed. The sooner morning came, the sooner he could start on his errand of mercy.

But he had to get through the night first. He willed it with all his strength but sleep would not come. He gazed at the cobweb around the light fixture on the ceiling. He tried to guess how many hooks there were holding up the folds on the yellow and brown striped curtains.

But most of all he thought of Ann. How futile, and unnecessary, for her to be in her bed, he in his. Was she in pain from the cancer? He prayed not. How blind he had been recently. Her hollow cheeks, the losing weight, which he had put down to worry and dieting had been the cancer. And he had rejoiced at seeing her regain a semblance of her old appearance and figure.

How ironic and stupid!

For a detective he didn't seem to see or understand much, he scolded himself. Self-doubt grew in him as it had ever since he'd failed to crack the Slattery case. Maybe his past successes were down to luck or a cruel, vindictive streak in him which lately Ann had softened.

Perhaps he'd better become that old, hard bastard again. If it took that to save Ann's life, he would. Even if it meant alienating her affections. He gulped. Yes, even if it meant that. She had to live. He didn't matter. His twisted nature was probably beyond unravelling and saving anyway.

The next morning despite his weariness Hood dressed with more than his accustomed care. He gave his grey, worsted suit a quick brush and chose the muted striped shirt with matching blue tie. He wanted to make a good impression with these bank managers.

Taking an extended lunch break from work he began doing the rounds, starting with his own bank. He had invented a cover story. As Slattery's accountant he was thinking of setting up in business for himself. But he soon realised he needn't have bothered. No matter how he put it, the answer was always the same: no. No assets, no collateral, no loan.

He tried again the next day, and the day after that. Time was running on, his lunch breaks had become total fictions, and he had achieved nothing. Disillusioned and angry each time, he returned to the office.

Finally after the failure of all these attempts he left work again to try his second string - the loan sharks. It meant driving to dingy end terrace offices by council estates. 'Loans without security' was blazoned from their windows in red lettering, while inside lurked hardened men with balding pates, distrustful eyes, and sharp vicious tongues.

After the preliminaries, they went for the jugular in terms of income, property, ability to repay. It took only minutes to discover that at their rates of interest he couldn't begin to repay the loan. Hood sweated and wondered whether to risk it anyway, just to get his hands on the money. When he defaulted, to break his legs they'd have to find him first - and he was a policeman. Though even that wouldn't prevent them: he knew of cases.

But they had their own system of checking. A couple of phone calls and Hood's own retail business collapse of years ago, with debts outstanding, came to light. Once that was known they backed off visibly and showed him the door.

As he reeled out of the last one on his list, he leant against the car, shaking. He'd tried everything he knew and got nowhere. He faced the stark truth: he was credit black-listed. That meant it didn't matter how many banks, finance houses, loan sharks he tried, the answer would always be the same.

How could he tell Ann? He'd been so certain he could bring her some good news. And then he remembered Slattery. Perhaps because he disliked the idea of approaching him so much, he'd placed it at the back of his memory.

One last throw. Slattery had to deliver. He'd appeal to old times sake, guilt, altruism, any damn thing to make Slattery shell out at least part of the money.

Slattery lived in a large, white house with three dormer windows, and doors at either end of the building. This gave it the curiously elongated look of a farmhouse or private school. It was set behind a high privet hedge interspersed with conifers to ensure maximum privacy.

Hood swung his Volvo through the gateway and around in front of the house. He climbed out and paused in the driveway. Beside him was a small circular pond with algae floating on the top.

The whiteness of the house was quite dazzling as if newly painted and in sharp contrast the gutters and down-spouts were a shiny tarmac black.

The window frames were oak brown and fitted with slatted shutters which gave a continental appearance. Behind the building's expansive, cultivated façade Hood sensed a hidden message of reserve and retreat, the faint aura of a secluded nursing home or sanatorium. Hood used the polished brass knocker and a couple of minutes later Slattery appeared at the door. He registered surprise.

Hood began: "Sorry to trouble you at home but I've something most urgent to see you about."

Slattery filled the doorway and didn't seem inclined to move. "Can't it wait until tomorrow morning at the office?"

"I am afraid not. It's personal."

Slattery gave him a wondering, assessing stare, his chiselled features set in a line of enquiry and then he made up his mind. "Very well, you'd better come in. We can talk in the study."

Slattery led the way into a book lined room which also contained a white computer stand with monitor. There was a leather topped table at the far end overlooking the lawn.

On a small, inlaid, occasional table stood decanters of sherry and port and two glasses. However Slattery ignored this and motioned for Hood to take a high backed Queen Anne chair.

Slattery drew up another from the wall and they faced each other only yards apart.

"Well what can I do for you? Please keep it short as the family will be sitting down to dinner soon."

Hood looked at Slattery and wondered where to begin and the best tack to take.

Slattery was casually dressed in navy blue flannel trousers, sneakers, a monogrammed check shirt and a cream, v-necked lamb's-wool pullover.

Would Slattery's relaxed appearance make him receptive or alternatively reluctant to consider money outside office hours? But, Hood decided, no one who had reached Slattery's position ever found money an uninteresting topic.

Hood's face hardened as he began. He didn't like appealing to this man, for he knew what lay beneath the affability.

"I've come about money. I need a lot of money urgently for a friend."

Slattery pursed his lips. "This friend - he's in some difficulty I take it? By the way to save time: this friend isn't yourself is it?" Suspicions of a police trap flitted through his mind.

Hood shook his head. "No. You have a right to know; the friend is Ann Renshaw. The fact is she's got cancer and the only available treatment is in America and costs four hundred thousand pounds."

A glint came to Slattery's eyes. "And you expect me to pay towards it? What do you think I am: a charity?"

"I don't expect anything. I came to put the situation before you. What you decide to do about it, is up to you. But Ann and I can't raise that kind of money. Believe me, I've tried."

Slattery looked at Hood's tired, worn face and saw the truth of his statement.

"Why come to me? I'm very sorry about Ann's condition but

it really is nothing to do with me. I hardly know the woman. I can't be helping every sick person I've ever met. I'd have no money left."

Hood had watched him edging back on the hard chair and saw he was in a quandary. He must press him. "Ann came to you for help before. That must mean something."

Slattery rose and went to stand by the table, looking over the lawn . The flower beds needed tidying, he noted absently. "You're mistaken. We've barely exchanged words." He was tight lipped.

"That's not what I heard. Very close, was my information. Don't you two go way back?"

Slattery swung round. "Are you contradicting me? I'd watch your mouth if I were you. I only take so much from my employees. And I particularly don't like this sort of innuendo in my own home with my family down the hall."

Hood stared back at him, the ridges under his eyes prominent. "I bet you don't."

"You . . . don't try and threaten me in my own house. If you've any money matters to discuss in the future keep them for the office. Neither you nor Ann are getting a penny, d'you hear that? I've come across some cheap blackmail stunts in my time but this . . . it's laughable. I bet she's as healthy as I am."

Hood's face became dark, the eyes brooding and fierce. He stood up, taller than Slattery. "Why don't you see her and tell her that. Then you'll believe me. The face never lies." His voice rose then thickened. "You go and take a damn good look. Then tell me I'm wrong." He swung away and pulled the study door open. He could feel Slattery's angry yet perplexed, cautious stare behind him.

"I might just do that. Now you're in this state you'd better go. I've family waiting."

How nice, Hood thought bitterly, as he was shown out, down the hall and to the front door. He pictured the scene: the adoring family circle around Slattery. Dining off the finest china, drinking from cut crystal. All the fruits of dishonest toil. And he couldn't spare a few thousand to save a life. It made Hood want to spit.

Chapter Seventeen

After leaving Slattery's house Hood called in briefly on Ann to make sure she was all right. He didn't have the heart to tell her of his failed efforts, that he was credit black-listed.

Instead they chatted about inconsequential things - or tried to. But Ann's attention kept wandering until she had to admit that she was very frightened of the men with the torches coming back.

Hood begged her to stay at his flat or let him stay with her in her house but despite her fear she was adamant.

"No Bill, it's so tempting but I can't. I mustn't. Once they make me too afraid to live alone in my own house, they've won. I won't let them. Down to my last breath I won't."

Hood wondered whether she saw death on the horizon and was determined to hold out in her house till it overwhelmed her anyway. Then he decided maybe that was too melodramatic. More likely she had a gut feeling which told her to hold on to what was hers.

He kissed her but a kind of pathos was entering their embraces, however they might fight it. Passion and pathos didn't quite mix. After a while they mutually and gently released each other and Hood made his way to the front door.

"If you're all right . . ?" Still he paused on the threshold.

"Go on, will you get out of here?" she managed to scold him, with a surface brightness.

"I don't know, throwing a poor man out onto the street," Hood joked and then blew her a kiss as he left.

Slowly he drove home in his huge battered Volvo. Majestic, even in a scrap-yard it would stand out.

He let the car pull at its own pace while he chewed on a wine gum and let his mind drift. It was comforting for a few minutes to escape into this muffled night-world of empty pavements, closed shops, diffused light from the street lamps. It was like being wrapped in gauze.

But no matter how slowly he drove, eventually he reached his flat. He switched off the engine. These car rugs could do with a clean, he thought, as he stretched out his legs.

His chair and his thinking lay waiting for him, inexorable. Putting it off wouldn't help, only make him more tired. Reluctantly he climbed out of the car and entered the flat. He clumped, bad temperedly up the stairs and let himself into his flat.

It smelled cold and damp. Quickly he made a coffee and switched on the fire in the living-room.

For once he rebelled against the easy chair under the spotlight of the standard lamp and plonked himself down on the sofa. He stretched out full length and propped his head up in the corner. His mug of coffee rested, between his fingers, on the steel buckle of his belt. He took a sip, careful not to choke himself, and then gingerly placed the mug on his lap.

So much for the preliminaries. Now for the thinking. But of what? He knew beforehand that when he started there would be this blank. He'd tried every known avenue to finance and been rejected at every turn. Maybe there was nothing to think about - the money could not be had and that was an end to it.

But he couldn't accept that. A mere few days of looking and he was prepared to consign Ann to a terrible cancerous death. What sort of paltry attempt was that?

All right, he told himself, but what alternative was there? More banks, more loan sharks? Making futile gestures wasn't going to help Ann. And he didn't have all the time in the world. He couldn't waste weeks, months going down the wrong track. It was Ann's life he was dicing with.

No, he needed a sure fire thing, and he needed it now. Where did people find money, when all the usual avenues were closed?

He knew the answer; all the time it had been in the wings waiting to be summoned, recognised, but he had evaded it till now. It must be faced: they stole it.

If they were desperate enough. He ought to know that better than most, the number of bank clerks, estate agents, even bank managers he'd convicted.

So it had come to that: he had to steal four hundred thousand pounds. Child's play!

The mug slipped from its perch and burning his fingers he quickly transferred it to the floor. Then he swung his legs round, sat up, and rubbed his eyes. The room looked the same; in the seaside picture the gulls still wheeled overhead. He hadn't been sleeping: he had consciously become a criminal.

He must be crazy. He was a policeman, damn it, there to uphold the law not break it. There was nothing worse than a bent policeman, he knew that. It was a betrayal of peoples' trust.

Anguish ripped him apart. Betrayal of Ann if he didn't steal, betrayal of his trust if he did. What the hell was he going to do?

He jumped up and began walking frenziedly up and down, dragging his hand through his hair.

He must have got it wrong. The choice couldn't be as stark as that. There must be a third way - another attempt at appealing to Slattery or maybe to some other rich benefactor.

Hood swore: damn it, he didn't know any. He didn't mix in society where the rich could touch each other for a loan - "just to tide me over till the stocks move."

In his world four hundred thousand pounds was as distant as the moon. Only pools winners saw that kind of money in one lump.

No, there was no way out. He paused and thought of Ann. Was he ready to consign her to agony and death for a principle?

Then he thought of the alternative. Steal the money. If he succeeded he was committed to living a lie: the "dedicated police officer" who inside was corrupt, hollow. If he was caught, no money to save Ann and a life in jail, hated and despised, alone.

Whatever the outcome, once the money was taken there was no going back, it was irrevocable.

He paused, his two hands gripping the top of the drop leaf table. The curtains were drawn. As if mesmerised his eyes fixed on each thread, each stitch. Just to bury his head there, shut everything out, make it all go away.

Then he raised his eyes as another thought assailed him. With her principles Ann would never accept stolen money from him. What then? She must never know, never suspect, the money was stolen. He'd need a cover story she'd believe.

The chances of success were incredibly slim. So much could go wrong. Hell-fire, that's how he caught so many criminals himself. Because so much could go wrong: he repeated the words grimly to himself. The only advantage he had, was that from the other side of the fence, he knew all the pitfalls.

An immense sadness filled his heart. Instead of righting an old wrong, and nailing Slattery, he was contemplating a worse crime himself. The world seemed turned upside down, a hellish place.

But then it always had been: wanton cruelty had driven his father to that fatal heart attack.

It was a bad, black world, getting blacker every minute. He lay down again and watched the shadows seem to move over him, layer of darkness upon darkness.

Chapter Eighteen

When he awoke the next morning the rough, hemmed edge of the blanket was tickling his chin and light was filtering through the cotton curtains. He turned over for a minute but then decided he didn't need any more sleep. For once he felt clear headed and wide awake.

He quickly dressed and padded through to the kitchen to prepare some breakfast. Plugging in his electric razor to the adaptor on the wall socket, he pulled a small mirror from a cupboard. While the toast browned he shaved and hummed to himself.

Things looked a whole lot better in the light of morning. There was surely no need to go to extremes the way he had last night.

He put away his razor, buttered his toast, made the coffee and carried his breakfast through to the living-room.

Setting it down on the occasional table he went to draw the curtains. There was a light drizzle, but the cloud seemed to be clearing and it might be fine later.

He plumped down in the chair and ate his breakfast. It was funny how routine could banish one's dark forebodings. In a few minutes he would be off to work and resume his relentless dogging of Slattery's footsteps. He was still the dedicated, honest policeman. No one would ever know the thoughts he had had, the temptation he had suffered. He was all right, he could go on with a clear conscience.

For no one, not even Ann, could expect him to throw all this over and begin a life of crime, however worthy the cause. There were other, legitimate ways of raising money, like the ones he tried, and no one could ask more of him than that. In fact Ann had never asked him to raise the money for her at all. He had assumed the responsibility entirely of his own volition. Well, he was exercising his right to limit that responsibility to what was legal.

He munched his last piece of toast with satisfaction. It was good to get all this cleared up, and thought through.

Besides, suppose he was able to obtain the money and induce Ann to take it, there was no guarantee the treatment would be a success. Alternatively, Ann might be cured without such expensive treatment. Magazines were full of stories about people who through changed diet and positive thinking had survived even apparently inoperable cancers.

In other words there were so many imponderables attached to the situation, it made no sense to ruin his life on the chance he could buy Ann a cure.

Brushing the crumbs off his shirt he rose and carried his mug and plate back through to the kitchen. Then he doused them under the tap and left them on the draining board to dry.

Yes, he felt a lot happier. It was reassuring to rise and in the simple act of getting ready for work, put everything in perspective. With a light step he took up his coat and went down to his car.

At lunch time he decided to drive over to see how Ann was feeling. He didn't have to, he told himself, but it would be a good opportunity and more low-key than an evening visit.

As he parked outside her house he noticed that the boards had gone and the window was replaced, but the curtains were only partially drawn back. The other marks on the house remained and the pieces of broken slate still lay about.

He knocked and there was no answer. He tried again and was about to give up and go round the back, when the door opened. Ann's face, puffed up and swollen as from crying, peered through a crack.

"Go away. I don't want to see anyone."

"Ann," Hood appealed to her and pushed gently on the door.

After token resistance, Ann let go of the door entirely and retreated down the hall in carpet slippers. Hood followed her into the living-room.

She still had on her nightie and serge dressing gown roughly tied at the waist with a tasselled cord. Her hair was a tangle, with dark roots showing through.

"I didn't want you seeing me like this. I know what you're

thinking: midday and still not dressed."

Hood came and embraced her gently. "I'm not thinking anything. You've had a rough night, I can see that. What happened?"

Ann pulled away from him, and dragging a damp handkerchief from her pocket blew her nose. Then she dabbed her eyes. "Those bastards were back again at three in the morning. Foul language and stones against the windows. I thought they were going to break in any minute."

Hood nodded in sympathy as she sank down in a chair.

"But that's not the half of it. I haven't had a wink of sleep all night. If it wasn't them, it was this awful pain I've been getting in my belly. Sometimes it seems to move round to my back, and then to the front again. I can't begin to describe it. It's an awful griping as if all my stomach muscles are being torn and twisted." All colour had drained from her face while she was telling Hood this. The memory tormented her.

She leant forward and grabbed Hood's hand. "I'm so frightened of the pain coming back. I can stand anything else but that."

"Hasn't the doctor given you anything for the pain?"

"Doctors - pah!" Her tone was one of disgust. "He's given me some pain killers but they do no good - only give me indigestion on top of everything else. Oh Bill, why did all this have to happen to me? As if I hadn't had enough to contend with in my life." Her expression was baffled, uncomprehending, angry.

"I don't know. I wish I did."

Hood's sad expression became fixed and talk languished. Ann fiddled with her dressing gown cord, kneading it between her fingers. She wanted Hood to take her in his arms, tell her everything would be all right, give her some hope of an end to this appalling agony.

But he just sat there, not looking at her. He was probably thinking about something else, wondering how long he had to decently stay before he could leave.

What was he thinking of? Why didn't he say something? Here she'd been on her own all night with no one to talk with or turn to, and now he sat there dumb. Just one word of reassurance, one promise that something would be done, was that too much to ask?

But men were repelled when a woman was ill, she knew that. No point in expecting help in that quarter. Men were only any

110

good when the going was fine. Otherwise you couldn't see them for dust.

She looked at him again, defensively, as he averted his gaze to the floor. "It embarrasses you, all this, doesn't it? I can tell. Men are no good when it comes to suffering. You want to get away. Anything just to make your excuses and leave."

Hood did not answer at first, did not look at her. Finally: "It's not like that," he said in a low voice.

This only seemed to rile Ann more. "Look at me, why don't you? I'm not a skeleton yet to make love to. You hate the sight of me. Well no more than I do you, sitting there all smug with your fake concern."

Hood looked at her in guilt and reproach. "That's unfair, totally uncalled for."

Then Ann was standing over him. Slapping him on the back of the head. "Is it? Fake, fake, fake. Go on, get out of here."

Hood raised his arm to protect himself and slowly rose. Then he pinioned Ann's arms behind her.

He looked into her eyes; there was no recognition only pain, fear, agony, and despair, lashing out at anybody. Her pupils were tiny black balls of hate. She quivered, a sort of electricity running through her, as she struggled to free herself.

Hood turned with her imprisoned till he was near the doorway. Then releasing her, he sprang down the hall and out of the still part-open front door.

Then he was down the path and into his car.

Ann appeared in the doorway, gasping and heaving, her face purple in sullen fury. She waved two fingers at him. "Scum," she called out. "Worthless scum of a man." Then she withdrew herself back inside and dragged the door quickly shut. Sobs came as she hobbled back down the hall.

For Hood, sitting in his car, it was as bad. He was breathing quickly, horrified by what had happened to Ann.

Letting in the clutch he drove off. Then a sigh of relief. He was out of there, and Ann had made his decision for him. By throwing him out, she had made things so much easier and more clear cut than he could have hoped.

111

Chapter Nineteen

Suddenly weary and deflated Ann slumped into one of the arm chairs. She fingered the hem on the blue floral cotton cover. She had tried so hard to make this room nice, friendly and welcoming, and it had all been thrown back in her face.

The profusion of lights, all unlit in the daytime, struck her as unnecessary and pathetic. What did she need with all these spotlights, the corner uplighting, - was she expecting a party?

All the efforts she had made to jolly her life along, rang hollow now, hollow and futile.

She rubbed the sleep from her eyes, dry now, all cried out. She'd move away only she couldn't face getting another home together in the time left to her.

That Hood. She grunted. Then sighed. Why was it that the ones who seemed most dependable let you down? She could have sworn he would have stood by her, but then she'd thought that about better men than he in the past and they'd run out on her.

Well this was the last time, only she wasn't going to sit back and take it like before. What had she to lose this time? No, Hood was going to pay, for his own callous treatment of her and for all the other men before him who'd betrayed her.

Vigour seemed to return to her as she decided this. She tossed her head back and passed her hand through her tangled hair. She'd dress, sort herself out, while planning Hood's retribution.

A snarl passed her lips, as she leant forward looking into space. Hood might think he knew about hate, but he'd discover he'd seen nothing yet. What did they say about a woman scorned? He didn't know what he'd taken on, messing with her.

He thought he could be rid of her, with no come-back, when she became a liability. Well he'd discover very different. No wonder that wife of his had given him the push. No doubt he'd welshed on her too.

Men never understood a woman's pain. As long as she kept quiet about it, a man would go on ignoring it. And if she revealed her pain, the man was gone. Well Hood was going to feel her pain. She would make him suffer the way she was suffering. There was no walking away scot-free.

She had risen and gone running upstairs. The thought of revenge seemed to have energised her. She felt alive and in control again.

In her bedroom she rummaged through her closet. With the white wood doors wide open and several outfits flung on the bed she stopped, stock still. This new energy had set her thoughts in another direction. She'd show Hood that she had never needed his help in raising the money for her treatment. She'd do it herself, and the obvious source was Des Slattery. She could use her feminine charm on him to raise the money, and then she'd thumb her nose at Hood.

In that case she needed to take extra special care in dressing. As she tried to choose what to wear, her thoughts returned to years gone by, when Des had helped her out of a scrape. They went back a long way together, she and Des. He had a soft spot for her. She could be very appealing when she wanted. But he would never help her if she looked dreadful, incurable.

Among the pile of clothes on the bed, she found a long, green dress with a flattering, scooped neckline, well padded at the shoulders, with three-quarter length sleeves and pleated at the bottom. Yes, green, a friendly, non-aggressive colour. She mustn't put him off.

White court shoes with a good heel went well, and she took her pearls from their box and roped them around her neck. She looked into the mirror. Well, the rest of her was all right but her face needed working on. That pasty, washed out look was still there with grey under the eyes. She set to work with moisturiser, blusher, and powder to paint some life onto her face.

Finally she inspected herself again in the mirror and found a person transformed, almost blooming. She turned profile each way, and then full face again. Had hate and anger and desire for revenge brought about this transformation? Was her cancer concealed under powder and paint? The thought bewildered her but she mustn't let the magic wear off.

It didn't matter how she'd achieved the transformation. She was better, restored, if only for a few hours and that was all that mattered.

She was learning: short-term appearances were everything. Nothing lasted - not beauty, love, friendship, life itself. All was temporary, to be used up. It was a hateful philosophy but she was embracing it. Anything, to stop being a loser.

Coming to the centre of the room she paused. Here she was, ready and she hadn't even contacted Des. All dressed up and nowhere to go, so carried away had she been.

She ran down the stairs and phoned his office. After a brief delay she was put through to him. Her bubbling enthusiasm wouldn't take no for an answer. He refused a lunch date but she cornered him for the 'happy hour' at a classy pub they both knew.

Delighted she put down the receiver. Round one to her. Never before had she obtained a date with Des so easily. It must be a good omen that he was receptive to her.

What to do for the rest of the afternoon? She sauntered round, running her finger along the bookcase and pine bureau. But the roll of dust on the end of her finger did not discomfit her. No housework in her best clothes.

Instead she would pretend she was a lady of leisure. She snatched the cushions from the two armchairs and slotted them, an awkward fit, onto the gaping space in the sofa.

Then she stretched out and began flicking through the pile of magazines that had accumulated in the corner. This was the life, this was more like it.

At five fifteen Ann phoned for a taxi, and by half past was on her way. They were to meet at a pub called The Tavern in the city centre. Originally a bank, rationalisation had caused its closure, whereupon it was taken over by a brewery and transformed.

Ann climbed the sculptured steps and entered between two mighty concrete buttresses either side of the swing doors. Inside she was impressed by the maroon marble columns and the intricately decorated ceiling with its gold cross and medallion motif.

She crossed by the bar, where the service tills had been in its previous incarnation. A large floor area had been roped off for diners, and contained round tables with crisp white cloths and striped parasols. Flanking the dining area was a huge floor mosaic in concentric circles of green and turquoise.

Opposite her she noticed Des seated, lost in thought, incongruous beneath a parasol.

Ann walked energetically up to his table. She noticed how his grey hair was tightly cropped like steel wool. His aquiline nose, was strong and determined. She mustn't let him face her down.

"Hello Des."

He looked up quickly, as if surprised to see her. Then he managed a brief smile. "Ann, how nice. Well here we are. Do sit down. What can I get you?"

"Campari and soda, please."

Slattery nodded and attracting a waiter's attention gave his order for drinks.

There was a pause. To break the silence Ann said as gaily as she could, "I suppose I should feel flattered, you meeting me at such short notice."

Slattery inclined his head a fraction and replied, "It's always a pleasure to see an old friend."

Ann wondered how sincerely he meant this. Her drink arrived and she sipped on it.

"That dress is very becoming," Slattery flattered her, in his gallant but grave voice.

"Thank you. It's nothing new, but I like it." Ann took another sip of her drink and told herself not to overdo the bright, carefree chatter.

"You always look good." Then Slattery became serious. "I heard about your illness. I'm sorry."

"That's very kind." Ann smiled. All afternoon she'd been pretending away her cancer, but now she was jolted back to reality.

She tried to stop her voice from wavering, keep the smile fixed. "I have good days, bad days, nights." The smile slipped, and the terror and agony began to show at the corners of her eyes and mouth.

Impulsively she grabbed Slattery's hand and held it tight. "Des, we go back a long way?"

Reluctantly Slattery returned her grip. "Yes, we do."

"I know that doesn't give me the right to make demands, and we've always kept things on a business footing but . . ."

Slattery put his other hand on top of hers. "Ann, please don't say any more. Don't embarrass yourself."

Ann gazed straight back at him, bewildered, uncomprehending. "Why should I do that?"

"Bill Hood's been there before you. He came to see me with the whole story. Believe me, when he told me about the cancer, I was shocked. It's hit so many of my friends. I myself, a few years ago . . . but anyway that's not the issue."

Ann was trying to read his expression. The heavy eyebrows were knit in concern and his cheeks were flecked with red, from broken arteries.

"I told him, much as I'd like to help, I can't come up with such vast sums. I'm not made of money. Then Hood tried blackmailing me about our relationship, with my wife and family in the next room." He paused, his breathing now heavy. "That won't get the two of you anywhere. There was never anything between us. I'll squash anyone saying different. My family is sacred."

Ann leant across to try and make things right. "I didn't put Hood up to that. Believe me Des, I wouldn't try and pull anything on you. I just thought . . . for old times sake, some of the money?"

Slattery picked up a knife and began absently polishing it on the corner of the tablecloth. "How would you pay me back?"

"Pay you back?" Ann hadn't thought, her only horizon was the treatment and its limited chances of success. "I don't know. I could go to work for you again."

"What as?" Slattery couldn't hide his sarcasm.

"Oh I don't know Des. Does it really matter? Can I have the money or can't I? We can discuss paying it back another time."

Slattery shook his head. "I'm sorry Ann but I can't afford to. I've others to consider, you know. It wouldn't be fair to them."

"Des, what can I say? I'll do anything."

"Ann, please stop. Don't demean yourself. I told you not to press me. If you persist the answer has to be no. I'm sorry. That's final."

"Final! You bet it is, for me." Ann looked frenziedly to either side as if in escape of the situation. This couldn't be happening to her. A red mark was spreading across the neckline above her dress. "Do you know what you're doing? What you're sentencing me to?"

"Now Ann, don't be melodramatic. You can't put it on me. My family come first."

Ann's control broke and angry tears came coursing down. "Yeah, I know. I come second with everybody. Nobody gives a damn about what happens to me." She stood up, bridling, wondering what to do next. It all seemed hopeless. She felt trapped behind the ropes of this reserved table.

"Here," she said, "finish this drink for me." And she threw the remains of her Campari and soda in his face.

It was the first time she'd ever done such a thing and it gave her a moment of relief and satisfaction. Then instead of walking round, she climbed over the rope and flounced towards the door.

Angrily Slattery mopped his face and retrieved pieces of cherry and lemon from the lapels of his suit.

"Crazy woman," he muttered. "Four hundred thousand, she expects, just like that. Well she can whistle for it. Waiter, another drink. A large one."

Chapter Twenty

Hood sat, fists clenched, at his desk only a few feet from Slattery's office. Sometimes it amazed him that he was still tolerated there after what he'd said to Slattery. He felt more than ever an impostor, thinking his secret thoughts.

When he had left Ann's house he had known with total certainty and clarity what he had to do: steal the money and pay for the treatment that would save her life and her sanity. He couldn't sit idly by and witness the disintegration of her personality.

She hadn't been the Ann he'd known and loved, but some crazed stranger, her mind turned by anguish. When he thought of her previous joyfulness, spontaneity, so larger than life, the warm-heartedness - he couldn't bear to watch all that destroyed. Not when he could prevent it.

He toyed with some accounts on his computer screen while he tried to think. The obvious and pressing problem was how to get the money.

At first sight he was in the perfect position to embezzle it. He felt little guilt about stealing from a crook like Slattery. But could he get away with it? The audit controls were formidable and Slattery would pounce upon any shortfall in the accounts.

Besides, it was impossible to disguise the syphoning off of huge sums over such a short period. Time was against him. And Slattery knew he was desperate for money. His boss would be suspicious, on his guard.

Bitterly Hood regretted his openness with Slattery. It would have been much wiser to keep him in the dark.

No, he would have to look elsewhere. If only the banks had lent him the money - he wouldn't have to steal it from them!

What he needed was a cover and an alibi for the robberies. Then he realised he was sitting on one: while he was out collecting the takings from Slattery's establishments, he would do the jobs. Slattery trusted him to pick up these amounts and bring them back to the office. It was also his job later to retrieve the takings, total them up and bank them.

No one would ever suspect there to be too much money being placed in the safe. He could simply let the stolen money accumulate at the rear of the safe until he was ready to remove it. So long as the company takings didn't fluctuate suspiciously, no one had access to the safe except himself. It was the perfect hiding place.

But could he go through with the robberies? He didn't know. All his training, his background, his convictions stood in the way. However, he must force himself to do it. There was no alternative.

He knew that the more spontaneous and apparently amateurish the crime, the better its chance of success. Keep it simple. Mask on, into the building, take the money at gun point, run to a car well hidden, then away - ultimately back to the office as if nothing had happened. An undetected deviation from routine, that was what to aim for. Lose yourself in the crowd.

As he brooded on the possibilities he had a superstitious certainty that he would get away with it - at the time. He felt as if he could simply walk in and take the money and he would be inviolable. But in the end there would be a reckoning and they would catch up with him. Well that didn't matter, so long as Ann had paid for her treatment. They could do what they liked to him then. And if Slattery was the fall guy with him, so much the better. Hood laughed at the irony of it all.

People in the office looked at him, and wondered what was the private joke. Still, it was good to have Hood laughing at all. He tended to present a stricken grandeur which was exhausting to live with. It was nice to see him lighten up a little.

As the day wore on Hood decided that there was one more important move he should make to cover himself. After work he went to see Russell.

Hood found the Assistant Chief Constable in distracted and defensive mood, sitting behind his desk but gazing out of the window.

"Well?" Russell said, without looking at him. "I didn't send for you."

Hood was determined not to be riled and kept a calm and even tone as he remained standing on the other side of the desk.

"No, but there has been a new development. I've broken with Ann Renshaw. We won't be seeing each other any more."

Russell swung round on his chair to face Hood, puzzled and suspicious.

"Why now? I've been telling you to do that ever since this business began."

Hood took breath, and his eyes became guarded. "You did, sir, and I now realise that Ann could be an obstacle to my investigation. She's been seeing Slattery recently and I can't be sure what their relationship is, but anyway it's no good."

Russell's face broke into a self-satisfied smile. He stroked the fullness of his beard and pursed his lips. So Hood was jealous, that was at the bottom of this. The man couldn't stand the thought of Ann with someone else.

Then he stopped and his smile disappeared into a bitter line. Just like himself. Now Hood was finding out what it felt like. The joke was that Slattery was just using Ann. Wasn't he?

Hood was waiting for him to say something. Very well. "I'm glad you took my words finally to heart." Russell emphasised the last word, viciously.

"Perhaps now you will progress faster with the investigation since you can give it your single undivided attention."

Hood frowned at the slur on his efforts then gave up in disgust. After all, soon it wouldn't matter, when he crossed that line from law-enforcer to law-breaker.

He looked straight at Russell. What right had he to despise, condescend towards him, when the man was only doing his best to be a good policeman? He felt a sudden, brief surge of sympathy and pity for the uncomfortable man opposite who always seemed to wear his uniform like a costume. He was wriggling in it now, as if to try and be at ease and failing. Russell lacked self-belief and without it in a position of authority he was lost.

"I'll do my best," Hood assured him.

"Right Hood. Hurry things along. The Chief Constable is becoming impatient for results, and I can't stall him much longer. We need a conviction soon or I'll have to pull you off the case." Russell could barely conceal his pleasure.

Hood twitched at this reversal. Before he'd been pleading to be

120

taken off this hopeless assignment. But now with the robberies planned, he needed to stay on the case. All he could do was brazen it out.

"I've several leads sir, and I'm following them up as fast as I can. Just a few more weeks . . ."

"You'll get a few more days, more like," Russell continued, enjoying seeing Hood sweat under pressure.

"Yes sir."

"Right. Well there's nothing else is there?" Russell concluded the interview, assuming an impatient, busy air.

"No sir."

"Good." He had the braid. He would win. Hood was finished.

f

Chapter Twenty-one

Ann was drinking alone in The Newsroom. The bar staff had given up trying to draw her into conversation. She even ordered another drink by a simple gesture. Her appearance was a shocking contrast to her former gaudy outfits.

She wore a shapeless black wool dress with tassels hanging from the long sleeves and a v-neck. There was a vent in the side and the dress hung in two great flaps around her ankles. She could have been wearing widow's weeds.

No bubbly drink enlivened her gloom, only refills of gin with a trickle of tonic. She was staring blankly in front of her and then sometimes her head would slump down facing the table top.

Lifting her ahead again she forced herself to look around her, blearily. This was where the rat Hood had met her. Bitterly she remembered the glad hail they had exchanged and her invitation for him to join her at her table. She regretted it now, that cruel chance meeting.

How many times in the past years had she sat alone in a pub after a man had deserted her? It didn't bear counting. She had shrugged and put it down to bad luck or mens' faithlessness.

Her fist clenched and she banged it upon the table, making her glass jump and spill. Well no more. She would not be put upon or discarded again. Her time was short and Hood was going to pay, the fall guy for all of the rest.

She would never have thought that possible before. He had seemed so dominant, enduring, unassailable. But lately she had seen a new, craven side to his character. He was a backslider. Put him under pressure and he cracked, backed off, ran away. She should have realised when she learnt he'd fled his wife and the city because his business failed.

Her mouth filled with saliva. God, how she despised him. She'd like to ram all those caring, supportive words of his back down his throat. How he'd stand by her, never leave her, fight her enemies. What bunkum. He was running scared.

Well she'd hunt him down. He'd wish he hadn't been born by the time she'd finished with him. She gulped down the remains of her gin, relishing the relief and excitement that the thought of vengeance brought.

The angry words fell over each other in her mind for a while, but then lethargy and depression took over. Maybe she ought to cut back on the gin. Oh what the hell. She'd be dead soon anyway.

The horror struck her fully again at that moment. To die alone, unloved, in her home or a hospital bed, with only uniformed nurses left to fuss around her. No doubt they'd be secretly thinking what an inconvenience she was, and why couldn't she hurry up and die.

She looked up, misery standing in the tears on her face. Maybe she should do it now, commit suicide, and forestall all the agony, the drawn out suffering.

What was the use of going on, of revenge on Hood for that matter? But she balked there. She wasn't to be done out of that. Her last defiance against a cruel male world.

Oh but Bill, and her mind drifted against her will back to years past and their recent reunion. He was so handsome in a sort of battered way that spoke of the suffering he'd been through.

Why couldn't they have seen this thing through together, found a kind of beauty with each other? There she went again, romanticising. Would she never learn, never drop these illusions? She could never build anything with another person; it just didn't work that way.

She thought of all the lonely people she'd helped as a councillor. Everyone was alone. It was the law of life ultimately. But still, deep inside, she rebelled against this. Oh what was the use?

Glancing across she felt sorry for the bar staff. She was putting a real dampener on their evening. There at the end was the pretty sulky girl with whom Bill used to argue. Moving towards the cellar was the nervous, stringy man in his pin-stripe trousers.

She tried to smile towards them but they were avoiding her eye. The pub had seemed to blossom for her when Bill was there.

123

It had been like their own private club.

But the fun had gone out of it, now that Hood had disappeared from her life. That man had a talent for destroying her happiness. God, she hated him. Yes, she really did, she decided.

It was a new emotion for her, despite all the hate she had received. She felt her face become rigid under its influence, her eyelids constricted, her mouth tightened. So this was what hate felt like. She'd better remember, hang on to it, if she was to do to Hood what she had in mind.

Gathering up her handbag and coat she slithered across the seat and stood up. A sudden pain in her abdomen creased her and she bent over, leaning on the table. Just as the barmaid was moving to help Ann straightened up and managed a quick, brave smile.

"It's all right. I feel better now. It just came on so suddenly."

The barmaid gave her another anxious look but already Ann was forcing herself towards the door.

The pain was so unpredictable. She'd feel fine for hours, even able to forget about the cancer, and then just when she was least expecting it, she would be laid low.

Well she wasn't giving way to it this time. She had Hood to see. Trying not to jolt herself or twist her muscles, she navigated past the stained-glass door and around the corner towards Hood's flat.

The night was overcast with ragged banks of dirty brown cloud scudding across the sky. Ann pulled her belted, tan raincoat closer round her for it now felt baggy. The purple wool scarf hung behind her, forgotten.

With determined steps Ann pressed on though gusts of wind buffeted her and it seemed to her that people gave her strange looks. From a distance came the thunder of the railway marshalling yards.

Ahead was Hood's flat, just like an old school building. As a child she remembered thinking that one day all her worries and fears would be gone with adulthood. If she'd only known.

She was opposite the doorway now, and paused undecided. It would be so much better, easier, if he came out. But she couldn't stand round all night on the off chance. Besides it angered her to think that he might have settled in for the night while she waited here chilled and miserable.

She had to push hard on the swing door, taking all her strength

124

to gain admittance. Once inside, in the no-man's-land of the hallway she gained her breath. She saw the pigeon-holes and curiosity led her to look in Hood's but it was empty.

Swinging round she headed along the hallway and clattered up the chill, stone stairs. Then she was along to his room and knocked. There was no answer.

She tried again. Could he be in and ignoring her, hoping she'd go away? But he didn't know who was calling or why. She tried again but still there was no answer.

Was he lying low, the craven coward? She called out now, risking everything, her patience gone. But it was to no avail.

She listened for a few minutes at his door, but could hear nothing. Eventually she retreated, all the way downstairs, through the hallway and out into the street.

This was too much. If he'd been in, maybe she'd have let him off with a lecture, but this was unforgivable, demeaning. What was she supposed to do, hang around on street corners all night until he deigned to put in an appearance? All her life she'd waited around for men at their beck and call. Tonight was meant to be different. She was supposed to be turning the tables on Hood. A fat chance, with him nowhere to be seen.

She was exhausted, depressed, her head ached, and the gin lingered sickly in her stomach. So, should she go home and leave it for tonight? She started to retrace her steps then stopped.

It was no good. If she went home now, she'd never find the courage again. It had to be tonight. But where was he? She felt desperate, lost.

Casting around, she slumped back into the doorway of a closed-up shop. Empty shelving had been dragged to the middle of the bare floor. Dead mail lay inside near the letter box, last futile attempts to get in touch.

Two men passed by, glanced at her, and exchanged smirking glances. She knew what they were thinking.

"What are you looking at?" she snarled.

They quickened their pace down the street to the pub. No doubt they'd have a good laugh with their mates, about the old bag still on the game.

That wasn't her. She had constituents now, who depended upon her. She'd been neglecting them shamefully too. That was Hood's influence, always selfish. So her vocation was gone, along with everything else. Was nothing sacred?

There was the culprit. At the far end of the street she could see Hood's unmistakable outline.

He had on that same discoloured sheepskin coat, which he'd forgotten to button all the way up. He looked tired, his eyes downcast.

Now he was quickening his step, perhaps relieved to be almost home. She leapt off the step and hastened back up the street to intercept him.

He was just at the doorway when she placed her body in the way, barring his entrance.

"Ann! what are you doing here?"

"I came to see you."

Hood looked up and down the street, and then yearningly at the way through to his flat.

"I thought we had nothing left to say to each other."

"That's what you think, you two-time loser."

Hood was looking for a way to dodge round her. "Don't Ann. You'll only work yourself up, and it's not good for you."

Ann blocked his way, her hip jutting out aggressively. "You're always so concerned about my health. Until it involves doing anything. You heel."

Hood's eyes were becoming weary, the cheeks grey, with a five o'clock shadow.

"Whatever you say Ann. I'm too tired to argue. Get it out of your system."

"So now it's 'let's be patient with Ann. And then she'll leave me alone.' Well I've news for you Bill Hood. I'll give you no peace until the day I die."

Her eyes blazed at him. "See, I'm not afraid to say it, though you are. That's the difference between us. I don't know why I ever bothered with you."

"All right," Hood interrupted her. "That's enough. Go and shoot your mouth off some place else. I'm going inside." Hood was genuinely angry with her in her present mood.

"Oh no you don't get rid of me that easily. Remember you once told me how you dogged your criminals' footsteps, never let them be, gave them no peace? Well I'm going to do the same to you."

Hood's face registered how appalled he felt. This could ruin everything, his chance of getting the money and helping her, and she couldn't realise it.

"You mustn't. I forbid it. You . . ."

Ann laughed, excited at the success of her threat. "You should see your face. It's a picture."

"Seriously Ann, you must let me alone. We're finished. There's no good you hanging around me."

Ann looked down quickly. Her eyes had, unaccountably, been about to moisten but they hardened as she reminded herself of her hate. "But there is, for me. I can enjoy torturing you. I want to see you put through it, the way I've been."

"Ann, you don't know what you're saying. This isn't the real you. Stop before it's too late."

Something seemed to wrench inside Ann, as if a final transformation was taking place. "But it is - the brand new me, tough. No more hard luck stories."

It did almost seem to Hood that she was changed, into someone like that sulky Newsroom barmaid.

Ann sidled forward her coat open and said in a harsh whisper, "I'm going to leave you with something to remember me by, till the next time."

Hood braced himself for the kiss. Her lips, like poison darts, drew close to his cheek, and for some reason he shuddered and drew back.

It was too late. A knife in her hand, Ann was slashing his chest. Hood yelled in pain under the flurry of blows and grappled with her. Deep gashes were torn in his hands and arms as he fought for the knife. Blood spurted from the wounds to his chest. Then with a hard blow to her wrist he knocked the knife to the ground. Ann stood there gloating as the blood poured down his shirt and coat sleeves. She was exultant.

Hood was groaning and trying to stem the flow with his coat. Ashen he looked at her. "Go on, clear out now. You've done your worst." And he waved her away.

But Ann stayed a mite longer, savouring his agony. Then even she had had enough and turned on her heel satisfied.

Hood watched her go, horrified and disgusted. Then he dragged himself inside and staggered up the stairs to his flat. Every step was torture. His chest seemed about to burst, and his coat in ribbons tripped him up.

Trying to keep his clothes wound tight around him, he fumbled for his keys and let himself in to the flat.

Then he lunged for the bathroom. Dried blood was congealing all over his hands and arms. And suddenly this gave him hope.

He peeled back his coat and let it fall from his shoulders. Fortunately it had borne the brunt, saving his arms.

His chest however, felt ablaze. He opened his shirt. Rivers of blood were still pumping and would not be staunched.

He knew he had only minutes to summon a doctor before he bled to death. Wrapping a towel around his middle and tying it hard, he stumbled through to the lounge and found the phone.

He located a doctor's locum who seemed more asleep than awake, but agreed to come. Hood didn't want the hospitals or police involved.

"Thank God," Hood cried out, and then retreated to the bathroom.

The towel around his middle was crimson now. He had to risk untying it, and then quickly substituted another.

But his strength was failing and it took him all his efforts to tie the other towel in place.

Then, spent, he sank down and sat on the edge of the bath. Finally he succumbed and slipped down till he lay stretched out on the floor.

"Please hurry," he muttered. "There's not much time left."

Chapter Twenty-two

Hood lay there, propped against the bath. His chest hurt as if a hot iron was pressed against it. He tried to shallow his breathing and clutched the towel hard to him, knowing his life depended on staunching the flow of blood. But still it gushed down from his chest, onto his trousers, and then snaked along the creases until it congealed in black pools on the floor.

The doctor couldn't be long, he told himself. But then he remembered how dozy the man had seemed and began to panic. He couldn't die like this, simply bleeding his life away. He tried calling out to the neighbours but his voice was weak and it strained him to make any noise. The sound echoed around the bathroom but did not seem to carry anywhere else. How pathetic, he fumed. Then his anger turned on Ann who had done this to him. What a person to seek to help! It was like caring for a rabid animal.

Maybe he should get up and try to reach help. He tested the strength in his legs for a kneeling position. But his limbs were wobbly, as if he'd been in the water for hours, and wouldn't support him. He fell back exhausted from the effort. So he must lie here helpless. He thought of the phone, his life-line, in the lounge. It might as well be miles away for all the use it was to him.

Then he heard distant footsteps. Hope leapt up inside him and he began calling out till he was forced to subside into coughing. Please let them come nearer, he prayed.

There was a clattering along the corridor. Sweat appeared on his brow: had he left the front door open when he stumbled inside? His mouth was working with the strain of hoping.

The steps came closer, and paused. "Come in, come in, damn

it," he cried. Then they resumed. By their lightness, and the tell-tale tap tap he knew it was a woman.

His mind raced at the possibilities. If it was Ann, had she returned from remorse to check he was all right? Or had she come vindictively, to finish him off? Involuntarily he pictured her appearing round the door with the bloodstained knife in her hand, ready to slash him to pieces.

He slunk against the bath. He didn't know what he hoped or expected now. Was it better the front door barred entrance to whoever it was? But things couldn't be much worse than they were. He hung his head in despair.

"Bill? My God."

He twisted his head round to see Monica's anxious and appalled expression. She was coming through the doorway and kneeling down beside him.

"Careful you don't get blood all over you," he warned her.

"Never mind that. What's happened to you?" Her small, sharp features looked into his, her eyes behind the narrow rimmed spectacles alert and intense.

"I've . . . been stabbed," he got out as his fingers pointed inwards clutching the towel to him.

"Oh Bill, who did this?" She was angry now, and distraught at the sight of his suffering.

Hood turned away. "Don't know," he whispered.

Monica felt helpless. She knew little first-aid and it seemed unwise to remove the towel however much soaked with blood.

"I bet I do. Still that can wait. I'll get a doctor."

Hood put out his hand to detain her. "Already have. One's on his way. Be here soon."

Monica grasped his hand with hers. "Sure." She looked over his crumpled form, so different from the tall, powerful figure she was used to.

She'd had to come back to see him. Even though she had nothing new to tell him, she couldn't stop herself. Any excuse to be with him for a few minutes. When she'd heard that Ann had returned home it was like a starting pistol.

She flinched at the memory of her own jealousy of Ann. To win Hood so easily, and keep him on a string. How she would love to be in that position. Instead she had Charlie, and felt a sudden squall of disgust.

What had they done to Hood, between them? She couldn't stand the guilt. She had to say something.

"Was this about Ann again? Who worked you over? I'll bet you were trying to protect her."

Hood tried to think what to reply. He shook his head violently, but without total conviction. Monica's words were like a mirror version of the truth.

She put her hand to her forehead. "I'm sorry Bill. Be calm. I shouldn't be exciting you. It's just . . . I had nothing to do with it. You do believe me, don't you? All this violence, it's out of my hands. I have no control over it."

As she said the words the bitterest recriminations against herself were starting up inside. Why hadn't she control when she was leader of the Council? She could snap her fingers and have council officials running - and frequently did. She was a little autocrat and yet she couldn't put a stop to this intimidation. Worse, it was escalating into stabbing now. How long before someone was killed? And she stood by and proclaimed her innocence. At that moment she hated herself so much, she found it hard to live with herself.

But she couldn't inflict all this on Hood in his weakened state. That would be too selfish for words, only piling on his agony. So she knelt beside him, trying to cradle him in her arms.

She took off her grey blouson jacket and wrapped it around his shoulders.

"There, are you warmer now?"

He shivered and nodded.

It eased her conscience to be able to comfort him, and relieve a little of his suffering.

Another footstep was heard coming along the corridor and then over the threshold to the flat, pausing impatiently.

Monica called, "In here."

A moment later a young doctor with a severe hair cut and swarthy skin came into the bathroom.

"So. Mr Hood? Let's have a look at you. Will you excuse me please," and Monica was eased aside. "Are you his wife?"

Monica looked down. "No, just a friend."

"Well could you leave us for a moment, to make room. It's very cramped in here."

Hurt, Monica said, "Of course, yes," and withdrew.

She paced the hall, wondering what was going on in the bathroom. Was it worse than either she or Hood had feared? Her hand went to her throat. Suppose he died in there, his last minutes spent in that sordid, dirty bathroom on those bare floorboards.

Biting her lip, she crept back for a peek. The doctor was peeling back the towel, and tearing the shirt away from the wounded area of chest. Then he replaced the towel and sprang up. Brushing past her he said, "I'm ringing for an ambulance, to get him to casualty. He's lost a lot of blood."

Monica sat down with Hood to keep him company while the doctor phoned.

Hood smiled in a tired way at Monica. "You're good to have here."

Monica forced a smile, to prevent tears. "Don't say that. You know I don't deserve it. But I'll make it up to you."

Hood's head lolled back, and Monica gripped his hand. The doctor reappeared in the doorway. "The ambulance will be here very soon. There's not much more we can do for him here."

He knelt down and felt Hood's pulse. "What happened, do you know?" he asked Monica.

She shook her head, glad to be ignorant of the details, but still feeling guilty. She was sure that she was blushing and that the doctor must notice.

But he only nodded and went back to his patient. A few minutes later ambulance men carried Hood downstairs into the ambulance. Monica hung around uncertainly outside the van.

"Can I go with him?" she asked.

But the doctor dissuaded her. "There's nothing you can do. Leave him to us, we'll look after him."

Monica nodded, and watched shivering in the roadway as the ambulance roared away, siren wailing. Then she turned and wandered in a daze back to her car.

She prayed that Hood would be all right. But then so many things depended upon that. Changes had to be made. She couldn't go on like this, confronting the victims of political violence, apologising all the time and never knowing if she was believed. It was eating away at her self respect and she couldn't stand it any more. She had to speak to Charlie tonight.

Leaving her car outside the flat, she walked across the city centre to the Labour Club. Rushing up the steps she ignored a couple of members coming down, and heard their muttered, "Stuck up cow." But she didn't care. She had more important things to worry about than her reputation.

She accosted the man on the door: "Where's Charlie?"

He nodded towards the committee room. She hurried along the corridor and went in. Voices fell silent; she had gate-crashed a meeting. There was not a woman in the crowded room except herself.

"Monica," Charlie called out from behind the bar. "What an unexpected pleasure," trying to ease the situation.

There was a murmur of dissent. Monica, ignoring this, went up to the bar and hissed, "Charlie, I have to speak to you now, in private."

"But darling," Charlie tried to mollify her, "how can I? I'm on bar duty tonight. They'll go spare if there's no one to serve them ale."

"I don't care. We have to talk and it won't wait."

Charlie noticed the black bloodstain on her clothes and her generally dishevelled and agitated appearance.

"OK if it's serious."

Asking Trevor, one of the regulars, to cover for him, Charlie led the way out and through to the pool room The pool tables were deserted at the moment and the bar stood empty. They walked across the maroon carpet of the large, empty room. A huge gilt mirror hung on one side, over a begrimed green and gold patterned wallpaper.

Threading their way between the tables, Charlie and Monica found some matching green beige seats.

"Well?" Charlie's small frame was perched on a stool, his scalp glistening under the lights, his waistcoat stretched over his pot belly, like a mischievous gnome.

Monica breathed out. It was hard to know how to begin without antagonising Charlie. She passed her hand across her tight-knit blonde curls.

Charlie grinned aggressively at her. "Come on slow coach. I've thirty thirsty men in there. And when that meeting breaks up which should be . . ." he consulted his watch - "in about fifteen minutes time they'll be clamouring for beer."

"I know Charlie. Don't go on." She hesitated then plunged in: "I went to see Bill Hood tonight."

Charlie's eye glinted with malicious satisfaction. "I thought so. You've been acting very suspiciously. I can always tell. I can read you like a book. Did you enjoy yourselves?" Charlie enjoyed playing the innocent.

Monica gritted her teeth. Charlie was going to make it hard for her. "No, as it happens. But I didn't go for that. When I got there he'd been stabbed. There was blood everywhere. It was awful."

Charlie was becoming restless. He had an impulse to comfort Monica, but then contempt for her in visiting Hood at all held him back.

"They carted him off in an ambulance. Oh Charlie, you should have seen him."

"Why, what good would that have done?" Charlie's tone was cold, abrupt. He knew what to expect from her and it wouldn't wash.

"You liked him too. You told me once he was good for a laugh."

"What if I did?"

Monica moved closer to him, her tight, check skirt riding up. "We can't go on crucifying him like this. It's got to stop."

"So he told you I was behind it?"

Monica clicked her tongue at his apparent wilful misunderstanding. "No of course not. Why would he suspect you? He thinks you're an amiable buffoon trying to keep me in order. I'm the villain of the piece."

"So he accused you."

"Charlie," Monica raised her voice and then quickly lowered it again to a harsh whisper, "he didn't accuse anybody. He didn't need to. One mention of Ann Renshaw and he acted like he'd been kicked. You can't go on taking out your vendetta against her on him."

Charlie's eyes narrowed and his mouth became small, twisted in disgust.

"Now you listen to me," he said in a very quiet, threatening voice. "Don't you ever take somebody else's side against me again. You assumed I was behind it without even asking. For your information my boys didn't lay a finger on Hood tonight. Maybe Slattery's men did it. Maybe Ann herself. Who knows? Who cares? If it put him in the hospital, all to the good. I'm not going to cry over him."

Monica recoiled. "How can you be so callous?"

"Listen, don't go soft on me now. This is a rough business. We're playing for big stakes. You never used to complain about my methods."

Monica squirmed. "I know and I was grateful. But stabbing, torching Ann's house, this is beyond the pale. I can't go along with it."

Charlie moved with a fighter's speed and gripped her wrist. "You'll go along with whatever I tell you to. Or else." Then with his other hand he slapped her twice across the face. "Understand?"

"Charlie!" Monica tore herself away from him, kicked over her stool, and fell sprawling. She picked herself up, and stood shaking with fury. "You bastard Charlie. Try that again and I'll . . ."

"You'll what? You need me. There's not a man in this ward would lift a finger for you without my say so. Just you remember that."

Monica, her face crimson, her glasses framing her angry eyes, was beside herself but she knew it was true and that only made it worse.

Baffled, she withdrew to a safe distance. "So you won't call off this witch-hunt?"

"Not until we've cleansed the Party. They've got to learn they're either with us or against us."

"And who decides that?"

Charlie looked genuinely hurt. "I have my orders too. It's hard for me as well. I don't enjoy playing the fool, people patronising me. I have my pride."

Monica's breathing was slowing down now, and she was calmer. A desolate disappointment hung over her. She moved back to Charlie. "Oh yes, your pride. Oh Charlie."

She stretched out her arm half way towards him. "What am I going to do with you?"

Charlie swept her hand away. "Stop chasing other men for a start. Bill Hood's not for you. I'm the only man for you. Don't you forget it."

"I know Charlie." She felt very tired now. "Let's talk about it another time. I'm bushed. All the excitement I guess."

"Yeah, you go home and get some rest. I'll try and leave early and we'll have a cosy evening together, just the two of us. You won't have to do a thing."

"I know Charlie. You'll take care of everything." Then she went off, hobbling as one shoe came adrift.

Charlie watched her, small awkward but a little firebrand when she got hold of an idea. He'd have to watch those ideas of hers and make sure they didn't get out of hand. The bosses wouldn't like it and he didn't fancy answering to them for her. Better keep her under close wraps.

Chapter Twenty-three

It was late that night when two ambulance men helped Hood up the stairs to his flat. His face was haggard, eyes great shadowed gouges. His slashed sheepskin coat was pulled round him and his mouth was contorted as he negotiated his painful way, step by step. The cold stone seemed to jar his footsteps and turning the corner at the top involved an agonising twist of his torso. His chest muscles strained against the tight wrapping of bandages.

"Here, take it slow and easy," one of the ambulance men told him, a burly, friendly fellow with a light beard. "You don't want to re-open those wounds. I'm not sure they should have let you out at all," he tut-tutted.

Leaning on them for support Hood ploughed his way down the corridor.

"I'll be all right. Just get me inside, that's all."

"You're the boss," the other ambulance man answered, and they waited as he placed his key in the lock.

Then with a great effort he pushed the door and it swung slowly open. Hood peered into the darkness and was suddenly afraid. He had an irrational premonition that someone was going to leap out at him.

He paused on the threshold, the sweat going cold on his forehead.

"I can't go in," he muttered. Then he turned his head away.

"What's the matter, mate?" the burly ambulance man sympathised. "Got the jitters? Heaven knows it's enough to give anyone the shakes, coming into an empty home at this hour." Boldly he stepped forward and fumbled inside the doorway for a light switch.

After a few seconds scrabbling the hallway was illuminated,

and Hood could see the familiar chipped blue and white paint on the interior doors.

"There you are, it's all yours," and the ambulance man strode about confidently in the hallway to dispel Hood's anxieties. "Snug as anything." Privately he was thinking 'what a mausoleum' as he rejoined his colleague in the corridor.

"Well if you don't need us any further we'll be going." He kept up the cheery tone.

In the hallway Hood turned with a grim smile. "Yes, of course, thanks. You've both been a big help."

"Take care of yourself," the burly one's mate called as they disappeared along the corridor and down the stairwell.

Hood was left alone in the hallway. Gingerly he pulled off his coat, one sleeve at a time and hung it up. Habit, he told himself, considering the state of the coat.

Then he paused, uncertain. None of the rooms was particularly inviting. In the end from weariness he picked the living-room and putting on the light flopped into his usual chair under the standard lamp.

Sitting for a few moments he realised he was cold and would have to move. He strained his hand against the chair arms to press himself up on to his feet. Then he stumbled across the bare carpet and pulled the curtains. They snagged and he had to disentangle them. Then it was down to switch on the electric fire. Irritated he kicked it but the coal effect still refused to illuminate. It remained its dull, lifeless self.

Back towards his chair, he stood in thought. Was there anything he'd forgotten before he sat down again? He didn't think he could manage rising again for a while yet. His mind was tired, and giving up on the question he sank down again. The hessian covering tweaked and scratched under him.

At last he was at rest of a sort. That was what the doctor had advised, ordered. "The only way I'm letting you home at all, is if you promise to rest," he'd said. "It's a miracle the knife missed an artery. If one had been severed, well you'd be a goner now. As it is you've lost too much blood. So go to bed and stay there. We'll send for you in a few weeks to take out the stitches."

Still, what did these doctors know? He was strong as an ox, he told himself. He'd be up and doing tomorrow.

But for tonight, at the moment all he could do was sit there. He tried dragging the occasional table across and then resting his foot on it. However the sharp edges cut into his calf and it felt in imminent danger of collapse, so he left it.

How could Ann have done this? He gnawed on the side of his hand just below the stitches. Whatever she thought of him - and it was clear she had formed the lowest opinion possible - to lunge at him with a knife! Imagine carrying around that flat table knife she used for paring carrots and green beans. She must be sick in the head.

All the more reason for getting her treatment as quickly as possible. She was changing out of all recognition into a cruel, vengeful termagant. If he didn't move quickly she'd be irredeemable. But how could he, his chest slashed to ribbons?

He thought back to the attack - the surprise, bewilderment at first, then panic as Ann seemed to go berserk. And then later lying down in the bathroom and thinking he was dying.

The life had been oozing out of him. If he hadn't made that phone call when he did, if Monica hadn't appeared, he'd be gone.

The light in the room seemed to flicker, with an electricity surge. The chocolate curtains for a second looked a shade darker, like black-out drapes. He passed his hand in front of his face.

So close to death. He'd had brushes with it during his police career but nothing that close and drawn out. Usually they'd been sudden dangers and then gone. But this time death had been stalking him.

Ever since his return to the city things had been closing in on him. Fate, destiny, was toying with him on its course. Doom was all around him yet he had been preserved - to save Ann. He was indestructible, until he had served his purpose.

Always the same: if he escaped one duty, he was trapped by another. Anger flared up inside him. Why should he go on, knocking himself out, ready to sacrifice everything for a woman who plunged knives at his heart. He loved her and she treated him as scum. How dare she? He'd never put up with that from anyone else, so why from her?

He'd like to pay her back, punish her, that was his way, the way he'd brought with him to the city. But he couldn't strike back at her; pity and love held his hand.

He was a prisoner struggling against his beloved jailer. Anger and love alternated in his mind till he was weary. It was a merry-go-round and he couldn't get off.

For relief he turned to the thought of Monica and her unselfishness. From the outside she appeared so brusque and unprepossessing but she had hidden qualities of concern, delicacy, warmth even.

Or was it simply guilt? She thought that her political heavies were responsible, while he was protecting Ann from them.

Monica was strange, so urgent and sincere, so breathless and a little awkward. She'd be hard work for Charlie, he conjectured. But easier than Ann was for him.

Ann: a one woman crusade against himself, the man who could save her life. It was symptomatic of how the city turned people crazy.

Maybe he was barmy himself, with his hate obsession raking up the past, his criminal master plan, his vain hope to somehow bring down Slattery. None of it made sense. How did he ever get into this situation?

At that point he stopped, exhausted. He couldn't review his entire past life now. He was so tired his eyes could barely stay open. The bookcase and drop-leaf table opposite were just blurring shapes now.

Dragging himself up, he plunged for the door, and then pressing along the walls of the hallway he reached his bedroom.

The door. Again that irrational fear that Ann might be waiting inside with a knife poised. He could see the blade, hovering.

Mouth dry, breath heavy he leant against the door jamb. He couldn't go on like this, jumping at shadows. He twisted the door knob. The door slid open. Darkness beckoned.

Sighing he went in. Doom might be comforting. He couldn't be bothered any more. He was just too tired. The shape of the bed welcomed him and he flopped down on top of it, in the dark. Somehow that seemed to suit him better than the light. He slept.

The next morning Hood dragged himself into the office. His face was ashen, cheeks gaunt, and he held himself tightly, in an uncomfortable bundle, to prevent the chest lesions opening up.

Slattery, coming across the room to check some figures, stopped at his desk. "My God, you look awful. What's been happening to you?"

"Nothing. I've just got a bad gut. That's all."

"That's all, nothing. Come into my office."

Reluctantly Hood followed Slattery through. Once the door was shut, Slattery perched on the corner of his desk. "Now come on, what's the story?"

Hood sighed. There was no keeping things from Slattery. "I was set upon. Some burly bloke . . ." He began to improvise using the physical description of the ambulance man.

"So how bad is it?"

"I got some nasty knife wounds, though I managed to fend him off in the end. I wound up in casualty."

"I'm surprised you're not still there." Slattery scratched his head in perplexity. "You seem to attract an awful lot of trouble."

Hood let his anger boil up. "It's not my fault. I was walking along the street minding my own business. It's this city - the streets aren't safe to walk." The irony was not lost on him, but he strove to hide it.

Slattery became impatient, and slid off the corner of his desk. He went to look through the window. There was a distasteful-looking amusement arcade opposite, with cheap plastic stars on its walls and the poster painted word 'Amusement' inscribed in a rainbow over the entrance. What a way to make his living, he sighed, cheap and nasty. Then his thoughts came back to Hood.

"Well that's as maybe. The point is, can I trust you to do the rounds and pick up the takings in your condition? Suppose you were mugged?"

Inwardly Hood panicked. It would ruin his plans if he was taken off the collection round. It was to be his alibi.

"I can do it. Have I ever let you down?"

Slattery managed to look embarrassed. "No, that's true. Well, if you're sure. But for God's sake be careful - it's my money you're responsible for."

Hood grinned, but his mouth was twisted bitterly. No concern for him, his welfare, only the money. Still, what could you expect from a man like Slattery.

"Is that all?" Hood asked.

"Yes, you can go," Slattery told him, suddenly tiring of the conversation, and again he turned to the window.

There was no fun in winding up Hood at the moment, in his condition. Who had put the knife in? Not one of his boys, surely. They knew better than to go freelance. Who else? A stranger, a psychopath who just happened to be passing? It was unlikely, but who knew?

Hood returned to his desk. He managed to swivel on his chair without hurting himself too much and switched on his computer screen. For a few hours he could take his mind off his pain with brain work.

But inexorably the hours went by till it was time for him to begin the takings collection round. He went to the safe and took out the large, empty, gaberdine pouches.

He could tell that Slattery was watching him, doubtful, from his interior office window. Quickly Hood closed the safe and emerging from the storeroom, walked to the office door, praying he would not be recalled. But Slattery had apparently not thought better of sending him, and he was allowed to proceed

Once in his car he checked he had everything he needed. Beside him on the floor was the lightweight car maintenance overall that would cover him head to toe. In the glove compartment was the black, woollen balaclava helmet with holes for his eyes and mouth. Hidden behind it was the gun.

He had it all planned. He'd do the pick-ups as normal till he came to the fourth one, from the Highgate betting shop. Just two streets away was the bank he'd targeted. They were all in isolated pockets of the city, where security was light and lackadaisical.

The first two collections tired him more than he'd expected. Each time the staff had sympathetically commented on how washed out he looked and he'd struggled to carry the money out to the car. How on earth was he going to manage when he came to the robbery?

He sat behind the steering wheel, shaking in reaction to all his exertion. He'd never make it. He'd either collapse in the bank or be unable to carry the weight of money to the car. It had to be called off.

Part of him gave a great sigh of relief, while another sternly reproved him and told him he had to go on with it.

"You can't string yourself up to this again. You know you can't. It's now or never. Oh hell, what am I going to do?"

He stared in an agony of indecision through the windscreen, till a passer-by gave him a worried look and he drove off.

The next two collections were easier. He was learning how to pack and lift the money without twisting too much, and the staff seemed to notice his disability less.

Perhaps he could make it after all. Hope sprang up in him. But what if the bank staff noticed his painful movements? Those sort of things gave one away. On the other hand his injuries were another alibi. No one would ever consider him possible of committing armed robbery in his condition.

So it was a toss up again, an impasse. Should he go through with it? He sat there, doubts gnawing at him. Then came the image of Ann, like a deranged wild cat setting about him. Something had to be done about that and fast. This was no time for dithering.

"Oh what the hell." He let in the clutch and drove down one terraced street, then across by the park. He drew the car up behind some disused garages on waste ground.

The bank lay through an entry and just beyond the fish and chip shop and the off-licence. Very salubrious.

Gulping he struggled into the overall and then grabbed the rest of his equipment. His hands trembled and the gun fell with a clatter on to the car floor.

"Damn these jitters," he cursed himself and picking it up, glanced around him through the windows. But no one was about to notice.

Climbing out of the car he had the balaclava and gun in a bin bag. So this was it. He was crossing a point of no return. Farewell an honest and respectable life. Oh well, would he really miss it? Of course he would, but it couldn't be helped. Ann took priority. Respectability made poor company; you couldn't love it.

He set off trying to maintain a quick but normal pace so as not to attract attention.

Two children were playing by the kerb, floating bits of paper down the water to the grid. They didn't even look up as he passed. They had more engrossing things to do. He sighed and carried on.

Through the entry and he was behind the corner. Now speed was of the essence, but he forced himself not to run. He was outside the bank. He knew what to do. But his hands refused. They hung there, useless, in front of him.

He was standing in full view of the street. What was he up to? He asked himself. Forcing himself he took out the balaclava. He mustn't tear the seam, he reminded himself, furiously as he pulled it on. Then he was ready.

He marched into the bank and pulling out the gun strode up to the desk.

The woman cashier screamed. This threw him. He said nothing. The video camera's eye was on him from the top corner of the room.

The seconds ticked on, by the clock on the wall. He could just walk out again now. It was becoming like a dream.

Suddenly a strangled Irish accent said, "bring fifty thousand pounds out here this minute or I start shooting." It was him, he'd amazed himself.

Two elderly customers were standing stupefied by the wall. Then as they sidled along towards the door he said, "Don't either of you move."

They nodded, terror in their eyes, and stood still on spindly legs.

The woman reappeared moments later and threw some packets of notes on the floor.

"That's not fifty thousand," Hood growled. "You've ten seconds more then they get it." He motioned to the old couple who visibly jumped at the threat.

"We haven't any more," the woman wailed desperately.

"Find some."

She hurried away and Hood saw her in urgent conversation with a young man in spectacles and a pin stripe suit.

The next moment together they appeared with some more packets and threw them on the pile.

"That's better," Hood grunted. "Now lie on the floor - everybody." While they obeyed he scooped the money into the bin bag.

Then he rose and moved to the door. "Anyone coming out of here in the next five minutes will be shot."

With that he was gone. He yanked off the balaclava and stuffed it and the gun into the bin bag on top of the money. He was down the entry now. The children had gone. It was all working out perfectly.

He jumped into the car and drove off. After two miles, he pulled into the kerb and struggling in the driver's seat, removed his overall. Then he transferred the money to one of the gaberdine pouches. He couldn't believe it. Things had gone more smoothly than he ever expected. It was having the initiative, taking them by surprise, that made it work. The staff in the bank were too taken aback to resist. Oh if all robberies were like this.

He was euphoric, and told himself he must calm down and be careful. Pulling up outside Slattery's Leisure Club in a leafy pleasant suburb he forced himself to walk sedately inside. The only comment he received was that he looked cheerful, which was innocuous enough.

Then he had only one more collection to make, and back to the office. His conscience hadn't bothered him once. Robbery was just a job of work to him now.

Back at the office he struggled in with the pouches, dragging them across the floor to the storeroom safe.

Cobham appeared as if by magic at his side. "Here let me help. I'll put them in the safe for you." His sleeves were as usual rolled up in eagerness to help. His face was florid with embarrassed good intentions.

"No, Stan. No. Please." Hood extended the word in strained anger. "I don't want any help. This is my job. The safe is my responsibility."

Cobham sprang back as if he'd been stung. "Well all right. There's no need to take that attitude, old man. Some people are so sensitive," he muttered to one of the clerks as he retreated to his own desk.

Breathing heavily and relieved to be left alone, Hood opened the safe and began loading in the pouches. He was carefully arranging them so that the one with the stolen money was secreted at the back behind a metal shelf.

"Everything all right?"

Hood jumped involuntarily. Slattery was standing over him, his long nose pointed inquisitively towards the fumbling going on in the safe.

Hood withdrew his hand and knelt back. "Yes, fine. Just packing in the pouches. There's some weight in them. Takings must be good this week."

Slattery gave him a beady, suspicious look. "They are every week."

Hood knew that Slattery was for a moment considering whether Hood could be trusted. He looked straight back at Slattery. "Good job we have strong audit controls here, with all this money."

"I'm all the control we need . I know exactly how much should

145

g

be there. No one's ever pulled the wool over my eyes."

"I'm sure."

Hood finished locking the safe, and then walked slowly back out of the storeroom to his desk. Had Slattery become suspicious all of a sudden?

But it seemed a passing fancy of the boss's, for the next moment Slattery had patted him on the shoulder and was chatting genially.

"You're the main one I rely on, I trust," Slattery suddenly confided in him.

"That's my job, making sure the books balance."

Slattery nodded thoughtfully then wandered back to his office.

Hood wondered if he resented having to trust and rely on other people. Probably he wanted to do everything himself.

Just so long as he didn't start counting the pouches and emptying them all out. He'd find that the takings were thirty or forty grand up. That would take some explaining!

Two hours later Hood retrieved the pouches full of takings from the safe. He totalled them and then watched as Slattery checked his calculations. There was no discrepancy.

Satisfied Slattery announced: "Right, get this lot banked would you? We wouldn't want any to go missing."

Chapter Twenty-four

All the other staff had gone. Slattery had asked him to lock up. Still he hung on, as the afternoon lengthened into evening. Somehow he could not tear himself away from the money. Despite himself he was drawn back to the safe. He had to see the stolen proceeds one more time. The money held him under a spell.

An inner voice warned him that he might be discovered. Slattery might return and catch him at any moment. But he did not move.

He was in a kind of trance. Putting out his hand he steadied himself against the safe. That felt comforting, reassuring. Then quickly he locked it again, and retreated into the main office.

Breathing out through his nose he snuffled. It was stuffy with all the windows closed. An evening chill was descending over the room as the heating went off.

The light was out inside Slattery's office. Half-heartedly Hood thought of going through Slattery's papers again for incriminating evidence. But he couldn't be bothered now that he was on the criminal side of the fence.

How would people regard him if they knew? A figure of fun? He'd never have peoples' confidence and respect again. That was gone for ever. So was his job: whether he was found out or not his days as a policeman were finished.

Outside of the stolen money, he now had no function and was empty like this room. Hood felt like a wraith, a shadow flitting ghostly about, affecting nothing. The plants stood closed up in corners. The computers were inert, the screens dead.

An invisible dust sheet lay over everything, keeping it in mothballs until morning. Perhaps that was it. While he stayed, time stood still.

The reason for taking the money was suddenly unimportant. A fortune lay there in the safe for the taking, but his will seemed gone. He just wanted to lie down beside the money.

Ann herself seemed distant, lost to him. Maybe she would still always hate him. Some people could never forgive their benefactors. She might go off with someone else. You could never tell.

The office was unbearably lonely. The money was no company. He must tear himself away now. He had lived through the worst. The day was moving inexorably on; tomorrow was beckoning.

Then the phone rang. It sounded unbearably loud like an alarm going off. For a second Hood panicked, full of guilty suspicions. Who was checking up on him? They would want to know why he was still at the office so late.

Better not to answer it. Then he scolded himself: "Don't be stupid. Slattery knows you're here. That would look suspicious, deliberately not answering the phone."

He stared at the handset, heart beating wildly in indecision. Finally he grabbed the receiver.

"Hello?" He couldn't keep the anxiety from his voice.

"Hello Bill? It's Ann. Thank God I've tracked you down."

He held the receiver away from his ear, suspended in mid-air and was ready to bang it down again on the handset.

A voice, floating it seemed, cried out, "Don't hang up, please, whatever you do."

Slowly he brought the receiver back to his ear. But his face was set, determined. He forswore all emotion. He mustn't betray himself.

"Bill, I know I've no right to ring you after . . . what I did. But I just had to check you were all right."

"Rung to gloat, have you?"

"Bill, listen to me. I was out of my mind. I don't know why I did it. I'd never hurt you."

"Some chance."

"Please listen. Let me make it up to you. I know it won't be easy for you to forgive me, but if I could just see you. Then in time . . ."

Hood was bristling. What was she trying to do to him? He couldn't trust her, or himself with her. It was taking all his energy and concentration to get the money. He could only cope with one thing at a time. He was furious with her and yet would have given anything to see her.

"No," he said gruffly but emphatically.

"I understand how you feel," Ann gabbled desperately. "But please think about it, give it a chance."

"I told you Ann. Can't you take no for an answer?"

"I never could."

"Well you'd better start learning how." This time he did bang down the receiver. It relieved his feelings, to give her a little of his own back. See how she liked rejection.

Why this impulse to hurt the woman for whom he was sacrificing everything? It wasn't simply to repay her for stabbing him. It was this whole situation.

Since he met her again after all those years, his plans had been totally changed, turned on their head.

It was now Ann, her survival, fighting the men who hated her, which was occupying him to the exclusion of everything else.

He thumped the side of the chair. "Damn it, that woman has taken over my life."

Well there was no escape now. He had chosen the treadmill.

Over the next few days he carried out his routine collections of Slattery's takings. Twice he deviated for a few minutes, donned his car overall and balaclava. Straight in, straight out, his car hidden down a side alley or back street. Cash transferred to an empty company pouch, and then on with his regular collections.

No one could tell he had departed from his regular schedule.

His struggling with the heavy pouches now went barely noticed, put down to his slowly healing wounds. In fact he was regarded as quite a hero, for the way he carried on with his normal duties without complaining. He never seemed to let his injuries interfere with his work.

The money was accumulating in the safe. He must have over one hundred and seventy thousand in there. It was very satisfactory. He felt proud of his achievement. Exultant - and sick at the same time.

He never felt free of the money, even when he was away from the office. It was as if he were a miser obsessed with his hoard. He felt suffocated, buried along with the stuff.

He couldn't seem to get past all this, and envisage a time when

Ann would be well and the two of them together. But why? That was the reason he was doing all this.

Sometimes the combined weight of his guilt and his doubt was too much. He longed for the old certainties. But they were beyond recall.

Chapter Twenty-five

Hood was vulnerable when Ann rang again. This time he couldn't contain the relief, excitement even, when he heard her voice.

"Ann?"

"Yes, it's me. You knew I'd call again, didn't you?" She could sense the receptiveness in his tone.

Hood tried to sound guarded. "I guessed you would."

"Well don't make me do everything Bill. Help me a little, please."

"How?"

"A bit of tenderness. I need that more than anything. Show you don't bear grudges, that you've forgiven me."

Hood took a deep sigh, and then his voice dropped: "I suppose so."

"What? I can't hear you."

Exasperated Hood moved the receiver to his other hand. "I said I forgive you."

There was a slightly stunned pause at Ann's end, then, "So where do we go from here?"

"I really don't know what's best for us, Ann."

"I must see you."

Hood was about to protest but then saw the futility. Unless he told her the truth about the stolen money, how could he reasonably put her off? Besides he wanted to see her.

Warily he said, "I could come over."

"Oh, would you Bill? That would mean so much to me."

Hood wondered if Ann was being over-effusive, but she had always been open-hearted, spontaneous.

"I'm on my way."

"Great. Have you eaten?"

"No, why?"

"Have a meal at my place. I want to do something to make amends."

Hood was touched by this simple gesture. "Fine, but don't go to any trouble. Nothing fancy."

"Just take it as you find it."

"OK, I'll be over in an hour."

"Hurry."

"I love you."

"Me too."

"Bye." Hood rang off.

Ann's invitation seemed to relieve some of the pressure he felt. Even if he could not tell her about the money, they could at least share a meal together.

He changed into a pair of blue, linen trousers, green cotton check shirt, and a cream, v-neck lamb's-wool pullover. Then he shaved carefully, and even buffed his best, hand-stitched leather shoes. Ann was getting the full treatment.

Less than an hour later Hood stood in the doorway as Ann appeared. The charred wood had been replaced and a gleaming new red door fitted. Only the faintest trace of black remained on the edge of the surrounding brickwork.

"Bill, come in." She beamed at him. They kissed quickly then he followed her inside.

She wore a pink halter dress, with tucks at the middle and pleats in its full skirt. This revealed her slim legs, and white court shoes. Hood noticed how brown she was looking as if she'd been using a sunray lamp. But most amazing was her transformation from being overweight to that almost gauntness of top models.

With her blonde hair gathered back under a gold clip, her face was a gentle sun, radiating well-being. Here eyes were expectant, quivering, emphasised by pink eye-liner.

"Sit down," she invited him.

The three piece suite had been recovered in a pale rose and green pattern, and a new sheepskin rug covered the black mark on the carpet.

"Everywhere looks lovely," he complimented her.

"Yes, it's better isn't it? I think I would have changed things even without the damage. Some of those lamps will go next."

Hood nodded. It felt as if they were on their first date. "You're

152

looking tremendous." He didn't try and disguise the admiration in his voice.

"Well thank you. That deserves a kiss." Playfully she rose from her chair and went across to him. They embraced and Hood pulled her down beside him. After a few seconds she tapped him on the shoulder. "This isn't getting the meal served."

"Damn the meal," Hood growled in fun.

"Now don't say that. I've been to a lot of trouble. Let go," and she gave a gentle karate tap on his hands.

His interlaced fingers were released and she jumped from his grasp.

"I'll just check the casserole and then we're about set. Would you like to open the wine?"

"I thought you said you weren't going to any trouble," Hood called after her, as he followed her through to the dining room.

"It's a woman's privilege to change her mind," Ann told him, as she fastened around her a brown apron decorated with cooking utensils.

The table was set with a white linen tablecloth, flower decorated table mats, and green and white napkins.

A bottle of red wine stood on a silver gilt coaster in the middle.

"You'll find a corkscrew on the sideboard," Ann called from the kitchen.

As he pulled the cork, Hood looked around him. Despite being freshly painted, it had an air of being forgotten, unused.

"Here we are," she announced and brought in two small earthenware casserole dishes. "One for you, one for me."

"Very cosy," Hood commented in sarcastic amusement.

"Well I know you. You'd have the lion's share if I let you."

"Aren't you taking off your apron?"

"Of course, how silly of me," and Ann yanked the apron over her head, catching the string on the gold clip in her hair.

"Here let me help," Hood offered.

"Leave me alone," Ann responded in a flash of anger and then covered it with a smile. "Sorry, I just hate getting all mussed up."

Disentangled from the apron, she regained her poise and sat down. "There, everything is fine now. Bon appetit."

They clinked glasses and drank a little of the burgundy. Hood dug into the beef casserole.

"This is delicious," he spoke with his mouth full. "I've never tasted anything quite like it."

"My own special recipe," Ann told him, her eyes gleaming. "I'm so glad you like it. Have some more wine."

"Thanks I will." Hood was really letting go. He hadn't felt this good in ages.

When they'd finished, Ann picked up the plates with a flourish. "There's baked Alaska to follow - courtesy of the supermarket."

Hood's eyes lit up and soon he was demolishing a generous helping.

Ann looked a little disgusted with him, and he told himself to watch his table manners. He didn't want her to think him a pig. But he was just so happy and the wine was making him carefree.

He finished the last mouthful and then pushed his plate back. "That was marvellous. Thank you - from the bottom of my heart."

"Thank you. I'm very happy. Shall we go through?" She indicated the living-room.

"Certainly." Hood did his best to stifle a burp as he followed her.

They sat together on the sofa, hands clasped.

"You don't know what this means to me," Hood confessed.

Ann nodded, her eyes fastened on him. Was she less drunk than he, he wondered? Yes, considerably he decided. Oh well, that was her affair. So much the worse for her. He felt terrific.

Next they were kissing and Hood was holding her tight. His hands moved over her dress feeling her body beneath them. She moved in response to his touch, pressing back against him.

"Let's go upstairs," she suggested.

Hood nodded, and watched her curvaceous body swaying as she walked ahead of him.

In the bedroom they both sat down on the bed and held each other again. But their balance was awkward and they fell back. Hood had Ann spread-eagled under him and was clutching her hair, her mouth. The gold clip fell out and her hair spread out behind her, golden.

"Let me get out of this dress," Ann told him, and pushed him back.

Hood withdrew and stood up to undress.

Ann had pulled back the fluffy, flower patterned duvet and lay naked, her head on the satin pillow. Hood joined her, pressing his body down on hers.

She held him almost viciously tight, and they entwined as if they were trying to mould themselves to each other. Ann bit his shoulder and Hood cried out in pain before grinding his mouth into hers.

"You bitch," came out in a husky voice.

She scratched his back with her nails, digging in like a cat. He arched his back then fell on her, penetrating her. She cried out too and they fought with each other for ultimate pleasure. The wrangling went on, twisting, turning so that first Hood was on top then Ann, then Hood again. Finally he released all the pressure he had to give and sank back exhausted.

"I'm done," he croaked.

Ann stroked his chest thoughtfully, and the tears formed in her eyes. Hood touched her head, praying she wasn't disappointed in any way. He couldn't remember such a savage, passionate, exultant love-making before. It made everything worthwhile.

"Oh God, you don't know how I love you Ann."

Suddenly Ann turned away, bitterness adding to her tears.

Hood reached for her shoulder. "Ann, what's the matter? What have I said?"

"It's nothing. It's . . . just too much."

Hood desisted. He turned over onto his side and went to sleep.

In a cellar someone was burning him with red hot irons. He looked up at the figure looming over him, but couldn't make out the face. He twisted all ways to escape but it was impossible. His body was bound to a table and his naked chest was being seared. He knew he couldn't restrain a scream much longer. He'd have to . . . now . . . he woke up.

Lying on his side, his face still held the horror of the dream. He was contorted in pain. His chest was all knotted up, and he was crouched in a foetal position. He really was in red hot pain.

Scrambling out of the side of the bed he stumbled doubled over to the bathroom. He tried to be sick but only a little came.

He leant against the sink, and his face was twisted in agony. He'd never felt pain like this before. It was tearing him up inside as if someone was taking a knife to his intestines.

"Oh God," he cried, "I can't stand it. Help, anything. Only take away the pain."

But it built and built, an embroiling inferno. The heat seemed to be getting greater all the time. His fingers felt his stomach and the warmth radiated onto his hand.

He sat on the edge of the bath and put his head between his legs, hoping this might alleviate the pain. But it made no difference. He raised his head, and stood up. He tried walking about rubbing his tortured abdomen, but the pain throbbed away, spreading in waves.

Desperate he went to the toilet but nothing happened. He returned to the bathroom. Sweat was streaking his brow. He'd have to wake Ann, get a doctor. This was agony and he couldn't endure any more of it.

Ann was standing in the bathroom doorway. She looked cool, aloof in a white silk reclining outfit. Her hair was once more neatly held back by the gold clip. Her eyes were detached, large ovals almost transparent.

"Ann, thank goodness. I'm in agony. It must have been something I've eaten."

Ann watched him without speaking.

"Ann, don't just stand there, do something."

She leant against the door jamb, dreamily. "There's nothing I or anyone can do."

"What do you mean?" Hood was swaying about, still trying to massage away the pain.

"You're dying. I've killed you."

"What? Ann don't joke. You must be crazy. I've just got a stomach ache."

"You've got food poisoning. I should know. It won't be long now. Then you'll be finished. Dead."

Horror spread across Hood's features. "You mean you've done for me? You cow, you . . . why? After bed together . . ."

"That had nothing to do with it." Then she seemed to rouse herself from her dream and went and sat on the bath rim. "Stabbing you didn't work, and I couldn't leave it there. Credit me with more determination than that. And you thought I wanted to make up."

But Hood was barely listening any more. He was staggering about, wondering how long he'd got, whether there was an antidote. What poison had she used?

Ann tilted her head up sternly. "I'm not dying alone, I'm taking you with me. Understand that. When you walked out on me I knew I couldn't let you go."

156

Hood half heard her, and knew she wasn't talking sense. He decided to dash for the phone and a doctor but Ann was ahead of him and unplugged it.

"No Bill. There's no way out. You're going ahead of me, that's all."

Hood breathed in; he knew he had to plead with her. "Ann, please, plug in the phone. This is no time for messing about. Be serious. This is my life. We can talk about everything later. But I have to have a doctor."

"No. Besides I told you it won't do you any good."

A fresh eruption seemed to have been set off inside him, and Hood rushed for the bathroom.

This time he was violently sick, his head almost crashing down into the basin with the force of his vomiting. His stomach muscles were opening and contracting in massive spasms.

His body was exhausted. He hung on to the basin, then collapsed onto the floor. His head was lolling, his tongue hanging out. So this was what it felt like, he vaguely thought. He hoped he'd pass out.

But that wasn't to be. Instead he twitched on the floor while his stomach seemed to be turning itself inside out. He thought of animals with blocked insides and turned away in self-disgust.

He seemed to lie there for hours, with burning rods implanted inside him, being dragged about. He longed for the end.

Chapter Twenty-Six

They sat on as if oblivious of each other, him on the floor, her sitting on the edge of the bath. Hood's eyes were sunken, his head now lolling forward onto his chest, his breathing fitful and difficult. He was exhausted.

Ann's eyes were barely focused and her hands kept fiddling with the cord of her silk lounging suit. It kept falling open and she would irritably pull the sides together. Her hair had slipped from its clip again and was falling into her eyes. She gathered handfuls and pushed them back.

Hood coughed and moved his leg which was going to sleep. His gaze moved to Ann. After a few seconds he croaked, "Why?" But then his hand went up, disclaiming the question, too weary to listen to the answer.

Ann didn't seem to hear him at first and then slowly swivelled in his direction. "I wanted to kill you."

Hood nodded. He understood so far, too well. "After all I've done for her," he muttered mostly to himself, shaking his head.

Ann licked her lips and sighed. Her attention had moved to the green tiled wall of the bathroom. She noticed a couple were chipped and needed replacing. Then she seemed to home in again on what he was saying.

"No one's ever done anything for me."

Hood's head snapped up as if a puppet on a string. "I've been such a fool. The meal, then bed, everything; taken in completely." Again he shook his head over his own folly. How could anyone be so stupid?

'Call yourself a detective?' he inwardly scolded himself. 'You couldn't detect your way out of a paper bag.' He gazed at Ann hard and evenly. "Look in my coat pocket." When she stared back at him questioningly, he said, "Just do it, - please."

The urgency of his tone convinced her and reluctantly she rose and walked slowly along the landing and downstairs.

Hood waited, his body tense, not knowing what she might do. The seconds lengthened to minutes and he wondered if she had found it.

Then she was in the bathroom doorway again. "Is this what you wanted me to find?" She pointed the barrel of his gun at him.

Hood nodded. "I was going to give you it for protection." His throat became hoarse. "I'm so sick of all this." Then his voice came out tired, harsh, cracked. "If you want me dead so badly go on, pull the trigger."

Ann's eyes widened and then a sort of vicious calm came over her. "You asked for it."

Hood twisted his torso from side to side, his legs splayed out. "Well do it then." He was angry now. "I've wasted too much time already." He was thinking that he should have used the gun on himself, that first night back in the city. It would have saved a lot of grief.

"Stop giving me orders," Ann shouted back at him. "I can't think

Exasperated Hood broke out: "Oh for God's sake!" Then seeing her confused, unsure, he gave way. "Stop, wait a minute."

Ann watched him, suspicious. Was this some trick? "Well?"

"Before you shoot, you must know: there's money for you. It's in Slattery's safe." He couldn't bear dying and her not knowing about that, after all his trouble and sacrifice to steal it.

"Money, what do you mean money?"

"The folding kind. Maybe two hundred thousand, enough to start buying that treatment in America. I want you to have it."

Ann's hand tightened around the gun. He must be lying, buying time to save his life. "Where would you get two hundred thousand?"

"I stole it."

Ann stared at him. The Bill Hood she knew would never do a thing like that. It was inconceivable.

"You must think I was born yesterday. How did you steal it? From Slattery I suppose - and then left it in his safe."

"No." She might as well know the whole truth. "Not from Slattery. I've been working under cover for the police in his office. No, I stole it from banks and hid it there."

"You're an undercover policeman who robs banks? You'll have to do better than that."

"It's the truth, damn it. I did it all for you. There was no other way."

Could this fantastic tale be true? Who would invent a story like that? But she was desperately afraid of being duped. It was so hard to take it all in.

The gun was no help. She tossed it to one side. Then she panicked: but there was only a thud and a clatter, no explosion.

Shaken she turned back to Hood. "You mean it? All of it?"

Hood nodded.

Bending down beside him she tried to help him up. The knife scars on his chest were livid and rubbed against her. She pulled at him twice trying to raise him then collapsed against him in tears. "Oh Bill hold me. What have I done to you?"

She smothered his face with kisses so that he could hardly breathe. She brushed back his tousled hair. "I keep trying to kill you and you come back for more. That's insane, you know that. But then we're two of a kind, aren't we?"

She tried to brush away her tears. Some had fallen on Hood's cheeks. She dabbed at them with her silk.

"You'd do anything for me, wouldn't you?" Men had treated her so badly for so long, she could hardly believe it. "I feel so ashamed. I should have known. We're . . . part of each other aren't we? How could I have doubted you?" She kept asking herself this as Hood leant against her.

"You see, I hated you. I had nothing to live for and I was determined I was taking you down with me."

She nestled Hood more comfortably in her arms. "But it's all changed now. Forget the money. I'm going to beat this cancer on my own. I'm not dying, not by a long chalk. You've done that for me." She looked at him, and checked herself. He was almost unconscious.

Holding him under his arms she dragged him along the landing and back to the bedroom.

"Come on try, for me," and she coaxed him onto the side of the bed, and finally onto the mattress. Tenderly she pulled the duvet over him.

Then she scampered downstairs to the living-room. Picking up the phone, she dialled. Seconds later: "Doctor, yes it's an emergency. Food poisoning."

Later after the doctor had left, in bed she cradled Hood's head in her arms. "Thank God I've got you back. I don't know what I'd have done if you'd . . . gone."

Hood was still sleepy. "You'd have managed."

"I'd have gone crazy in a prison cell for life. As it was I could tell the doctor was highly suspicious."

Hood eased his head round to rest more easily on the pillow. "Just what did you put into that casserole?" Then quickly he changed his mind. "No don't tell me. I don't want to know. With my delicate stomach it might set me off again."

Then he lay further back and clasped Ann around the waist. "I think I see now what was going through your mind. I should never have left you. I didn't dare tell you about my plans. Keeping you in the dark was the biggest mistake I ever made."

Then a terrible lassitude crept up on him again. He was sinking back against the mattress. Death had crept too close, for both of them. How many more reprieves could there be?

Then Ann's voice warm, tender, throaty cut through his thoughts. "I love you."

He couldn't restrain himself: "Say it again, I just need to hear you say it."

Ann kissed him on the forehead. "You'll hear it many times again. I love you."

Maybe things would be all right after all. He just wanted her to keep saying it.

Chapter Twenty-Seven

By morning, after a few hours fitful sleep, Hood was able to move about. His stomach still felt as if it had been scraped raw but the nausea had all but gone. He felt weak, legs rubbery, and could only manage half a cup of luke-warm tea.

Later Hood phoned into work sick: 'food poisoning'. It seemed to put into perspective, normalise, the horror. Ann watched him tenderly, guilty but trying not to show it.

"When shall I see you?" she asked suddenly as Hood dragged on his jacket.

"I'm going home to change my clothes, and then I'd better show my face at work this afternoon."

"You're never!"

"I'm over the worst. I can manage."

"Oh Bill. Couldn't you stay here, with me?"

"Shouldn't we really keep apart until I've got the money to you?"

Ann turned away trying to disguise the hurt. And yet she knew he was only thinking of her. She held together the loosening folds of her purple kimono style dressing gown. "I don't see why?" she blurted out. "What does it matter, now I know. Anyway I can't take the money. It'll only land you in terrible trouble."

"Now don't talk like that. What am I supposed to do with the money? We've been through all this. I can't give it back. You need it."

Ann clasped his hands. Her face was turned up to him, shining, eyes moist like a summer sun after the rain. "But do I? I feel better now, just having you here. I can beat this thing myself, with you to support me. People have. There are homeopathic remedies, all sorts of things to try."

Hood bent down and kissed her. "Try them by all means. Anything is worth a go. But the money's there, as a last resort. You said yourself, the American treatment was your best chance."

She grasped his hand again, so hard she hurt him. "Sorry Bill. Oh I wish you'd never taken that money." Hood pulled away from her. Ann stretched out her hand towards him. "I know, you did it for love."

Hood turned to face her. His eyes were shadowed by concern. "It's there for you. Just one job will do it."

Ann ran across to him. "Oh no Bill, no more. I forbid it. They'll catch you and what good will that do? No, it's out of the question."

Hood held her two arms in his. "I must. There isn't enough money yet. One last job, I promise you."

"Bill, Bill why will you never listen to me? I never wanted the money in the first place. Stop before it's too late."

"You say that now, but you'll thank me in the end."

Ann pressed her face into his. Her blonde waves fell across his cheek.

"I am grateful now. But it's too risky. I couldn't stand it if you were caught and taken away from me in prison. I need you here. You're the only reason I think I could fight this thing. Without you I'd go under."

"No you wouldn't. We said all this last night. You're tough, a survivor."

"I only look like that to you. Oh Bill hold me close. I need you so much."

They clung together in a violent embrace, their lips seeking each other.

Slowly Hood extricated himself from her grasp. "I'd better go now. Things to do. It won't be so long until tonight. We could plan our future together."

With that he went into the hall and found his coat draped over the banister rail. Putting it on he felt a weight dragging it down at one side. Reaching in the pocket his fingers closed on the gun. His eyes met Ann's.

Grimly he nodded to her, and then his features relaxed into a warming smile as he went to the door.

"See you."

"See you. Please don't do anything . . . rash." There she gave up.

Hood was through the doorway and onto the path. "I won't. I promise." Then he was gone.

Ann felt very alone as she shut the door on him. She was so tired she simply sat down on the bottom step of the stairs, and rested her head in her hands. What was to become of her?

Hood was bound to stretch his luck and get caught. All for her. It warmed and angered her at the same time. Did she really want to stop him? A pain had started in her side after breakfast. If she was truthful she longed for that treatment. If only it could magically guarantee to cure her. Imagine: to be free of all this and able to live a normal life with the man she loved.

She bit her lip and then substituted her thumb nail. "Please God, let it work out," she prayed. And then felt guilty. God didn't condone armed robbery.

Things were never easy or simple. She'd suffered for years and years for no reason. She'd done bad things in her life before. So what was so different now? Sometimes you had to be bad to survive. Even the good were punished.

If Hood were more of a scoundrel she'd find it easier to take the money off him. She'd always had a weakness for shameless, handsome devils.

She looked at herself in the wall mirror. Better slap some make-up on, she thought. This was the face Hood was selling his soul for.

Hood sat at his desk that afternoon and wondered what to do. He'd promised one last robbery. Could his luck hold out? Already it was the talk of the newspapers, the apparently casual rapid raid - straight in, straight out, and then the thief disappearing without trace. So far he'd been able to hide the car and not be spotted, but that couldn't go on. And once they had the car number he was finished.

He braced his arms on the desk top and rested his head on them. Office staff looked on sympathetically, after he'd struggled into work despite his food poisoning. Even Slattery had given him a pat on the back and asked him if he was OK.

Gritting his teeth he knew he had to risk it. There was simply not enough money yet. One more robbery should do it. And it had to be soon. He found himself often peering in the direction of the storeroom and the green safe. Suppose someone, Slattery maybe, decided to have a clear out or check its contents. Again he'd be finished. His head went giddy sometimes when he thought of all the chances he'd taken and not been caught out. It was all down to keeping his nerve. Most criminals were caught through cracking, being informed upon, or sheer bad luck.

He almost felt there was a power somewhere working for him, a charm or spell that kept him undiscovered. Well Ann deserved that, after all the relentless ill-treatment life had dealt her over the years.

One last throw: the excitement bubbled up inside him. He'd do it today. All the equipment was still in the car. The relief of getting it over with outweighed every other consideration. So what that the sickness and vomiting had taken it out of him?

And then he remembered: he'd done the first robbery after Ann had knifed him with intent to kill. Now he was contemplating the last theft again after her final murderous attempt. The world was certainly a crooked and bizarre place.

Slattery came out of his office. "Bill, you look terrible. All washed out. I'll get Bristow to do the collections today."

Hood's face came up determined, angry. "That's all right Mr Slattery. I'm fit enough to do it. I don't like entrusting the collections to anyone else."

Slattery looked at him hard, his eyebrows arched. "You take your work seriously. Very well. I appreciate you not trusting the money to anyone else. I'd feel the same."

Hood forced a smile. Now he could carry out the robbery as planned. The relief was intense. But he bitterly resented Slattery's comments that they were the same. Crime wasn't a way of life for him as it was for Slattery.

Their common corruption made Hood blazing angry. At moments like this he hated himself.

Still he withdrew the pouches from the safe and set off. But his cruel self-contempt was relentless.

He had his target picked out: a bank on the edge of a run-down estate to the west of the city. Should he go through with it? He was so agitated he was bound to make mistakes. But he drove on, seemingly unable to stop. Black hole entrances to multi-storey car parks beckoned, down which he could have bolted. Instead he

165

pressed on and began the first collections as if in a trance. Maybe time would run out, forestalling the robbery. But only minutes had elapsed and he was on his way again.

Up the hill he passed one of Slattery's night clubs. White stucco, smothered with plastic stars and topped off with a cupola. Hood grimaced. Ahead stretched grey council houses and overgrown waste ground.

The bank was to his right, down a busy through road. He carried on past the junction, and then worked his way round looking for a place to hide the car. On a back road he found a children's play ground flanked by a block of flats. He parked the Volvo behind the flats and climbed out. The car was effectively screened and yet the bank was only a couple of minutes walk away. He had the bag and his balaclava in his hand. Just one more robbery. He took a deep breath, and then walked steadily forward and almost tripped over an uneven flagstone.

He was all on edge now, his balance disturbed. His steps slowed. He could still veer away, and call the whole thing off.

Oh Ann, he thought, what shall I do? It wasn't like him to be indecisive, but their whole future was at stake.

Then a coldness settled upon him. If he didn't go through with it, Ann would die. It was as simple as that. Nothing else mattered. He pulled the balaclava over his face.

He was a different person now, unswerving, implacable. Nothing was going to stop him. He was ready.

He went in. "This is a gun and I'm ready to use it. Move. I want eighty thousand pounds. Now."

Chapter Twenty-eight

Tonight was the pay off: he had it all. Enough money to cover Ann's treatment and make her well again. He longed to see her face when he gave her the money. And if he was honest he would be glad to see the back of it. He was sick of the contaminated feeling it gave him.

With everyone gone, Hood crept back into the office. Along he stalked to the storeroom and clicked on the light. There was the dusty green safe, a massive ton in weight. Opening it was always like entering a cold, dead cave.

Stretching far into its interior over the empty pouches and piles of old ledgers - nothing. Panicking, he stretched full length, fingers scrabbling about on the chill metal floor of the safe. Further in he penetrated: he must be at the back-plate now. Supposing someone had run off with it all. Insupportable. What could he tell Ann?

Then his fingers felt a wrapper, one crisp packet of notes. Furiously he delved further and reassured found a mountain of packets stacked against the back-plate where he'd left them.

He cursed himself for giving way. He should have remembered he had pushed them that far back for safety. It was the occasion, putting all the money together for Ann, which had momentarily thrown him.

Withdrawing he crouched back on his haunches and mopped his brow with his handkerchief. He didn't need any more frights like that. He must compose himself. In a few minutes he would be walking out of the building and down the street with four hundred thousand pounds under his arm. He mustn't draw any attention to himself. There must be no slip ups with success so close.

"Hold it right there. Don't move a muscle."

Turning his head to one side Hood looked up. Slattery was standing there, in a long tweed overcoat, collar pulled up, and in his hand was a gun. His steel-wire hair seemed to bristle under the harsh strip electric light.

"Close the safe, then sit on the floor," Slattery commanded.

Shaken, Hood obeyed and then leant his back against the storeroom wall.

"I knew you were up to something." Slattery shook the gun impatiently in Hood's direction. "All your concern that no one interfere with the collections. And then those bulging pouches."

Slattery's face broke into a dismissive grin. "Some days I thought you were going to have a hernia, dragging them in. But you were clever, I have to admit that. The money always tallied, was never short."

Slattery eased himself against the storeroom wall, his head cocked to one side. "The hours I've spent trying to figure it out. All that working late at the office or coming back after everyone else had gone. Oh I knew about that. I thought you were trying to incriminate me."

He waited for the word to register with Hood. "Oh I know you're an undercover cop - did right from the beginning." He enjoyed Hood's discomfiture.

Rattled, Hood came back: "Give me the gun. You're under arrest."

Slattery's eyes became hard beads. "Come off it. I've caught you, cop turned robber. They'll give you twenty years for this."

Hood tried edging along by the skirting board but Slattery's gun halted him. Hood tried again: "The stolen money is in your safe. You'll go down for it."

Slattery scratched his nose with the gun barrel. "Sort of a stand off? But if we turn each other in, no one gets the money. It's confiscated. Ann doesn't see a penny of it."

Hood was grim. "So you knew about that too?"

"It didn't take much figuring out. Both of you came to me desperate for money. Next thing you hide a fortune in my safe."

The fight seemed to suddenly go out of Hood. "So where do we go from here?"

Slattery eased himself off the wall and stood nimble on his feet. "That's more like it. Think positive. How much money is there?"

Hood considered lying, but Slattery would only check. "Around four hundred grand."

"Around four hundred give or take," Slattery muttered to himself. "Well that's fifty for you and three hundred and fifty for me."

"What?" Hood was shaking with anger.

"That's fair isn't it? After all I'm the banker in this little affair. I'm the one holding the money."

Hood half staggered to his feet ignoring Slattery's gun. "Listen you weasel. That money is all for Ann, understand? Not a penny less. She needs it for her cancer treatment."

Slattery retreated so that Hood could not jump him. "Take another step and I'll shoot."

Hood stopped, wrong footed. "So? What I said still goes."

"You can't be serious. Hand over four hundred grand to Ann? She really has conned you."

Hood suffered in silence Slattery's withering gaze.

Slattery was contemptuous: "There is no cancer. She'll just take the money and run. You'll never see the money again."

"I don't believe you. Ann's on the level."

"Rubbish. She's been on the game so long, she'd sell her own mother."

Hood's fists were clenched at his sides. "Take that back you scum."

"Please, no insults. All right, I'll be generous. Keep a hundred grand and do what you like with it. Give it to Ann."

Then Slattery's mouth became a hard line. The gun pointed fixedly at Hood's heart. "But I'm keeping the rest - for my trouble."

"Don't you understand?" A hundred grand's no good. The treatment costs four."

"Then do some more robberies. Bank it here. After my cut you'll soon have four hundred grand again."

"I've four now. Give me my money and I'll go."

"No. I'm putting it all in the vault where no one can get at it."

Hood stared at him in disbelief. "I can't steal any more. I've stretched my luck so far. I'll get caught."

"No you won't. You've an excellent cover. They'll never suspect you."

h

"Don't you believe it." The duplicity sickened him. Cosying up to Slattery made him crawl.

"Are you bottling out?"

Hood scowled back at him. "No. Unlike you I'm thinking of Ann. I can't let her down."

"Let's not argue about it. We're agreed then? Now if you'll walk ahead of me, we'll get out of here."

His gun poised, with his other hand Slattery scooped the money back into the safe and locked it. Then Hood preceded him out of the storeroom. Slattery was too cautious to be taken off guard and Hood believed him when he said he'd use the gun.

As Hood headed for the way out Slattery told him, "I'm glad that's all settled. Don't worry about me. I'll lock up."

Frustrated Hood stumbled, empty handed, out into the street. He had no where to go but home.

What a fool Slattery had made of him! More robberies, worse risks. All for Ann. She was true, wasn't she? She couldn't fake all those symptoms.

Damn Slattery for putting doubts into his head. If she was lying he'd kill them both. But she couldn't be - could she?

Chapter Twenty-nine

Hood was tramping up the back stairs at Police Headquarters. Another of Russell's urgent summonses, no doubt to berate him over lack of progress in the Slattery case. Hood no longer even grinned over the irony of the situation. A draught blew past him from above, bringing with it a damp, mildew smell.

At the next landing he met Russell rushing down, a pile of papers in his hands.

"Ah Hood. We'll have to talk here. There's a flap on and I have to see the Chief Constable in five minutes."

Hood noticed the way Russell's flushed face still expanded with pride at the information, even as anxiety creased the edges of his eyes.

"I'm taking you off the Slattery case. Those upstairs have decided we can't wait any longer for results."

Hood guarded his reaction, but inwardly he felt as if all the breath had been knocked out of him. How was he to obtain the money now? The collections, the cover for the robberies, had all been snatched away from him on a whim.

Russell glared impatiently. "You don't look too pleased about it. I thought you were tired of the Slattery assignment. Here, are you sick or something?"

Hood pulled himself together. "No sir. It just puts a different complexion on things. Takes some getting used to."

"Yes, well there isn't time to worry about that now. Report to Chief Inspector Pearson. Every free man is being put on these bank robberies. The Chief Constable wants us to give it top priority."

"Me?"

"Do you see anyone else here? Come on, snap to it. I'm under a huge amount of pressure to get results." Russell pulled at the collar of his uniform to ease it as if it were choking him. "You want to be thankful you don't get all that flak. What I do to cover your backs."

"Yes sir. What will be my role on Pearson's team?"

Russell began looking for an escape, annoyed with details. "He'll fill you in. The important thing is to visit these banks and talk to the eye witnesses again. The man's caught on video, so he shouldn't be hard to track down. At least you wouldn't think so." Russell saw only incompetence and betrayal in those below him.

"Do I give Slattery notice or what?"

Russell rounded on him. "No you do not. Invent some excuse and then don't go back. There's no time to waste. That's an order."

"Yes sir."

"Right. Well you know what you have to do. I'm expecting better results this time. That last operation didn't look good for either of us."

"No sir."

Russell paused, suspicious. "Are you a Mason?"

Then before Hood could answer, Russell stomped off down the stairs clutching his papers tightly, and muttering to himself about cliques.

Hood watched him go, a lonely, paranoid figure clinging to an ever more exposed position. Following orders he went across to the briefing room on the second floor. The place was packed with groups of officers buzzing with conversation, some in uniform some not.

"Right you lot," Pearson called out, an experienced business-like officer in his late forties, with a moustache, round face, and surprisingly slim build. Hood wondered if he was a keep-fit fanatic.

"All right, simmer down. Let's have some hush . . . shut it!"

All fell silent and took their places in the rows of seats facing the white board.

After two false starts interrupted by scraping chairs, Pearson was in full flow. "Right. You all know about this string of robberies. So far we've had no results, which is why you're all being drafted in from other duties. We're going to crack this case or the Chief Constable will want to know the reason why." He let this sink in. "Oh yes, the top brass are taking a personal interest in this. At the moment the newspapers are crucifying us, and when I say 'us' I mean them upstairs. It's getting too hot for everyone so we need results."

He began pacing up and down, taking an exact eight steps before turning.

"I am putting you all in teams. Each team will take a different bank. Somebody, some passer-by must have seen the man, his car. We want leads. I'm expecting an arrest by the end of the week." Over the howl of protests, he called, "that will be all."

As the meeting broke up Hood found the team to which he was allocated. While the groups were clustering he noticed two tall men in expensive suits button-holing Pearson and taking him to one side.

Hood turned to a colleague and asked, "Who are they?"

The other officer, an ex-marine with a permanently aggressive stare followed his gaze and said, off-handedly, "Special Services. The man had an Irish accent, so they're looking at the terrorist angle. Me, I think it's all horse shit."

Hood nodded and turned back to the team, where the bank to be visited was under discussion.

While he pretended to listen, his mind was racing, frantic. He had to get out of this. How could he interview eye witnesses and not be recognised? Or watch the video of the robbery, with himself up on that screen, and not be spotted?

He bit his lower lip, as the strain told on him. Fortunately his colleagues read only bitter determination in his anguished expression and took the whole thing more seriously themselves.

"It's really got under his skin," one said as they went out in a group to the car.

All the while Hood was wondering whether to feign illness or make a break for it, but he was hemmed in by the other three and to suddenly pull out would only draw attention.

Soon he was riding along with them, already feeling like a captured criminal being escorted to prison. Every second he wanted to call a halt, ask to be let out, but was swept along by the momentum of it all.

He tensed as the terraced streets came into view. Ridiculously he had hoped a wrong turn might postpone their arrival.

The railings around the park appeared, and yelping children

were running round the adjoining playground. He was cooked. The bank was only across the way now.

There, were the disused garages behind which he had parked. His tyre tracks could be matched. Furiously he told himself: 'don't betray yourself'.

They climbed out of the car, with Hood lagging at the rear, and entered the bank. For one second Hood froze on the threshold, remembering what it had cost him to go inside that last time. It took even more will-power to go in now.

While the woman cashier fetched the manager the detectives fanned out, examining the building, and checking the escape route from the doorway.

Then they worked in twos, interviewing the cashiers and the manager, despite protests about being questioned yet again. Hood with Johnson, a senior colleague, was speaking to the manager. It was the same youngish man in pin-stripe suit and horn-rimmed spectacles who had helped the cashier pile up the money on the floor.

Hood tried to leave the talking to Johnson, a shortish, dry-toned man with a slight stoop who always wore a belted gaberdine raincoat. But for naturalness Hood had to make the occasional monosyllabic interjection. He hoped his normal speaking voice was distant enough from the Irish accent he'd assumed, to prevent recognition.

However the strain made his voice croak on occasion as if he had laryngitis. The manager shuffled awkwardly at the strange sound and gave Hood a peculiar look.

Hood felt his face burning, under the inspection. Surely the man must be comparing his features with those of the disguised robber.

The manager was now describing the man he saw carrying the gun. Along with Johnson, Hood appeared to be listening intently, his eyes never leaving the manager's face. But inwardly he was wondering how long he could keep this up, listening to himself being described in exact detail.

Then suddenly it was as if Hood were listening from far away, in another room. The manager was talking about someone else who seemed to have no connection with Hood. He could listen to the manager now quite dispassionately, for it didn't seem to concern him at all.

174

They concluded the interview and were moving off to join the other detectives. The manager made a tentative movement to detain Hood.

It was tempting to pretend he didn't notice and go, but Hood knew he must avoid anything suspicious. Very unwillingly he moved back a pace.

"Yes?" he growled.

"I . . ." the manager faltered.

"Yes, what is it?"

"I . . . oh, it's nothing, but . . ."

Reluctantly Hood encouraged him. "Well?"

"The man, the robber, he held himself funny, as if he had stomach ache or something. Unless it was my imagination."

"Right, well thank you. Every detail helps. I'll remember that." Hood tried to imply scepticism without saying it, and moved off again. He didn't want the manager remembering any other useful details.

As the detectives gathered in a huddle to compare notes, Hood could see between their heads the nervous figure of the woman cashier lingering by the counter. He was desperate not to catch her eye and yet he felt, unreasonably, that all the time she was watching him.

"Right," Johnson, the Officer in Charge, announced, "Thank you for your co-operation. We'll take the videotape away with us if we may. Now we're going to scour the area and see if anyone saw anything, a car in particular. Something may turn up."

"I sincerely hope so," the manager returned. He was thin, and his delicate pale skin quivered, unnerved by the whole experience. "It's been a terrible shock. We're only a small branch you see, and . . ."

"Yes, it's terrible I know. You have our sympathy. But we must press on and catch the thief."

"Yes, of course," the manager agreed sadly. He felt deserted as the detectives spread out from the doorway to comb the nearby streets.

Hood was working his way alone up one side of the road, having fled in the opposite direction on the day of the robbery. He needed time to think. The relief of not being immediately discovered was making his hands shake, and his insides turn over. He wanted to stop and lean on a garden wall, but daren't, for it

175

might appear suspicious. Johnson was on the other side of the street, beginning house-to-house enquiries.

Appalled at having to go through with all this, nevertheless Hood forced himself to make a start. He must act normally, and not give away how dreadful he felt.

He knocked on the first door and waited. A dog was yapping from inside, and then its owner was telling it to be quiet.

Hood rubbed his brow. They couldn't have seen anything, at this end of the street. The meaningless conversation might even take his mind off things.

A scrawny, middle-aged woman in a green check overall and fluffy slippers opened the door and peered at him. "Yes?"

"Mrs . . ?" he had barely uttered the word, when she sprang back.

"What do you want?" she snapped, half shielded by the door.

"I'm detective Hood here to ask you about the bank robbery. Here's my warrant card. Did you see anything?" He felt he was gabbling, terror of detection flooding back inside him.

She looked slowly at the warrant card and then at him, and relaxed a little.

"No, I mean I'm not sure. Was it that day I saw a man in a balaclava helmet? Bit like you in build. You gave me a shock just now standing there. I don't see many people . . ."

Hood let her ramble on, desperately hoping she'd lose her thread and he could conclude the interview.

"So you might have seen him? Description?"

Hood wrote down her words, hoping anxiously that this wouldn't put her on the track of himself.

But instead she began to complain of her nerves, and how events like that upset her.

"Yes, it's very worrying I know. Well if there's anything else, please contact us," and Hood let her close the door on him.

As he moved to the next house, he glanced across the road. Johnson gave him a sympathetic nod. Palpitating, Hood lifted the door knocker. Please let this be over soon, he prayed and no one recognise him. He let the knocker fall with a hard, metallic rap.

Chapter Thirty

As Hood approached Ann's house, it still bore the scars of the siege, but no further damage was visible. Opening the door to him, her brave face revealed she had been in pain that day. He clasped her close to him and she buried her face in his chest. Then she tilted her head back and he kissed her.

"I'm so glad you've come. I needed you here so much."

"I know." He touched her head, wanting to smooth away the pain and fear.

Ann moved away from him and stood, listening. "It's gone so quiet."

"No more mob attacks?"

Ann shook her head. "But the silence - even that's getting to me. I keep expecting something awful to happen."

Hood tried to reassure her. "They saw they couldn't frighten you away and they've given up."

"Maybe," but Ann looked unconvinced. Then she was keen to change the conversation. "How about you?" her voice lowered, the tone darkened: "What have you done about the money?"

Hood hesitated. Should he spare her, and save himself embarrassment? But secrecy had been so disastrous before.

He looked down at the carpet. "Slattery caught me red handed, taking the money from the safe. He held me up at gun point."

"Slattery!" Ann was appalled.

"The nerve of the man: he demands a cut. I told him you needed it all but it made no difference."

He remembered Slattery's accusations against Ann, and then tried to dismiss them from his mind.

"Oh let him have it all Bill. I don't want you doing deals with him for me."

177

"Never. Look at you - how much longer can you go on like this? Pain-killers and more radiation treatment."

"I don't know Bill. I'm too tired. I can't think straight anymore. It's still stolen money."

"Trust me."

Evasive and anxious to change the subject, Ann suddenly rummaged in her bag.

"Look at this." She brandished a letter. "Would you believe it? The local Party ask if I'm standing again at the local elections."

"Of course you are."

Ann's eyes opened wide in amazement. "Me? I'm a wreck. How can I?"

Hood clasped her hand. "You must. Think positive. Remember the people who depend on you. You're not going to let the hate brigade win are you?"

"But Bill, be reasonable. I haven't the strength for canvassing and making speeches."

"You'll find it. We'll enlist help. Oh do it for me Ann. It'll give you something to . . . care . . ."

". . . Live for, you were going to say." She smiled at him. "Well maybe you're right. I never was a quitter. They've not beaten me yet."

A knock at the door interrupted their conversation.

"Who can that be? I'm not expecting anyone."

"I'd better go and answer," Hood offered.

"You sit where you are," Ann told him. "I'll answer it."

Hood conceded and Ann went to the door. Outside stood Monica. She wore a tight calf-length red wool coat with a black bag over her shoulder. Black leggings emphasised her slight build.

"May I come in?" Monica asked evenly.

Ann glared at her and then without a word opened the door wide to admit her. Ann followed her inside detesting the brisk, prim way she walked.

"Well you'd better sit down I suppose," Ann told her ungraciously.

"Hello Bill." Monica looked at him and tried to stop herself blushing.

"Monica," Hood acknowledged her.

Monica set herself on the edge of a chair. She undid the top two

178

buttons on her coat.

"I suppose you're wondering why I've come."

"You could say that. You're not popular around here," Ann informed her.

Monica lowered her head. "I know. And I understand. I've come to make amends."

Then she raised her head and looked directly at Ann. "You've been through a lot and it's my fault. I'm here to warn you, so that you'll be spared any more."

"Why? Are you changing sides? I don't believe it."

"Listen, there's a lot you should understand. Charlie pushed me onto the Council. He controls what goes on, not me. I just take orders."

Hood felt he had to intervene.

"You're telling us as leader of the Council you're not in charge?"

Monica nodded. "More than you can ever know. I live in fear too. Behind Charlie are some very heavy people. Well you've seen that for yourself. Believe me, I've tried to stop them. But Charlie either laughs or is nasty with me. I've been threatened and battered."

Monica turned away, the release of her bottled-up secret too much.

Hood rose and bent over her. His hand hovered in sympathy. "It's brave of you to tell us."

"No, it's you two who've been brave, standing up against them. I went along with it. You see I love Charlie, even though half the time I think he despises me."

Hood went back to sit beside Ann. "So where do we go from here?"

Monica stiffened, her sense of purpose returning. "Of course, that's what I really came about. I've some vital information and you must believe it. Charlie doesn't know I'm here. He'd kill me if he found out."

"Yes, well what is it?" Both Hood and Ann were becoming impatient.

"It's about the elections. You're too much of a liability to them, Ann. You're to be snatched and kept in cold storage till the nominations have closed."

Ann looked incredulous. "Kidnap me?"

"That's about the size of it. I don't know when exactly. Soon. In the next few days."

Ann turned to Hood. "Oh Bill, what am I going to do?"

Hood put his arms around her. "They won't get you," he spoke viciously.

"There's nothing they won't stoop to," Monica warned.

"So what do we do, sit around waiting for them to pick Ann up?"

Monica crouched determined. "No. Ann needs a hideout, a safe house where they can't find her. I have the place."

"Of course, what a coincidence. I smell a trap, Ann."

"That's not fair. I've warned you what Charlie's up to, haven't I?"

"To put us off guard," Hood responded, grim.

Monica despaired of Hood for the moment and turned to Ann. "Ann, woman to woman, surely you can see I'm telling the truth. I only want to help you. I haven't been able to live with myself, knowing what they were doing to you." Then to pre-empt Ann: "I know you don't like me. Maybe you hate me. That doesn't matter. My brother has a flat. It's yours to use if you want it."

Ann listened, her anger simmering. How she resented being vulnerable, dependant on this other woman's help. "Thank you," was all she managed to say.

"You can't stay here," Monica urged her. "You're not safe."

"Oh I believe that," Ann responded. Could she trust Monica? "I'll have to think about it," she prevaricated.

"Don't be long, or it will be too late."

"What do you think Bill?" Ann appealed to Hood.

Hood looked at both of them. He couldn't be with Ann twenty-four hours a day protecting her.

But Monica's sudden change of heart was very suspicious. Was there some deeper motive involved? To collude with Monica in betraying Ann to her enemies would be unbearable. Was that what Monica really wanted?

Chapter Thirty-one

While Ann packed, Hood sulked.

"Please reconsider."

"No."

"Stand down. You're health comes first. You've been through too much."

"You've changed your tune. Before, you were telling me I must stand. And you were right. Otherwise what am I living for?"

"For us."

"Yes. But I must be doing something as well."

She didn't know how many clothes to take or for how long and threw a jumble sale assortment into a suitcase.

The strain of parting was telling on both of them. Each wondered if the other was secretly relieved. So they clung together in a tight embrace of desperate reassurance.

"Oh Ann. If anything happens to you . . ."

"Don't. Nothing will, now."

An urgent rap on the window pane split them apart, and Ann opened the door to Monica.

"The car's outside. Are you ready?"

"Yes. Bill - what will you do?"

"I'll follow in the Volvo."

Monica raised a sceptical eyebrow. "Well drive well back. We don't want a convoy."

"All right Monica," Hood said testily. "I do know how."

"Well all right then," Monica replied, not liking his rebuke. "Don't just stand there. Let's go."

Hood tailed Monica's white Polo as it headed to the outer city suburbs. Ahead lay a business park, all Securities Holdings companies. Very high tech and hush hush, it seemed an appropriate area for a safe house.

Behind the business park was a street of semis. Monica dodged her Polo around the parked cars, and it came to a halt at the kerbside. Hood pulled in behind, and they all met in a huddle on the pavement.

"Here we are," Monica announced eagerly, proud of her initiative. "You'll be quite safe. No one knows about this place, especially not Charlie. Come on, and I'll introduce you."

Monica led the way up a cracked concrete path to the front door of a solid looking fifties semi. She rang the bell and they all stood awkwardly on the threshold.

Eventually the door was opened by a fat man in his thirties wearing a dirty purple T-shirt, corduroy trousers, and trainers. His hair was long and straggled down towards his shoulders. He wore a lazy, shiftless expression.

"Malcolm, this is Ann, the woman I phoned you about. She wants to stay for a few days."

Malcolm nodded, unsurprised, and without a word led the way inside, his trainers flopping down the hall.

Monica pulled Ann to one side. "He's a slob but perfectly all right. He won't bother you."

Ann nodded, distastefully. Hood carried her suitcase upstairs and then rejoined her in the hall.

"Well Ann, I have to go." He looked around him at the strange surroundings. Was he safe leaving her alone with this man Malcolm? Monica had vouched for him, but he might still turn nasty.

He kissed Ann, while Monica, embarrassed, stepped outside onto the doorstep, and checked again that no one had followed them.

"I'll be in touch darling. You take care in here. And if there's any trouble," with his head he indicated Malcolm in the kitchen, "you ring me straight away and I'll get you. I don't like leaving you."

Ann smiled at him. "Go on with you, I'll be all right. Now get off, I need to unpack." But inside she desperately wanted him with her.

Hood followed Monica outside. "Thank you," he made himself say. "I know what you're doing for us. I appreciate it."

Embarrassed and ruffled Monica replied, "Well I hope Ann

does." And she climbed into her Polo. "See you around," and with that she drove off.

Thoughtfully Hood walked back to the Volvo and started up the engine. He prayed Ann would be safe and he could stop worrying about her all the time. He still felt he shouldn't have left her there. Things always seemed to go wrong when they were apart.

As he drove he tried to put it out of his mind. Instead he concentrated on one last desperate gamble: that afternoon's robbery.

It was madness he knew. Already he was investigating his own thefts. How much longer before he was recognised? But he couldn't sit by and watch Ann's downward slide without one last attempt. Each day she was losing ground. He chewed his lip. Suppose her case was hopeless, terminal. It couldn't be; he wouldn't allow himself to think like that.

He drove in a sort of trance. Almost before he could see it he knew that the bank he wanted was ahead on the corner. He steadily gained on it and then was past turning right at a squat chapel with its services plastered on blackboard in front. Now he was searching for a parking spot; near enough to the bank to be easily walked but far enough to avoid identification. The pavement almost disappeared at one point as a builder's merchants wall billowed out into the road. He pulled up just beyond. It provided a perfect curtain obscuring the view of people from the top end of the road towards the bank.

He stopped the car, breathed in for a moment and then gathered his equipment together in the bag. It was a ritual by now. He felt something for each item which had served him. But then again he would not be sorry when he disposed of everything which could incriminate him.

Now he was out of the car and into the street. In his overalls he lounged by the car pretending to struggle locking it while he waited for the street to clear of pedestrians.

Then he quickly circumvented the wall and pressed along the street sheltering beneath the scaffolding and blown polythene sheeting which covered the Co-op building to his right.

The bank side was visible at the corner, and its colonnade jutted out like a greek temple.

He was almost upon it now. One last time; his nerve mustn't

fail him now. With trembling fingers he pulled out the balaclava and then dropped it. Hastily he retrieved it from the pavement looking round to see if he was observed. Then he hauled it over his head, and clasped the gun tightly inside the bag. He was ready, it was time, he strode forward, despite a terrible warning voice inside telling him it was all about to go wrong.

His step faltered, picked up, faltered again. Then he mastered himself and the old calm settled on him. A totally surprising devil-may-care confidence took hold of him. He was in charge; he sauntered in.

Bells ringing, minutes later he ran out in panic. He had the money but left pandemonium behind him. People were running about, shouting and gesticulating. Faster than he ever remembered running, till his lungs seemed to be bursting, he hared round the corner and down the street. He could see the car bumper now, jutting around the builder's merchants wall. If he could just reach it. He looked over his shoulder; figures were gathering, buzzing, at the top of the street, uncertain. He grabbed his keys, jammed them into the lock, yanked at the door handle. He was inside. The relief seemed to pour in streams down his face. The overall was dragged down his body till it snagged on his waistband. The money in the bag lay on the floor behind the seat, the gun underneath it with the balaclava.

Then he heard a rapping on the car window. Terror-struck he looked round - a uniformed policeman was sternly attracting his attention while two colleagues surrounded the vehicle noting its number plates.

Hood wound down the window.

"Step out of the car sir, please, if you would. Straight away." The words came out edgy but determined.

Instead Hood risked reaching inside his jacket. The policemen converged on him in seconds and the first tried a grab. But Hood was too quick for them. He brandished his warrant card. "Get on you loons. I'm detective Hood. I've been on look-out here for the bank. The man's just roared past me, in a green Maestro. For God's sake get on the radio."

Dazed they listened. Hood was all impatience and belligerence.

The first constable made up his mind; "Come on lads," and Hood watched them run to their patrol car and radio in the message. Then with sand and dust flying, they tore off in the direction which Hood had indicated.

Dragging himself into action, Hood started the Volvo and made himself follow in pursuit. It was a wild chance but he might just get away with it. Head singing, he pressed hard down and the Volvo roared.

Chapter Thirty-two

Discovery threatened every minute. Soon Hood would have a lot of explaining to do - about the green Maestro and its complete disappearance from the scene of the crime. He prayed no eye witness at the previous robberies had identified his gunmetal Volvo. If that happened he was finished.

He was riding round the city with a hundred thousand pounds stashed behind the back seat. Any minute he could be flagged down and arrested, or told to report immediately back at Headquarters.

He had to dispose of the money. But Slattery's office during working hours would be full of people to witness their transaction.

He was desperate. He couldn't roam around the city all afternoon with a car full of stolen money.

Then he thought of Ann, alone with surly Malcolm in that strange house, worrying herself sick. Then it came to him: he could use the safe house. No one, including the police, knew about her hideaway. It was perfect. He could lie low for a few hours and make sure she was all right. And then later he'd call on Slattery and divide up the money.

Encouraged he changed direction. Bypassing the city centre, he used the football stadium for a bearing and headed back down the dual carriageway.

Twenty minutes later he was outside the house. He found its ribbed tiles, red and white brickwork, arched bay windows, and privet hedge reassuring. It had a secure, unruffled atmosphere.

As he climbed out of the car he was undecided what to do with the money. It was tempting to simply hand it over to Ann as a down payment. But it was too little on its own. Slattery would want his cut before releasing the rest of Hood's share. The hundred thousand was his only bargaining lever to make Slattery give up the rest of the money. Reluctantly, with furtive movements Hood transferred the bag of money to the car boot and locked it.

Then he rang the bell. Nothing happened and he rang again. He sensed eyes peering from behind the curtains. Then after a delay the front door clicked open. He waited, then pushed but no one was behind it.

Suspicious he entered the hall, passed along the red and black carpet and then into the lounge. Ann was sitting in a corner chair, rigid and tense.

"What's the idea?" Hood asked. "I thought Malcolm was supposed to answer the door."

"Malcolm's out."

"I was worried."

Hood strolled uneasily about the room. A huge, black television dominated one corner. There was a long, teak sideboard against a wall, with a large copper bowl of fruit on top. A daubed painting of deer on a mountainside hung above a grimy settee.

Unnerved by Ann's silence, Hood broke out: "How are you?"

"You asked me that this morning." Ann would not meet his eye but kept focussing on the bowl of fruit opposite.

"Well I'm asking you again. You're acting very strangely."

He came over to crouch beside her, but she flinched and half turned away.

"Ann," he appealed to her.

"Why did you leave me here? That Malcolm, he's driving me mad prowling about the house all the time. There's nothing to do. How long am I going to be stuck here?"

"You were the one who wanted to come."

Ann folded her arms around her middle. She wore a straight blue dress with feeble white piping down the front, which hardly suited her.

"Don't remind me." She was becoming progressively more agitated. "Oh Bill, I'm so frightened of everything. Not just being kidnapped, but about you and me."

Hood put his hand on her arm. "We're all right. I thought we'd settled all that. I've levelled with you." Then he bit his tongue as he thought of the secret haul in the boot of the car.

Ann looked him in the face. "I know. But I'm left stuck here and you're out there free. I don't know where you are or what you're doing. I get so angry and resentful - sometimes I hate you. There I've said it. You'd be well rid of me."

"Ann, Ann," Hood again appealed to her, and took her head in his hands. "That doesn't matter. It's just nerves. I understand. Curse me if it will help."

Ann smiled back at him briefly. "You are good for me. I do love you so, really. It's just so hard to keep sane when you're not here. Then those awful feelings boil up again."

"It's bad for me too. I have my moments, believe me, when I think I must be nuts."

Ann stroked his head. "I'm sorry. I am selfish."

Hood clasped her hand in his. "Anyway I can stay for a while. I'm keeping out of sight." He hesitated then went on: "I'm waiting to make a final payment to Slattery. Then we'll share out the rest of the money and pay for your treatment in America."

"Oh Bill, what's the use?" The mention of America still seemed fantastical, like a prize dream holiday that someone else always wins.

They sat together for hours, fingers entwined, saying little but each trying to buoy up the other simply by their presence.

At five Hood suddenly announced, "Well I'd better be off."

"Must you go already?"

Hood checked his watch again. "I must if I'm to catch Slattery. The staff will be leaving soon, and I need him on his own."

"Be careful."

"Don't worry, I will."

They snatched a last kiss and then Hood let himself out of the house.

He knew now that it had to be settled tonight. Not only Ann's health but her state of mind wouldn't stand much more. Besides he risked being caught at any moment and then he and the money would be lost to her for ever.

The lights inside the Slattery office building were still on as Hood pulled the car up outside. Nimbly he strode through the doorway and into the familiar open-plan office. He looked over and around the screens but no one was there. The same cardigans were left over chairs. His own desk looked much as he had left it before he so abruptly resigned.

Hood could see Slattery in his office bending over some papers on his desk. As Hood rapped on the glass partition, he glanced up. He suddenly looked old, tired and lonely.

"I've a delivery for you."

Slattery nodded. "Well bring it in. No one saw you I suppose."

"You suppose right. What do you take me for?"

Hood stepped outside, retrieved the bag full of money from the car boot, and returned to Slattery's office. He dropped the bag on Slattery's desk, so that packets of notes slithered out and rested on his blotter.

"Go on, count it," Hood told him.

"No, you count it."

"There's a hundred thousand there I reckon. I want my share of the rest tonight."

"Tonight! But that's impossible. There isn't enough for either of us."

"It'll have to do." Hood's voice was grim.

"And I'm telling you that it can't be tonight."

"Let me persuade you." Hood pulled his revolver from his overcoat pocket.

"I must be losing my touch," Slattery reproached himself. "Put that away. Be sensible."

"I'm through being sensible. Come on, down to the vault."

Slattery lead the way down some stone steps to the basement. First he unlocked a steel door, withdrawing its heavy bolts. Then turning right they walked some yards under the floor of the office above. At the end of a narrow passage behind a grille was a huge safe with a steel lock.

With his keys Slattery opened the grille and then set to work on the safe, working the wheel and releasing the catches. On the chilly, stone flagged floor he began piling out the money till it formed a miniature mountain.

"Right, count out three hundred and fifty thousand," Hood told him.

"What? That's not an equal split."

"Just do it. Remember it's for Ann's sake. Be unselfish for a change."

As he began Slattery said, "You'd never use that thing," motioning to the gun.

"Just try me. Ann's sick and I'm desperate. Give me the

money."

"All right, stay calm. It takes time."

"Well don't stall."

"I'm not."

Slattery expertly counted out the packets of tens and twenties till all that was left of the mountain was a small residual pile.

"There, you can keep that for your trouble."

"Thanks," Slattery replied sarcastically and moved to rise.

"Who told you to get up," and Hood slapped him down.

Resting in a crouching position Slattery scowled at him. "I'll get you for this. Don't think I won't."

Hood looked down on him with contempt. "You're all washed up. It's over. Why don't you crawl away and die?"

"No one talks to me like that and gets away with it," Slattery snarled.

"Just watch me. I'm paying you back for all those years ago."

"What?"

"When you destroyed me, my business, everything."

"You must be crazy."

Hood raised the gun.

"It wasn't me. You've got the wrong man."

Hood looked at him impassively for long seconds. The light seemed to dance on Slattery's silvered hair. Then he lowered the gun. Stiffly he bagged up the money and walked away.

"See. You'll never know. You'll die wondering," Slattery sneered after him.

But Hood was through the office, needing the evening air, then into his car.

Forget Slattery, forget the past. Next stop was Ann, and then for her - America.

Slattery sank back sitting down on the stone flags. Robbed. He pushed his hands through his hair, and felt the thinning. He was getting old, past it. All he'd wanted was to stay ahead until he retired.

Russell's protection couldn't last for ever. How had he let himself become entangled with Hood and his mad schemes? That man was a jinx.

Hood was self-destructing, and he must fight or he'd be pulled down with him. The man must have a death wish. Well he'd have his wish and soon.

Chapter Thirty-three

As he drove along Hood could barely control his excitement. In a few minutes he would hand over the money to Ann and she could start the treatment to save her life. He pictured her gradually improving until finally she was completely well, blooming. Sudden doubt assailed him: would she still want him then? Who could tell? Gratitude didn't guarantee love.

He longed to be back with her, and reassured. The sacrifice would have been worth it so long as she loved him. Then he upbraided himself for his selfishness: the treatment was only a chance at best and this thought sobered him.

He breathed a sigh of relief as the sign to the business park loomed up and in the distance he could see its strange pagoda style architecture.

He was watching for the turning now, anxious not to miss it and delay being reunited with Ann. Swinging the Volvo round he drove a few yards then came to a halt outside the semi-detached hideaway. Quickly he jumped out, and then thought of the money. But he couldn't simply thrust the heavy bag full of notes at her without warning, so he left it in the boot for the moment. Soon enough he could present her with it.

Advancing down the path he reached the front door and rang the bell. Impatiently he peered through the frosted glass for a glimpse of her. No longer would she have to stay in a place which so dispirited her. Next stop for her was the USA!

The door opened and Malcolm stood there in a long grey sweat shirt that hung in folds almost to his knees. He pulled his hair out of his eyes. "Oh it's you," he said, sleepily.

"Yes, it's me," Hood repeated impatiently. "Where's Ann?" He looked past Malcolm down the hall.

"She's gone."

"What do you mean 'gone'? Where is she?"

Malcolm rested one trainered foot on the other, and perched like a bird.

"Like I said, gone. We had a few words and I took myself off to the shops. When I came back she had gone. Left her stuff though."

Hood's fists were clenching and unclenching. "What was said between you?"

"She did most of the talking. Downright ungrateful if you ask me. She blamed you mostly for leaving her here. She has a real nasty temper, hasn't she?"

Hood cut him off: "Do you know where she's gone? Did she say?"

Malcolm scratched his head. "No, she didn't either. Like I said it was a surprise to find her gone."

"Yes, yes, all right," Hood broke in. "Have you searched the area?" One look at Malcolm's lumbering posture told him the answer. Had Malcolm betrayed her? Hood couldn't tell and he didn't have time to linger and force it out of Malcolm.

Turning on his heel Hood walked quickly back to the Volvo. He didn't know what to think. Surely Ann wouldn't have simply walked out, whatever the provocation. Had Malcolm been pestering her? What if he'd tried to rape her and she'd run away? Hood told himself not to let his imagination run riot. There was probably a perfectly simple explanation.

The question was: had Ann walked out of her own free will or had Charlie's mob taken her? But Monica had assured him that Charlie knew nothing of the safe house.

Getting back in the Volvo he started up the engine. He thought of Ann, and then all that money, sitting uselessly in the car boot. He detested it, and near despaired of bringing Ann and the money safely together. Where was she?

The car was already moving and he still didn't know where he was heading. Instead of turning right, back the way he'd come, he tried left first and began searching the surrounding streets. Maybe Ann was walking round in circles, dazed, disorientated, not knowing what she was doing.

He covered the area, craning his head out of the window hoping for a glimpse of her, but she was nowhere to be seen.

Eventually he had to give up and admit defeat. She must be far gone by now. Where to try next? He travelled back down the main road towards the dual carriageway.

Her home must be the best bet. Perhaps she decided she couldn't stand the safe house and fled back to her own home, despite its attendant dangers.

His arm ached from twisting the steering wheel so much in the tight turns he'd made, scouring the area. All he wanted was to find her, and keep her safe. But what if she was crazed, and hated him again? She might even attack him, like before. He remembered the madness in her, the person he didn't recognise.

"Come on, come on," he urged the car, as he put his foot down on the accelerator down the dual carriageway. But he dare not go too fast and risk being flagged down for speeding.

So it was with frustration he maintained a middling speed always edging it up that little bit faster.

Finally he was outside Ann's house. He watched from the car. A couple of slates were loose and sparrows were darting about on the guttering, making nests. But otherwise there was no sign of movement, occupation.

Climbing out he ran down the path and knocked on the door. There was no answer. He pounded but still drew no response. What if she were lying dead inside? Suppose she'd killed herself, in a fit of depression? He peered through the windows and then ran round the back. There were still pieces of charcoaled wood lying in the yard, as he crossed it and knocked on the back door. He looked through the kitchen window, but still there was no sign of Ann.

Retracing his steps round to the front, he looked back at the bedroom windows. But there was no tell tale pull of curtains, no movement at all. He tried the neighbours, but no one had seen her return to the house that day.

Frustrated and angry he ran back to the car. "Where the hell are you Ann?" he called out. "Why are you doing this to me?"

He sat for a moment, shaking. He didn't know what to do next. If only he could be sure she was safe somewhere. But that was a forlorn hope. Wherever she had gone she was vulnerable: whether walking the streets or in the clutches of Charlie's mob. And there was her medication. She couldn't miss that, not even for a few hours. Heaven knows what suffering she might be going

193

j

through without it.

He had to find her. There was no alternative: he must enlist the help of his police colleagues. How bitter that felt, how ironical. But there was no help; it had to be done.

At Police Headquarters he found Russell deep in conversation with Pearson, standing beside a huge plan of the city. Little pinned flags denoted the various banks which had been raided. Hood walked straight up to Russell.

"Could I have a word sir?"

"Not now Hood, can't you see I'm busy? Why aren't you out catching this bank robber?"

Hood kept a straight face. "I have been. But if I could just speak to you for a moment sir. It is very urgent."

Reluctantly Russell allowed himself to be manoeuvred away from the huge wall map. He kept looking back at it, fondly. He loved anything like that, which involved paper strategy, planning, tactics.

"Well Hood what is it?"

"It's about Ann Renshaw."

Before Hood could continue, Russell erupted: "You drag me away at a crucial time to talk about that woman!"

"You don't understand. She's disappeared."

Russell half turned, on his way back to rejoin Pearson. "Good riddance. Is that all?"

"Sir," Hood halted Russell. "I didn't want to bring this up sir, but I have no choice. Ann is desperately ill with cancer. I think she's been kidnapped. If she doesn't get medication in the next few hours she's going to die."

The change in Russell was remarkable. The wall map was forgotten. A dreamlike look had come into his eyes.

"Ann, with cancer? it can't be." He seemed to find it hard to take it all in at once. "Kidnapped you say?"

"Yes sir. I received a warning it might happen from an informant."

"So why didn't you prevent it?" All his previous instructions to avoid Ann Renshaw, seemed now forgotten by Russell.

"I tried sir. We had her in a safe house but somehow her enemies must have found out. That is, unless she simply walked out of her own free will."

Gradually Russell was coming out of his daze. He picked his

beard thoughtfully. His large brown eyes were suspicious, hurt. "You mean you only think she's been kidnapped. She could simply have gone walkabout."

Reluctantly Hood answered, "It's possible."

"She's on drugs?"

"Yes sir."

"Then she may not know what she's doing." The realisation made Russell soften a little towards Hood. "All right. We'll put out an alert to find her."

"Sir, could I make a suggestion? Pull in Charlie Rigby. He's masterminded a hate campaign against her."

"Charlie Rigby? You must be joking. He's been one of our best informants."

"I don't care. He's a political crook and a thug."

Russell half opened his mouth to argue then closed it again. "Very well. We'll pull him in. But we'll have to tread very carefully."

Russell gave the orders then wandered back to his meeting. But the wall map seemed to have lost all of its appeal. He appeared distracted, his mind somewhere else. And occasionally he would cast a guilty stare up at the ceiling, as if somehow Ann's predicament were his fault.

Chapter Thirty-four

Hood didn't wait for Russell's instructions to filter down to the constables in the patrol cars. He wanted to collar Charlie Rigby now, himself, and get some answers.

He raced out of the building to his car and set off for Charlie's address. It was a quiet corner house in a cul-de-sac with a field behind and a school just across the way. Hood wondered if Charlie and Monica had children, and then decided it was unlikely. Their nefarious activities wouldn't give them time.

Slamming the car door he approached the house. It was a small neat bungalow painted pastel green, with a red tiled roof from which emerged the windowed dormer bedroom. A line of flagstones lay against the side of the house alongside a pile of sand.

Hood rang the bell, keeping his finger jammed hard on the button. He could hear the peal reverberating through the house. That should wake up Charlie.

There was a scratching sound as a chain was released from the door, and then it opened and Monica appeared. She was wearing a thick ribbed polo neck sweater which seemed to engulf her small frame. It came well down over her jeans. On her feet were the clumsy Doc Martins he remembered.

"Bill!"

Hood nodded curtly and pushed his way inside. "Where's Charlie?"

He was prowling the living-room, impatiently.

"Charlie's not here," she said in a low voice.

Hood listened suspiciously, and then searched the various rooms before rejoining her. "Very well, I'll start with you. Where's Ann?"

Monica moved away with stiff, pained steps. She picked up an

196

apple from the bowl on the table and began squeezing it spasmodically. "At the safe house isn't she?"

Hood lunged at her. "Now don't get smart with me. She's gone and you know it. You told Charlie where she was, didn't you?"

Monica looked away, her face anguished. Hood gripped her jaw with his hand. "Didn't you?"

Monica pulled away. "Yes, all right, I did. I can't stand it."

"You little bitch. Setting her up. I ought to . . ."

He wanted to lash out, the old cruel streak coming to the surface. She stood there, all withdrawn into herself, huddled together in misery and guilt. He wanted to let her have it, releasing all his rage, frustration. Raising his hand he yelled, "For the last time, where is Ann?"

"I don't know. Don't hit me Bill, I've been through all that with Charlie."

As she spoke, Hood noticed for the first time the dark purple bruising under her left eye and on her cheek. He also saw she was hobbling as she struggled to escape from him.

Shocked he dropped his hand. "Monica, I'm sorry. What did Charlie do - beat the information out of you?"

Monica nodded, her tough little mouth compressed to prevent herself giving way. When she was composed again, she answered, "He was suspicious. Someone told him that I'd been to see Ann and you. When she disappeared he put two and two together. It was awful." She shuddered and sat down. "You don't know him like I do. He's low down, vicious. I think sometimes he takes a perverse pleasure in hurting me. You should have seen that sick smile of his as he dragged the address from me. He's not human."

Hood put his hand gently on her shoulder. She winced, and he moved it, guiltily.

"So Charlie's got Ann. Do you know where he's taken her?"

"I don't Bill, that's the God's own truth. If I knew I'd tell you. No one is safe with him." Then she regretted her last remark.

"No idea at all?" Hood was desperate.

Monica spread her hands. "Believe me, if I did . . . but Charlie won't use any of the old places. He'd know I'd tell on him after this."

Hood looked hard at her. "Is there anything I can do for you. Shall I call the doctor?"

Monica shook her tousled head, the short curls bobbing. "No, I've seen one. In fact I've just come back from casualty," she finished bashfully.

"I'll get Charlie for this. We'll put him behind bars."

"No Bill, it's no use."

"Don't talk like that. But look, I can't stay any longer. Think about it. And if any idea where Ann might be comes to you, let me know."

Monica's eyes were bitter, sad, regretful. "I promise. I wish it didn't have to be like this. I hate letting you down Bill. You, of all people."

"I know."

She saw Hood to the door. "Ann will be OK. She's tougher than you think."

"I hope you're right."

Then, with his worst fears confirmed, he walked back to his car. All the way to Police Headquarters he wondered how at that precise moment Ann was feeling. Was she terrorised, were they hurting her, abusing her, or had the cancerous pain returned. In his mind he built up her suffering to intolerable proportions, but he couldn't help it. He loved her so much that everything seemed magnified. He had to have some hard information otherwise his imagination would only torture him.

Back at Headquarters he learned that they had pulled in Charlie. He wanted to go straight down and have it out with him but the officer in charge rebuffed him. "My lads are questioning him now. You can have your chance after them - if they don't get anywhere."

Chafing under this refusal, Hood wandered to the canteen and forced himself to drink a coffee from the dispenser. The plastic cup burnt his fingers but he barely noticed. Colleagues spoke to him, but he didn't reply. All his thoughts were centred on Charlie, and when he could work on him.

Then he shook himself. It would do no good to rough up Charlie. He must play this carefully for Ann's sake. Her welfare was what mattered now, not his own outraged feelings.

Finally after an hour and a half he received the go ahead to see Charlie in the interview room. It was cold and bare, with just two chairs and a table. A couple of posters about reducing crime were pinned to a cork board. A small, inadequate radiator hummed against the far wall. The paintwork was off white with some mysterious grey streaks appearing. The fluorescent light buzzed irritatingly, and one tube kept flicking off and on.

Charlie greeted Hood like a long lost friend. "Bill. Thank God you've come down. Set them straight will you? I don't know what they think old Charlie's been up to, but you know me. I steer well clear of trouble."

Hood sat down opposite him. He watched the eager, weasel expression, so fluid, manipulative. Charlie's bald patch was glistening under the light. Could it be anxiety? He was wearing a pin stripe waistcoat and blue shirt rolled up to the elbows, revealing his short, podgy arms.

"Where's Ann Renshaw, Charlie?"

Charlie looked away for a second in apparent surprise and exasperation.

"Not you too? They kept asking me that. How should I know? I've barely clapped eyes on the woman."

"Come off it Charlie. You can drop the act. I know you've been orchestrating the campaign to drive Ann crazy."

Charlie raised his hands. "Why do you say such things Bill? In the time we've known each other, have I ever put you wrong? This is all some hideous mistake. You know me and politics, like oil and water we don't mix."

Hood sighed. Charlie's clowning had palled long ago.

"Monica told me everything. You really worked her over properly, didn't you Charlie?"

"Me, you must be kidding. I wouldn't dare have a go at Monica. Have you seen her? What's she been saying about me? Bill, I warned you about her, from the start. She may be my wife and all but when she gets started on that political stuff . . ."

"Charlie," Hood interrupted sternly, "cut the crap. I know all about you, and not just from Monica. You're going down, old son. Assault, kidnapping . . ."

"Kidnapping!" then Charlie's mouth twisted in disgust. "And I thought you were my friend. Show me your evidence, go on. You've nothing on me, any of you."

Hood rose and glowered over him. "Where's Ann? You're not leaving here till you've told me."

"You'll have a long wait then," Charlie sneered back at him. "I want to see my solicitor."

199

"Where's Ann?" Hood's voice was ominous. Something was running out of control inside him.

Charlie sensed this, and his chair scraped back along the floor.

"I don't know I tell you. Hey, you outside. I want to go," he called, afraid.

Hood was over him now, reaching down. "For the last time do I have to squeeze it out of you? Where's Ann?"

"All right, Detective Hood. That will be enough. Leave this man now." It was the officer in charge standing behind him. To Charlie, the man said, "Very well sir, you may go. Thank you for your co-operation."

Charlie scampered up from his chair and circled round Hood warily. "You want to watch that temper of yours mate. It will land you in trouble one of these days." Then he managed to saunter out.

"You went too far then," the officer told Hood.

"I know. But is that what you call co-operation?"

"Well, you wouldn't get any more the way you were heading."

Hood nodded and walked, deflated, back out of the interview room.

Chapter Thirty-five

Charlie scurried to the nearest telephone booth. He was sweating. He reckoned he'd fended them off pretty well but with the police on the case, holding Ann was going to be a difficult, maybe impossible, matter. Much better to really put the frighteners on her and let her go. He had to admit she had more guts than he'd ever anticipated. She should have cracked months ago; most other people under the same pressure had. What made her different? Maybe it was Hood, always hanging around to give moral support. If only he could have separated those two.

He rang his contact. "Tom? Is that you? How are things going? Where have you stashed Ann Renshaw?"

There was a brief urgent explanation at the other end and Charlie's face exploded into anger. "What do you mean you missed her? She slipped through your fingers? You idiot."

Further apologies followed from Tom and then Charlie rounded on him: "Listen to me, you'll have to move fast. The police are looking for her too. So find her, put the frighteners on her - no for God's sake don't damage her - then let her go. It's too risky to stick to our original plan."

Then Charlie rang off. It was the best he could do in the circumstances. How could he have underestimated Ann?

As he walked down the road towards the station's taxi rank, another fear assailed him. What if his bosses heard about Ann getting away. Already they had become impatient with her intransigence. They expected results. The political complexion of the council could always change for the worse - unless steps were taken. If he didn't succeed, he would be replaced by someone who could.

His head went down. He couldn't face the ignominy of dismissal. After all, he'd worked his way up in the Party from nothing. He'd wheedled and cajoled, threatened and bullied, and taken on the dirty jobs which no one else wanted. Not for him the limelight. He'd worked in secret, in the shadows, maintaining a mask of political indifference. Patronised as a buffoon, a hen-pecked husband, he had maintained the perfect cover. All the while he despised the people who disregarded him, wrote him off, knowing that his day would come.

But when? His steps hurried on past the The Newsroom pub. Time and again he'd asked: why shouldn't he be the leader of the Council, instead of Monica, his puppet? But each time they turned him down. Stay in the background they told him, the unsung hero.

What if they were just using him, stringing him along? They'd find out he was no patsy. He'd outsmart them.

He pressed on down to the station apron and found a taxi. As it took him home he thought morosely of Monica. She'd betrayed him all along the line. Even a good hiding hadn't stopped her. He could never trust her again. He had to be rid of her.

But how? Arriving, he paid off the driver and stalked the last few yards to the bungalow.

"Charlie Rigby." He lifted his head to locate the speaker. Out from beneath the flowering horse-chestnut tree opposite, stepped Ann.

"I've been waiting for you," she announced. Charlie was stunned, and began thinking quickly. Was she deranged, he wondered?

"Have you? Why's that? Do you want to come in?"

Ann stepped forward. Her old yellow PVC raincoat was open, dwarfing her now. "No, what I have to say can be done out here. I understand your men have been looking for me."

"My men? I don't have any 'men', Ann. I'm a bar steward, that's all."

"Bastard, more like. Your cover's blown. I know all about you, you little weasel." She launched forward and scratched at him with her nails. She managed to claw his cheek before he fought her off.

"Have you gone mad? I'll call the police."

"You do that," she sneered. "All these months I've suffered, not knowing for certain who was behind it. And it turned out to be a contemptible little heel like you."

Charlie was stung by the scorn in her voice.

"Go on, you old bag," he retorted, "on your way, before I stick one on you."

"You would as well. You like beating up women, don't you? Poor Monica, what she's put up with."

"Leave her out of this."

"How could you? Do you get a kick out of it, or what?"

Charlie's face shut down, stonily. "You - leave," he said, in a cold, clipped voice, "while you can still walk."

"I can do more than that. Where's your phone?"

Surprised by her gall, Charlie watched as Ann rang the door bell. Monica answered and let Ann in. The door closed behind her.

Charlie, recovering himself, went forward and tried the door but it was locked. He took out his key and tried it but the lock had been changed. He hammered on the door, calling out, "Damn you Monica let me in. Do you hear?" Then he went round the back but had no more success.

Frustrated, he walked round the front again.

"This is ridiculous," he muttered. "Locked out by two women."

He battered on the front door again, calling out, "Monica, let me in this minute. Or I'll give you a right good hiding."

Then he stood back from the house, undecided. He was in a fury, pacing up and down the street. He couldn't stay out there all night.

Finally a gunmetal coloured Volvo roared up the street towards him and ground to a halt.

Charlie groaned. "Oh no, not you again."

Hood leapt out and ran for him. Instinctively Charlie swerved and headed off in the opposite direction. For a small man he was quite agile and desperation lent him speed.

But Hood was determined and angry. He leapt and grabbed Charlie round the waist, then thumped him behind the ear. Charlie flailed back and caught Hood on the collar bone. They were both sent sprawling on the gravel. Charlie was up again, searching for an escape route, when he looked down into Hood's gun.

Involuntarily Charlie let out a squeal. "Don't shoot. You can't. Murder!"

"So tell me about it," Hood growled back at him.

Charlie was hot footing up and down on one spot. "You can't," he wailed again.

Hood gave him the longest look, then slowly lowered the gun. "You're right. You're not worth it. I don't shoot bugs like you. I just step on them."

Hood replaced the gun in his pocket, and took out handcuffs instead. He clicked them over Charlie's wrists.

The two women who had been watching from the window, came outside, Monica leading. She glared at Charlie. "Put him away." Then she turned in disgust.

Hood looked at Ann. "Thank God you're safe. We've had a full alert out for you. Has he hurt you?"

"No, I'm all right. He got the worst of it." Ann grinned, her eyes shining to see Hood.

"Well if you'll share the car with this animal, I've orders to transport you to headquarters. It seems Deputy Chief Constable Russell wants to see you're all right in person."

Ann acquiesced and climbed into the car. As Hood drove, Ann tried to explain to him. "I hated that house and you. I had to get away. Then I saw Charlie's men converging on the house and I just ran. I was good and angry, enough to pay Charlie back." She turned and looked at him, the handcuffs chafing his wrists, and her face flushed with triumph.

Chapter Thirty-six

Hood ushered Ann into Russell's office.

"Thank you Detective Hood that will be all. Please wait outside," Russell told him and he withdrew.

Russell came from behind his desk and pulled out a chair. Gratefully Ann sat down and watched, perplexed, as Russell flitted around his office like a butterfly unsure where to settle. He straightened a notice on his wall-board, paused by the window, then sat down.

He seemed to find it hard to look Ann in the face. Finally he said, in a formal way, "I asked that you be brought up here to show how seriously I take the treatment of one of our councillors."

Ann's face hardened a fraction. "I hope you would have done the same for any woman."

Russell put his hand up. "Of course, that goes without saying."

He gazed at her now with those large, hurt eyes. His beard seemed like a bushy mask from behind which he tried to make contact.

Then again he tried to resume a controlled, authoritative tone. "Hood has been keeping me informed of your situation. I'm sorry you've been harassed. We've done everything we could."

Ann glared at him. "Well it wasn't damn well enough. It's taken until today to pull in Charlie Rigby. All these months he's been let off scot free to put me through hell." She blanched as she remembered the day-to-day terror, the intimidation, the jeering gang at midnight.

Russell pulled at his uniform collar. It was at times like this he seemed embarrassed of his uniform, as if wishing to be divested of it and all the responsibility that went with it.

"Yes, well, it takes time to build a case. I have to warn you we may not be able to hold Mr Rigby. I've warned Hood about this before."

"What! Are you telling me you're going to release him back on the streets to start all over again? Have you not been listening to a word I've said? My life won't be worth living after this."

Russell shuffled awkwardly. "Please don't distress yourself. We'll see you don't come to any harm. He won't dare pull anything now."

"Oh yeah?" Ann gazed back at him in disgust and scepticism.

She slipped the PVC raincoat from her shoulders onto the back of the chair. It was becoming clammy and oppressive in the room. Underneath the coat she had on a thick, ribbed red sweater and pleated black skirt.

Russell tried to disguise his responsiveness to her figure, and pulled some papers together on his desk. He glanced up quickly, risking a direct look at her. "Yes, believe me." Then somehow his gaze became locked on her, and his official reserve broke down. "Oh Ann why didn't you come to me over these last few months, years? You'd only to ask and I'd have done anything for you."

Ann looked puzzled, suspicious and leant back in her seat. "Why you?"

"Don't you remember . . ?"

Her hand went to her mouth. "Hey, wait a minute. It must be - five, eight years ago? I thought there was something. You used to buy me hot dogs at that little stand in the market."

Eagerly Russell took up the reminiscence. "And then we'd stroll down by the canal to the gardens. Do you remember that time you had a go on the swings?"

"Do I?" the memory came flooding back, of Russell a young, up and coming officer, so ardent in his attentions, embarrassingly so. Trying desperately to be romantic, do the right thing, showering her with chocolates and flowers. It was a pity she'd not felt the same way about him.

"We had some laughs."

Russell looked hurt. "It wasn't the laughs I was thinking of. That kiss, just near the weeping willow, I'll never forget it. We were going to meet for a meal in the evening, but you rang and cried off. That was the last I saw of you." The baffled pain still lay there, behind his voice.

Ann softened. "I know, I'm sorry. Seems silly after all these years to say that, doesn't it? But I am. I never wanted to hurt you. You were just coming on too strong."

"You don't know what it means to me to hear you talk like this, to say you're sorry."

"Well that's fine, but let's not make a whole big thing about it. It was years ago after all. Just a casual affair."

"Casual?" His voice almost screeched. Unable to sit still any longer, he rose and prowled by the wall. "Ann, have you any idea what you put me through? Do you know that not a day has passed since, that I haven't thought of you, wanted you?"

He turned urgently to her. "Hood told me about your . . . illness. Again, why didn't you come to me? I would have helped, done anything for you. Can't you see, I've never cared for anyone else but you."

Ann was left busy twisting in her seat, trying to follow his frenzied movements and over-wrought words. "I don't know what to say. I wish . . . I could have done something. But it was never like that for me. I was fond of you, but . . ."

At Russell's hurt, reproachful glance, she hurried on, ". . . But it was never more than that. You shouldn't have made more of it than there was. I didn't."

"Oh I know you didn't," he rounded on her. "I was soon forgotten, I could tell that. An endless procession of men after me, wasn't there? Only you didn't put them off the way you did with me."

Ann became alarmed. She wondered about Russell's state of mind.

"Now you're being insulting. I came up here . . ."

"You came because you were brought. And you're going to sit and listen to every word I have to say. You may learn something."

Excited, he paused to mop his brow with his handkerchief. He also tried to regain some self control.

"None of your . . . relationships, came to anything did they?"

Ann looked him in the eye, cross, not deigning to reply. Then though irritated she confirmed, "No, they didn't. Something always seemed to go wrong. Story of my life."

Russell seemed to gain a pained satisfaction from her reply. "They never stayed, did they? You'd meet a couple of times, then they'd stand you up, make excuses, drift away. The whole thing cooled off."

Ann was puzzled, angry. "Yes, that's the way it was. How come you know so much about it? Hey, have you been spying on me? You little peeping Tom!" She half rose in her chair, but Russell motioned her down.

His dignity seemed ruffled. "I didn't spy on you. I've better things to do. No, but a friend of mine kept tabs on who was with you. Then if it seemed to be getting serious, he warned them off, made them disappear."

Ann rocked in her chair. "I thought I was paranoid, the way they kept going. I used to torment myself with never being able to keep a man."

Then she glared in full fury at Russell. "Tell me who it was, or I'll tear you and this whole room apart. Who was it?"

Russell smiled. Why should he any longer protect the man, who was all washed up. "Slattery, Des Slattery."

"Him? That pimp?" She collapsed back into her chair.

While she was taking all this in, Russell came and stood over her, sympathetic.

"It was for your own good, Ann, do believe me. They weren't right for you, any of them. I had them checked out. They'd only have hurt you in the end. I hoped through all these years you'd realise that, and come back to me. I'm your only true love, body and soul."

Ann squirmed away from him in distaste. "I don't want your body or your soul, never did. Can't you get that through your thick skull? I don't want you. How could you do such terrible things to me? You, what are you, an Assistant Chief Constable? Strong-arming every man who ever cared for me. Ruining my life." She paused. She realised that Russell was the second man she'd accused of that today. She really could pick them.

Russell lowered his head. "I'm sorry you feel that. You're quite right of course. I should never have done it. It was unforgivable. But I was desperate. Do you know what unrequited love is like? It gnaws at you, destroys your peace of mind. You were killing me. I had to do something. You've no idea how lonely I've been up here."

Face suffused with anger Ann stood up, crashing her chair back against the wall. "Don't give me that, wallowing in your own self-pity. I know everything there is to know about loneliness. You saw to that. The evenings in The Newsroom, staring into a glass, drinking alone because the last man had left me. So don't tell me about it."

Russell strained his arm out towards her. "Don't go. Not like this. Say at least you forgive me. I can't go on otherwise."

"Tough. You get no sympathy from me." She moved to the door.

"Don't go Ann. I won't let you." Then his tone turned from begging to the hardness of threats. "Don't think you can throw me over for Hood."

She half turned at the door. "Why? What's to stop me if I want to."

"I know all about you two. Slattery told me, the cancer, the treatment . . . the money. You'll never get away with it, the two of you."

Ann tried to bluff it out. "I don't know what you're talking about." She was halfway through the door, but Russell grabbed the handle and forced her back.

All his politeness, courtesy was gone. "I'm talking about the stolen four hundred thousand pounds. Did you think you could just put it into a suitcase and walk off a plane with it?"

"This is crazy. I don't know anything about that amount of money. It's preposterous. Let me go."

"Not till you admit it. Hood is in love with you. He stole the money to pay for your treatment. Very touching." Then abruptly his tone changed again.

"Oh Ann, why didn't you come to me? I've savings. We could have worked something out. But this way he'll go down for twenty years you know. You'll never see him again."

Ann staggered from the door, almost crying. "I begged him not to do it. I told him I wanted no part of the money. But he just kept on. Oh Bill." The thought of never seeing him again was insupportable. What was going to happen to them?

Russell put his hand on her shoulder. "If you promise never to see him again, to go away with me, I might be able to fix it."

Ann shuddered. "What are you saying?"

"It's all within these four walls at the moment. I'm the only one here who knows about Hood and the robberies. I could protect him - if I had a reason."

Ann looked at him in horror. "You . . . slug. You'd trade Bill's

k

life?"

"I would. Think about it. I've waited all these years for you Ann. I want you. Nothing else matters. I'll do anything to get you - just like Hood did."

"And what if I die?"

Russell didn't pause for an instant. "Then I'd have had you, if only for a few months, days, or hours. That's all I want - you to myself."

Ann tugged away from him. "This is crazy. You can't barter over me. How do I know you'll keep your end of the bargain?"

"You'd have to trust me."

"Huh!" Ann spat out the word.

"Oh, and don't think you can warn Hood to dispose of the evidence. He's waiting outside. I can call him in anytime."

"You've really got it all figured out, haven't you?"

"I have."

Ann grabbed her coat. "It's a dirty bargain. But I'll think about it."

"Forty-eight hours. Then I pass Hood's case over to the Deputy Chief Constable. Once there it is out of my hands."

"You'll have your answer." Ann swung out of the door, straight past a surprised Hood who was sitting, bored, on the bench outside.

"The things I do for you men," she rasped as she swept past him and down the stairs, her heels clattering on the steps all the way down.

Russell mopped his brow: he'd made his final play. If this didn't work he was finished. And if it did? Elation swooped him up till he was dizzy and had to clutch the desk. Ann, Ann, her beautiful body, all his to enjoy.

But then he remembered her horror at his suggestion. How could he make love to her if she felt that way about him? It would be rape. "You slug," she'd called him.

He recoiled. What had he done, with his mad offer? Maybe his old romantic dream, loving her from afar, had been better. But that was forfeit, lost to him forever.

Suddenly he felt suffocated. If everything went wrong, where did he go from there? He needed another way out, and cast his eyes around desperately. Oh God, somebody help me, he thought. But there was no one.

Chapter Thirty-seven

Ann sat in the chair in Hood's flat while he faced her, standing in front of the electric fire. He seemed to be even more in a state of shock than her.

His eyes were baleful. "So Russell of all people figured out it was me?"

"Slattery told him."

"Oh well, that makes sense," Hood replied with bitter sarcasm. "Those two were in cahoots from the first. Can you believe it: Russell set me up with that gangster?"

Then realising he was getting off the point he began to pace. "It's all come crashing down. I feel so badly about it, for your sake Ann. I could be arrested at any time. The money's been confiscated. Russell even took my gun."

Ann ached to relieve his misery. "It doesn't matter."

"But it does," he rounded on her heatedly. "You can't pretend it doesn't. You need that treatment in America. We'd been relying on that to make you well. What do we do now?" And in his eyes lay the terror of having to sit around and watch her die, helplessly.

"There are other treatments," she reassured him.

"Oh come off it. We've been through all that. If they'd been any good we wouldn't have been looking to America." He came and knelt by her side.

"Ann, I feel I've let you down completely. To be honest I can see no way out. In a few hours they'll put me away and you'll be left to go through it all on your own. That hurts as much as anything."

Ann was touched and stroked his thick, black hair. "As long as you care about me the way you do, nothing else matters."

She clasped him close and then her self control went too. "Oh

211

Bill I can't stand it. Would they really give you twenty years in jail?"

Hood looked up at her, his heavy eyes solemn. "Fifteen, twenty what's the difference? Yes, I'm afraid so."

She drew back. "In that case we've got to shut Russell's mouth. I'll pretend to go along with what he wants. That will give us time."

"Oh Ann." Hood stood up and backed away. He leant on the empty bookcase for support. "You can't. It's like . . . prostitution." The word hung between them, a sick reminder.

"I don't mind," Ann said firmly. Then she realised what she'd said. "Of course I do mind, I mind like hell, a dirty little pervert like Russell trying to get his paws on me. But it's the only way out."

Hood moved in on her. "And I'm supposed to sit around and twiddle my thumbs while that leech makes love to you? All to save my precious skin. I won't do it."

Ann glared at him. "It's not your choice, it's mine. It won't mean anything. It doesn't affect us, the way we feel about each other."

"Oh doesn't it?" Distraught, his hands clawed the air. "I can't stand you and another man. How could it be the same between us afterwards?"

"Now you're just being adolescent. We can cope, we're grown up people. What have we both been through and come out at the other end? Do you really want to spend the rest of your life in jail? Because I'll be honest: it terrifies me. I've been on my own so long I don't think I can take another twenty years of solitary. We'd be old people by the time you came out."

Hood listened and realised how much he'd been thinking about himself, his own feelings, and not about hers. As usual he had underestimated her strength, what she was prepared to do for him, for both of them.

"I can't let you do it."

Ann gritted her teeth. "I'll have to pretend to go through with it. We've no other choice."

"But what if he still shops me? After he's got you, it would suit him to put me away for good."

"He knows I'd never see him again. Bill, his mind is warped. We must humour him."

212

"If you say so. What a gawd awful mess I've got you into."

"Don't you think I feel guilty? Sometimes I think I've ruined your life."

"Never. You're the only good part of it. It's those others - I'd like to see them dead."

"Don't Bill. You must stop hating them. You can't punish the whole world. Let them go. We only need each other."

She pulled on his arm to make him hold her close. "Who knows how long we may have together? Let's not waste it bickering. Kiss me."

Hood was overcome. "Ann, I love you so much."

Ann looked back at him. "I'll give Russell our answer then."

Chapter Thirty-eight

What Hood had been dreading and trying to put out of his mind finally happened: he received a summons to present himself before Deputy Chief Constable Greene.

As he sat among his fellow officers Hood saw his life crumbling. So Russell had taken the easy way out and shopped him to Greene. His offer to Ann had just been a tease, a pathetic attempt to force his attentions on her. Or maybe right and duty had triumphed with Russell in the end.

But the rightness didn't make it any easier to take. Fifteen years in jail at a minimum. And he knew how inmates and screws alike treated bent coppers in prison. His face was drawn with anguish.

He had done it all for Ann, and was now condemned to endless years of separation. To have found her, and then to lose her again was unsupportable. It was all his crazy fault. Why had he taken such a desperate gamble? He was a jinx all right: on himself, his own worst enemy.

His knuckles were white as he clenched his hands at his side. He must regain his self control, and not break down in front of the others. At least he could go with dignity, hold his head up.

Straightening his cuffs, he rose. He was wearing his herring-bone suit with a white shirt, blue striped tie, and brogues. In some ways he would have preferred to be in uniform but it couldn't be helped. At least he hadn't worn his shabby brown suit that day.

Slowly, head erect, back ram rod straight he walked out of the detectives' room and into the corridor. He decided to take the lift, so that he wouldn't appear breathless when he was before the Deputy Chief Constable.

As the lift rose he wondered how he would be treated. Greene was a stiff man from the north-east who brooked no argument. Nevertheless he had a reputation for being supportive to officers in trouble.

So: would he bawl Hood out, insult him, or ask for a reason? Hood sighed and for a moment lowered his head. In the end it didn't really matter how he was treated, the result must be the same. No extenuating circumstances could excuse a police officer stealing four hundred thousand pounds.

Hood reached the door. He lightly touched the polished mahogany for luck and then rapped firmly. All he wanted was to get the interview over. The tension was unbearable.

"Enter."

Hood stepped smartly inside, closed the door behind him, and saluted.

"Detective Hood reporting sir."

Greene, wearing full uniform, looked Hood straight in the eye. He had a long, rectangular face, and his grey hair was sharply cut. His hollowed cheeks had red gashes, and his mouth was tight but firm.

His fingers were laced in front of him on the desk. "I've ordered you here on a matter of the utmost seriousness. In all my years on the force I can't recall a situation more grave or distasteful. Whenever one encounters corruption at such a senior level in the force it reflects on all of us."

Hood remained at attention, his eyes focused just over the top of Greene's head. So here it came, the dressing down. Even though he had been expecting it, still it hurt to be demeaned by a superior whom he respected. Well, he'd brought it upon himself.

"I have some very hard things to say about a senior officer and it's not easy. But I must begin. Assistant Chief Constable Russell has committed suicide and left a confession. He shot himself with the same gun he used on the recent spate of robberies."

Hood swayed and then struggled to regain himself.

"Sir?" He was incredulous.

"I know it's terrible news to spring on you, who worked so closely with him. I have to ask you: did you ever suspect him of wrong dealing?"

Hood could only shake his head, trying to take all this in.

"You don't need to protect him, his memory, you know." Greene was grave but kind. "He wrote it all down in his confession. I've contacted Pearson and told the robberies team to stand down. We've found all the money, plus the gun and everything else he used, where he said he'd hidden them."

He leant back for a moment sympathetically. "I know this must be a hell of a shock for you." He paused then went on: "You look ashen. Sit down."

"No sir, it's all right. I prefer to stand." Hood was holding himself up by will-power.

"Very well. I blame the fact that Russell wasn't a team man. Too much time alone, brooding, then paranoia and bang."

"Is that all sir?"

Greene blinked and was curt for a moment. "There's more. Russell betrayed you to Slattery. Your cover was blown from the start. To put you in such danger, well words fail me. I'm only glad you came out in one piece."

Hood demurred and shuffled his feet. His head was whirling with each fresh disclosure.

"Russell had been protecting Slattery for years. But we'll get him now."

"I'm pleased to know that, sir."

"Good. I can see you don't bear grudges. You'll want to return to the Derbyshire force as soon as possible?"

Behind his words was a plea not to cause trouble.

Hood put up a token resistance. "I don't know sir. I trusted Russell. He told me it was a sealed operation: just him and me. He put me on the robberies detail too."

"I don't blame you for being angry. Between you and me I'm not sorry he topped himself. With that on his conscience what else could he do?"

Hood thought long and hard about that one. It was very near to home.

"Right Detective Hood, you may go now if you wish. I regret you've been treated in this shameful manner and we'll do everything we can to make amends."

"Yes sir. And thank you for putting me in the picture."

"Good afternoon Hood."

"Good afternoon sir."

Hood stepped out of the office and closed the door behind him. Then he walked in a daze along the corridor, and down the stairs. Flight after flight, to give himself time to think.

It wasn't a trick, was it, to lull him to catch him out? He shook himself. No, it couldn't be. He hadn't been asked any intimidating questions. Greene seemed genuinely appalled.

Russell committing suicide and taking the blame for the robberies: what a thing to do. It must have been for Ann. Perhaps the man needed to make one last romantic gesture. Anyway he was off the hook. But did he want to be off the hook? Yes, he didn't want to spend a lifetime in jail. But to get off scot free wasn't right. He should have been punished for his crime, he expected it. He almost felt done out of it by Russell's gesture. Maybe that was Russell's intention, to prove in the end he was the better man. Maybe he was, at that.

As Hood emerged from the final flight of stairs on to the ground floor he stopped in front of the double swing doors. Should he go straight back, confess everything to Greene, take the blame that was rightfully his?

But what good would that do? Clear his conscience? Maybe but there was Ann to consider. He couldn't help her much from a prison cell.

He'd been ready to be convicted. He'd accepted that risk when he'd embarked on the robberies, just so Ann could have the money. Well Ann couldn't have the money now. So what else could he give her but himself?

Anyway, he wasn't a martyr, he told himself. He wasn't going back upstairs to confess. Russell could have his moral victory.

217

Chapter Thirty-nine

Hood wandered outside in a daze. He didn't know where to go or what to do. Aimlessly he walked up and down between the rows of vehicles, caged within the perimeter fence.

Suddenly an image came to him of Russell sitting lonely in his high office waiting to pull the trigger. That first night back in the city it could have so easily been him putting a bullet into his brain.

Poor Russell, taking all the guilt upon himself. Ann had been his tragic obsession. Hood knew what Russell must have felt, to lose her. That prospect tormented him now.

He thought he heard his name being called but shook his head. He must have imagined it. However again it came, faint but frantic. "Hood! Hood!"

He turned to see a uniformed officer racing across from the building towards him.

Breathlessly the man said, "There you are. We've been searching all over. A phone message came in for you: Ann Renshaw's been rushed into hospital."

The words seemed to jump at him, sparking him into action. He skated across the car park, heading for his vehicle.

'Rushed in': did that mean she'd undergone a sudden deterioration? He began fearing the worst. Suppose she was dying and he was not there beside her. She might already be unconscious, unable to know he was there, to hear him tell her how he loved her.

He bruised himself struggling through a gap between the tightly parked cars to his Volvo.

His car was blocked in but by brutal manoeuvring Hood soon had the Volvo accelerating for the gates. Then he thought: where

218

was the hospital? Furious he slammed on the brakes. He wasted precious minutes checking the quickest route on the map.

Then he drove out, aggressively cutting in on the traffic, glaring at any driver who intruded into his lane. His face was grey, drawn, concentrating on making up lost time. He urged the car on, pressing round the ring road till he reached the poor district where old hospitals were always built.

Finally he saw ahead the chocolate brick edifice. He swung the car through the entrance. At the 'pay and display' car park he cursed and accosted another visitor for change. He angrily banged the coins into the machine and tore off the ticket.

Seconds later he was running across to the main door and stumbling inside. Several old people were sitting bemused, waiting to be collected. There were signs pointing in every direction. Bewildered he went to the enquiry desk and asked for Ann's ward number.

Then it was off down corridors, following arrows, finding doors locked and having to go round a different way. And all the while minutes ticking by for Ann.

What if they wouldn't let him see her? He sweated and his mouth had a bad taste. They had to. He couldn't be shut off from her, not now when she needed him.

He rounded the final bend and halted in front of some double doors. Trying to compose himself he pulled one door open. He mustn't give Ann a shock by appearing wild or unruly. He found the Ward Sister and was shown to Ann's bed.

She was sitting up, wearing a pink negligee with sashes running from the collar and lace at the top. Still flamboyant, Hood thought, as he approached. Her eyes were closed and he thought she might be asleep.

But when he whispered, "Ann," she opened them and turned with a wide-eyed, pained but loving look.

"You got the message then."

"Better late than never," he apologised and sat down. "I came as soon as I heard."

She nodded. "I knew you would. It all seemed rather melodramatic but I thought you'd want to know."

"Of course I would." Hood clasped her hand, gently. "How are you?"

"Not so good." She flashed him a bitter smile. "The pain has started to come on something awful. I rang the doctor in the end and he had me admitted."

"Quite right too. At least they can look after you here."

She gazed at Hood long and sorrowfully. "So I wouldn't have been fit to travel anyway. No flight to the USA. I'm afraid."

"Never mind all that. Just rest."

Then her mind went off at another tangent. "Oh Bill, I've done a terrible thing. I didn't ring Russell. I couldn't. And then I was brought in here and it was too late. I don't want to lose you. I don't think I can bear it. Why did all this have to happen?"

Hood stroked her arm to soothe her. In a grave, quiet voice he told her about Russell, the suicide and the confession he left.

Ann couldn't believe it. "You're kidding me. Making it up so I won't feel guilty - no? But why did he do it?"

"I suppose he came to the end of his rope. He knew he couldn't have you and had nothing left to live for. Perhaps his confession was his way of making up for what he'd done to both of us."

Ann gripped Hood's hand tightly. "But do the police believe it?"

"He had all the evidence. I gave it him myself. I feel guilty about it, but what can I do? What good would it be to tell the truth now?"

"You don't have to convince me Bill."

"No. I think I was really trying to convince myself."

Ann stroked his tired, battered face. "Bill you can't win. You did it for me. Forgive yourself."

"If only I could. I tell you one thing, Ann, after this I'm resigning from the police force. I'm finding it hard enough to live with myself as it is."

Ann nodded. "I understand. But you're not going away?"

"Just try and make me. We're in this together. What did the doctors say?"

"I'm stable at the moment, they tell me. They keep sticking needles in me and putting me on drips which isn't very pleasant."

Her eyes went down. Hood could tell she was holding something back.

"Please Ann, tell me. What is it? Have they told you something I don't know about.

For a horrifying second he waited to hear the worst.

"It's not good Bill." She grasped his hand again. "The cancer's not been responding to treatment."

He waited, a pain starting in his chest, heart pounding.

"But there's just a chance with a new drug. They're starting clinical trials on me."

She and Hood exchanged glances. "I know what you're thinking," she went on. "You read about a new drug every week in the newspapers and they're never the cure. But Bill I've got to take this chance."

"Of course you have. Grab it with both hands." At least there was hope, a way forward. Joy shook him for a moment. Then he tried to contain it, not get carried away. It was no use building up hopes too high. But then, why not? Everything else had been snatched away from them.

He reached over and held her close. The hate-filled past was gone. There was only now - and however much time they were given together. He prayed for a miracle. For once let him be not a jinx but a good luck charm warding evil off her.